I0602751

WEDGETAIL

A MIRANDA CHASE ACTION-ADVENTURE TECHNOTHRILLER

M. L. BUCHMAN

Copyright 2024 Matthew L. Buchman

All rights reserved.

This book, or parts thereof, may not be reproduced in any form without permission from the author.

Receive a free book and discover more by this author at: www.mlbuchman.com

Cover images:

Industrial cargo shipping tankers Singapore Harbor © joyfull

RAAF Wedgetail © Sergey Ryabtsev

PRAISE FOR M. L. BUCHMAN

Tom Clancy fans open to a strong female lead will clamor for more.

— *DRONE*, PUBLISHERS WEEKLY

Superb! Miranda is utterly compelling!

— *BOOKLIST*, STARRED REVIEW

Miranda Chase continues to astound and charm.

— BARB M.

Escape Rating: A. Five Stars! OMG just start with *Drone* and be prepared for a fantastic binge-read!

— READING REALITY

The best military thriller I've read in a very long time. Love the female characters.

— *DRONE*, SHELDON MCARTHUR, FOUNDER OF THE MYSTERY BOOKSTORE, LA

A fabulous soaring thriller.

— *TAKE OVER AT MIDNIGHT*, MIDWEST BOOK REVIEW

Meticulously researched, hard-hitting, and suspenseful.

— *PURE HEAT,* PUBLISHERS WEEKLY,
STARRED REVIEW

Expert technical details abound, as do realistic military missions with superb imagery that will have readers feeling as if they are right there in the midst and on the edges of their seats.

— *LIGHT UP THE NIGHT,* RT REVIEWS, 4 1/2
STARS

Buchman has catapulted his way to the top tier of my favorite authors.

— FRESH FICTION

Nonstop action that will keep readers on the edge of their seats.

— *TAKE OVER AT MIDNIGHT,* LIBRARY
JOURNAL

M L. Buchman's ability to keep the reader right in the middle of the action is amazing.

— LONG AND SHORT REVIEWS

The only thing you'll ask yourself is, "When does the next one come out?"

— *WAIT UNTIL MIDNIGHT,* RT REVIEWS, 4
STARS

The first...of (a) stellar, long-running (military) romantic suspense series.

— *THE NIGHT IS MINE,* BOOKLIST, "THE 20 BEST ROMANTIC SUSPENSE NOVELS: MODERN MASTERPIECES"

I knew the books would be good, but I didn't realize how good.

— NIGHT STALKERS SERIES, KIRKUS REVIEWS

Buchman mixes adrenalin-spiking battles and brusque military jargon with a sensitive approach.

— PUBLISHERS WEEKLY

13 times "Top Pick of the Month"

— NIGHT OWL REVIEWS

SIGN UP FOR M. L. BUCHMAN'S NEWSLETTER TODAY

and receive:
Release News
Free Short Stories
a Free Book

Get your free book today. Do it now.
free-book.mlbuchman.com

Other works by M. L. Buchman: *(* - also in audio)*

Action-Adventure Thrillers

Dead Chef
One Chef!
Two Chef!

Miranda Chase
*Drone**
*Thunderbolt**
*Condor**
*Ghostrider**
*Raider**
*Chinook**
*Havoc**
*White Top**
*Start the Chase**
*Lightning**
*Skibird**
*Nightwatch**
*Osprey**
*Gryphon**

Science Fiction / Fantasy

Deities Anonymous
Cookbook from Hell: Reheated
Saviors 101

Contemporary Romance

Eagle Cove
Return to Eagle Cove
Recipe for Eagle Cove
Longing for Eagle Cove
Keepsake for Eagle Cove

Love Abroad
Heart of the Cotswolds: England
Path of Love: Cinque Terre, Italy

Where Dreams
Where Dreams are Born
Where Dreams Reside
*Where Dreams Are of Christmas**
Where Dreams Unfold
Where Dreams Are Written
Where Dreams Continue

Non-Fiction

Strategies for Success
Managing Your Inner Artist/Writer
*Estate Planning for Authors**
Character Voice
*Narrate and Record Your Own Audiobook**
Beyond Prince Charming: One Guy's Guide to Writing Men in Romance

Short Story Series by M. L. Buchman:

Action-Adventure Thrillers

Dead Chef

Miranda Chase Stories

Romantic Suspense

Antarctic Ice Fliers

US Coast Guard

Contemporary Romance

Eagle Cove

Other

Deities Anonymous (fantasy)

Single Titles

The Emily Beale Universe
(military romantic suspense)

The Night Stalkers
MAIN FLIGHT
The Night Is Mine
I Own the Dawn
Wait Until Dark
Take Over at Midnight
Light Up the Night
Bring On the Dusk
By Break of Day
Target of the Heart
Target Lock on Love
Target of Mine
Target of One's Own
NIGHT STALKERS HOLIDAYS
*Daniel's Christmas**
*Frank's Independence Day**
*Peter's Christmas**
Christmas at Steel Beach
*Zachary's Christmas**
*Roy's Independence Day**
*Damien's Christmas**
Christmas at Peleliu Cove

Henderson's Ranch
*Nathan's Big Sky**
*Big Sky, Loyal Heart**
*Big Sky Dog Whisperer**
*Tales of Henderson's Ranch**

Shadow Force: Psi
*At the Slightest Sound**
*At the Quietest Word**
*At the Merest Glance**
*At the Clearest Sensation**

White House Protection Force
*Off the Leash**
*On Your Mark**
*In the Weeds**

Firehawks
Pure Heat
Full Blaze
*Hot Point**
*Flash of Fire**
Wild Fire
SMOKEJUMPERS
*Wildfire at Dawn**
*Wildfire at Larch Creek**
*Wildfire on the Skagit**

Delta Force
*Target Engaged**
*Heart Strike**
*Wild Justice**
*Midnight Trust**

Night Stalkers Reload
*Guard the East Flank**

Emily Beale Universe Short Story Series
The Night Stalkers
The Night Stalkers Stories
The Night Stalkers CSAR
The Night Stalkers Wedding Stories
The Future Night Stalkers

Delta Force
Th Delta Force Shooters
The Delta Force Warriors

Firehawks
The Firehawks Lookouts
The Firehawks Hotshots
The Firebirds

White House Protection Force
Stories

Future Night Stalkers
Stories (Science Fiction)

ABOUT THIS BOOK

Is an attack on the greatest shipping choke point in the world, the Strait of Malacca, a move for economic control...or something worse?

A Wedgetail, the most powerful surveillance airplane in the skies, goes down—hard. Miranda and her team race to investigate, unwittingly placing themselves in the crosshairs.

From the world's greatest shipping chokepoint at the Strait of Malacca to the Malaysian wilderness, from the Australian Outback to the halls of power in Southeast Asia, survival becomes the greatest challenge.

Can Miranda and her team unravel the crisis before it destroys global shipping and kills them all?

———

A list of characters and aircraft may be found at:
https://mlbuchman.com/fan-club-freebies
Scroll down to: People, Places, & Planes
And return afterward for a free bonus story
and a recipe from the book.

PROLOGUE

"Hello?"

"Hello, Shira. I need information from your benefactor." He pictured her, so pretty and perfect; so kept. Even now probably sunning on the balcony of that lovely Tel Aviv flat overlooking Geula Beach and the Mediterranean.

"My benefactor?" Her voice trailed off but he could hear the shift in tone from cautious to edged...and then into doubt. Smart woman.

"Benjamin. Aluf Benjamin Muntz." *Aluf* was the equivalent of a two-star American general. "Director of Special Weapons Research for the Israeli Defense Forces."

They'd all met during a dinner hosted by Muntz half a year ago. Muntz had brought this Shira as his date—more than. Not engaged but that couldn't be far off.

"I need to know the locations of all of Israel's aircraft equipped with the IB-weapon."

"Why would I—"

"Oh, that's simple, my dear girl. You have a past." A very dark one.

"I—"

"Roskovensky." The silence over the phone was complete. She had traveled through many changes since then. Perhaps in a prior age that would have kept her past hidden, but the modern one was data-driven and his people knew how to leverage that.

"You have your little claws into Muntz, and I'm sure you could talk even such an upstanding citizen around to your side." And, of course, Shin Bet's security goons would already know or they'd never have cleared her to be with their precious aluf. "However, I'm equally certain the Russians would still be most interested to have a chat with you regarding General Roskovensky's unexpected demise ten years ago. They have long memories for past wrongs. One question?"

She didn't acknowledge.

"Did you castrate him before or after you drove that kitchen knife under his chin and up into his brain?" He'd been the highest ranking death during the annexation of Crimea by Russia in 2014. All kept very hush-hush because the Russians couldn't admit to such a loss, especially at the hands of a pretty little Ukrainian Jew.

The silence continued.

"Ah well. I was merely curious. I'll call tomorrow at this time. You'll have the precise location of each aircraft for me, won't you, my dear?"

He waited a long moment before hanging up.

Step One: complete.

Step Two: find a crew.

Step Three: the plane.

1

---

4 WEEKS LATER

39,000' above the Strait of Malacca

"I hate this place," Nick grumbled over the intercom.

"Wouldn't be the strait without you saying so," she replied as always. Though Royal Australian Air Force Group Captain Rowena McCain couldn't argue.

She'd flown more than two hundred patrols in this claustrophobic 737 above the strait. Watching it not through her eyes, because the operational center of the plane had no windows, but instead at the ten stations of tactical displays. She knew the critical seaway below as well as her own hand, though she'd rarely seen it with her own eyes.

For the last two years, this roaring tube flying over the strait had become her home far more than the base housing at RAAF Tindal in the arid bush of the Northern Territory.

The Strait of Malacca was a tactical nightmare, which had become like that itch that no amount of scratching eased. It teetered on the verge of collapse at every level: sea, air, and space. Every minor problem could have global ramifications with the amount of trade moving through here.

"No, I *really* hate this place." Wing Commander Nick Nelson completed the ritual that had existed since they'd both been lowly flight lieutenants on their first patrol together along the distant Arafura Sea. When they'd first flown the Strait of Malacca, he'd taught her the sign language for *No, really!*—the Bruce Willis two fingers pinching down to the thumb, then a forefinger flicked outward from the point of the chin. As if the hand gesture made it more true here than everywhere else he'd ever served. He raised a hand from his keyboard to make the gesture without turning from his displays.

Nick, atypically dour for an Aussie but brilliant at his job, was a great hulk of a man. She'd chosen him to sit at her left hand as the senior Surveillance Officer the moment they'd bumped her to the command seat—all of last month.

The Wedgetail—technically the Boeing 737 AEW&C, Airborne Early Warning and Control plane—was the hottest flying command in the RAAF. It was the only plane in the Royal Australian Air Force staffed by a group captain, the equivalent of an American colonel. She had the responsibility *and* the power to order immediate action if needed.

"It's a bit of clutter, mates," Squadron Leader Grant Felton laughed. "But the place is bound to clear up one of these days." The diametric opposite of Nick, Grant would be chortling at some joke during his own funeral. Pity he wasn't as funny as he thought he was—though he was definitely as handsome. But she'd long since refused to fall for that.

Her promotion to group captain—raising her to be the highest ranked Black Australian in the RAAF—made her twice the target she'd ever been before. Especially in the eyes of a dog like Grant. His conviction of being the best dingo in a shaggy pack didn't make him the least bit more delightful. He'd hit on her the first day he'd joined the crew. To back him off, she'd finally threatened to recommend him for a lifetime of latrine duty in hisc next review. Which he referred to annoyingly often

—as if the year since hadn't worn the edges off it long ago. He remained convinced it was a bonding joke between them rather than an unvarnished threat.

They occupied the first three of the ten side-facing consoles in the main cabin of the E-7A Wedgetail patrol jet. Grant's role placed him at the forward end of the cabin closest to the main entry door and the cockpit. His job was to communicate with the two pilots forward and make sure that the plane stayed aloft and secure.

She sat next in the command seat, with Nick to her left managing the surveillance team.

Down the main cabin ranged seven more consoles, each wide enough for two screens, keyboard, keypad, and headset. Three along their port side of the plane and the remaining four to starboard. The count was split because of the large radio cabinets occupying the first two forward positions along the right side of the cabin.

Each station faced the hull. Not that there were any windows to see out of. Instead, each headset-wearing operator in their comfortable swivel seat stared at a bank of displays showing different aspects of the world around them. They could talk to a nearby jet or access anywhere on the globe via satellite with equal ease. Some flights only called for a few operators, but all ten stations were manned continuously when patrolling the strait.

Nick oversaw six of the seven down-cabin stations. He had responsibility for surveillance of everything that happened outside the plane. Somehow, he always managed to make sure that she was looking at the right thing at the right time. Nick had always done so, and now she had the absolute faith of experience in him.

Grant managed his own console and the tech who oversaw communications. Between them, they handled every aspect of the aircraft's operational integrity, including all the radars and radios that could be squeezed into or hung onto a 737's airframe.

Everything either Nick or Grant tagged as critical hit her display. At the moment, she was in overall command of far more than her plane. Security operations for the entire eight-hundred-kilometer length of the Strait of Malacca was hers for the duration of this patrol.

Which left her in the middle...again. Story of her life.

She'd been a middle sister with two gung ho brothers. One now a footie star and the other a world-class sailor. Not bad for a First Nations family working the big mines on the edge of the Great Victorian Desert. No longer in their shadows, she still sometimes felt stuck between her brothers' bigger-than-life personalities.

Always the quiet one, she now sat between the surveillance officer and the plane's systems officer. Not to mention being a single woman caught between a pair of RAAF bachelors. One with puppy-dog-sad eyes that saw the world all too clearly; the other convinced he knew far more about her than he did.

Nick tapped his screen, which highlighted a ship icon on hers.

Too fast for a fishing vessel, too small for a container ship.

"Satellite handy?" she asked.

"UK bird coming up over Sri Lanka. We'll have a visual five-minute window in three minutes."

"Roger that." Rowena returned to studying other shipping activity while waiting to see if some pirate was unlucky enough to commit his crime within her Wedgetail's long view of the strait.

In her two and a half decades of service, Rowena had seen plenty of ugly around these parts. Malacca wasn't going to be clearing up anytime soon, no matter Grant's prediction. The only thing that would stop this glut through the strait was war. She'd gamed that all too often at headquarters; one of the ultimate no-win scenarios no matter how they looked at it. Sink a handful of big ships across the gut of the strait and it would be closed. The only real shocker was that it hadn't happened yet; Indonesia, Malaysia, and Singapore might *need* each other, but they certainly didn't *like* each other much.

If the strait ever was closed, the only way to bypass it was a long haul south around Indonesia for the Strait of Lombok or on toward Australia and New Zealand. Ship owners most certainly didn't want to pay for their deliveries to travel an extra three thousand kilometers before turning north.

At the three-klick-wide choke point where the Malacca emptied out at Singapore, it wasn't unusual to have ships three hundred meters long that needed half an hour and six kilometers to stop, lined up two or three abreast. One kilometer apart, with the same passing in the opposite direction.

And that was merely the big trade boys. Add in more little boats than bugs in an Outback termite mound: local transports, fishermen, and world sailors, along with the occasional US Navy carrier group complete with submarines.

The real trouble came because where there were countries, there was squabbling.

And where there was congestion, there were pirates.

The pressure of eight billion people on the planet made for a lot of poor—near enough half a billion of them within shooting distance of the Strait of Malacca—and a lot of those feeling no qualms about taking from the rich and giving to themselves.

One poor freighter had been robbed four times in a single passage. The first time for the crew's cash and valuables. Then someone pulled alongside and cross-pumped a hundred thousand gallons of diesel at gunpoint. Another pirate took twenty thousand more gallons, leaving her almost dry of fuel for her engines. The final pirates, finding the ship stripped, had ridden along for two days eating as much food from her stores as they could before disembarking. Thankfully, that hadn't been on Australia's watch.

As there were no flotillas of military ships passing through at the moment, the pirates were the focus of today's mission.

Of course, from up here at thirty-nine thousand feet in the Wedgetail, they could also keep an eye on the pissing match China had turned into the next most likely war zone across much of the South China Sea. And not to forget Myanmar at the other end engaging anyone who'd listen to the latest military junta, which was no one with a pinch of common sense.

"Never two days the same," Grant teased.

"Each worse than the one before," Nick embraced his moroseness like an art form.

Unlike her prior commander, Rowena appreciated the banter. A standard patrol lasted twelve hours unless something bad kicked in. Then they'd get a midair refueling and often hit twenty hours aloft. She could rotate some of the operators to the comfortable crew rest seats in the rear, but she never took advantage of that herself.

That created its own kind of trouble. Being labeled as an overachiever pleased the top levels of command but irritated those immediately above her. They assumed she was after their jobs, which she was. The fact that she was smarter than most of them put together, and everyone knew it, didn't help matters.

The man she'd replaced had been aged out. Rather than making the grade to air commodore, he'd been grounded and was completing his final year from the ground. Angrier than a sack full of hornets, he'd turned over the Wedgetail to her command with only the barest of military protocols. She'd known he'd despised her for being better than he was—long since obvious to both of them as well as Command, who had promoted her—but she hadn't known how much until the handover.

Now off the plane and out of the No. 2 Security Forces Squadron, he was no longer her problem.

Neither Nick nor Grant despised her, that she could tell. And neither aspired, both glad to be in straightforward service roles.

Rowena, however, had her eye firmly trained on trading in the four thin stripes on her uniform for that one wide one of air commodore, equivalent to a US brigadier general. To achieve that, she had to hone her crew and her billion-Australian-dollar plane until they shone.

Under the Five Power Defence Arrangements—Australia's key military treaty with Singapore, the UK, New Zealand, and Malaysia—they helped to keep the trade moving as safely as possible throughout the region. Indonesia lay along the other side of the strait. Being too snarled in problems of their own, they cooperated, reluctantly, but did little to help.

Australia's Wedgetails had proven to be major assets in achieving smooth flow along this globally critical sea lane and she planned for her plane to be the most effective one in the fleet.

But now that she was here, sea traffic wasn't her only mission.

"Talk to me about the air." She hit the top right button on the soft-touch pad beside her keyboard to flip her view, relegating the sea to her secondary screen and showing her the surrounding air space on the primary.

Nick flipped his screen to match. His three maritime staff specialists would alert him if anything went astray.

"About the same sorry state," Nick groused.

They flew at thirty-nine thousand feet over two of the busiest airports in the world: Singapore's Changi and Malaysia's Kuala Lumpur International. The horizon lay four hundred kilometers away in all directions due to the Earth's curvature, and they could see out to nine hundred for aircraft at altitude. Everything from Ho Chi Minh City to Jakarta showed up on the screens—it almost made the clutter down in the strait look rational. At least the shipping remained on the surface of the sea, other than the occasional submarine. The clutter of the air routes crisscrossed at every altitude imaginable.

But the Wedgetail wasn't called the most capable AEW&C plane aloft without reason. It specialized in sorting the noteworthy from the mundane at sea, in the air, and in near space out to a thousand kilometers. They might be watching the sea and air today, but if someone lofted a ballistic missile from beyond the horizon, the Wedgetail could find it before it reentered the atmosphere.

Rowena scaled her view to the closest hundred kilometers in all directions and began identifying the patterns— something she did faster than anyone aboard. Always good to set a high bar for the staff.

The magic of her view was created in the back half of the plane.

Past the ten consoles and the small crew rest area, the aft half of the fuselage was closed off. From the wings back to the tail ranged some of the most sophisticated electronics anywhere. They controlled, fed, and watched through the Top Hat radar antenna. The antenna—like a fat-handled dough scraper jammed into the spine of the plane by a giant trying to split the fuselage in two lengthwise—ran from the plane's midpoint to close before the tail and nearly as tall.

This was *not* the thirty-foot-wide black-and-white spinning disk of the fifty-year-old E-3 Sentry AWACS planes. Those updated their radar view with one sweep every ten seconds. The E-7A Wedgetail's MESA radar—multi-role electronically scanned array—offered a three-hundred-and-sixty-degree view: sea low, airspace mid, and space high.

"What's the status on our stray boat?" Her internal timer

had gone off that the imaging satellite should have cleared the horizon by now and be able to see the boat they'd spotted earlier.

"Hang on. Hang on." Nick counted the phrase off in seconds, working his keyboard. "There. The boat's a service vessel. Registered. Called out to assist with a Saudi's broken Number Two engine. Liberian registry, of course." No accidental oil spill that could be traced to the Sauds, at least financially.

Rowena glanced over at his console and saw a low-angle satellite image, a static picture of the same boat for comparison, and basic registry information. It was one of many kept docked along the strait, like tow trucks pre-positioned on major highways during rush hour.

"Tell him to turn on his damn AIS." Ships were *supposed* to run with their Automatic Identification System transponder operating for just this reason.

After a quick radio call, the ship's ID blinked to life on the screen, reporting that the boat was who she said she was.

"Sounded hungover to me," Nick said in a voice that sounded that way himself. But then he always did, sober or not.

At her nod, he cleared the screen. One of his techs would keep an eye on it to make sure that it wasn't a false-flag operation or, if legitimate, that the ship they were assisting didn't break the traffic pattern in any dangerous fashion.

Back to studying the air traffic.

Commercial and cargo flights clustered in neat lines toward the major airports. Like a high-flying web that connected them to the wider world. Below them, feeder flights appeared like flowers, their predictable patterns blooming outward from major airports to smaller fields, then feeding back the other way.

Every pattern wove together on her monitor to make clear and predictable forms that—

"Who's this?"

She tapped her screen.

Nick glanced over at her console, squinted at it for a second, then turned back to his.

"Small plane," he reported. "Large bizjet class." Another pause. "Fifty-five kilometers out. Heading zero-six-zero. Crossing our course in one minute fifty seconds. Flight Level Four-Zero."

The Wedgetail flew northwest at thirty-nine thousand feet along the length of the far-below strait; they could sweep it from one extremity to the other every hour. The unknown flight flew northeast at forty thousand feet.

If it was a feeder flight climbing out of West Sumatra, Indonesia, it would still be far lower. To the southwest, beyond Sumatra, there was nowhere to come *from*. Nothing except the vast empty stretches of the Indian Ocean where the Malaysian airliner MH370 had disappeared, and not found even a decade later after the largest search-and-rescue operation in maritime history.

"Forty thousand should be a dead zone," she reminded Nick. "Verify."

"Flight Level Four-Zero verified. Ninety seconds out."

Eastbound aircraft should be at Flight Level Three-Seven or Four-One. With their own present westbound course at Three-Nine, it created a two-thousand-foot vertical buffer between planes going in opposite directions—or it was supposed to. Nobody should be at Four-Zero unless they were in transition between flight levels.

"Identity?" Rowena asked.

"No transponder. Radar shows..." Nick kept working his keyboard.

In seconds he'd re-tuned the big Top Hat radar from wide-area survey to threat-sector analysis in the direction of the unknown aircraft. Focusing the entirety of the

MESA radar on a single aircraft vastly increased the detail.

"Bogey is a Dassault Falcon 2000 business jet. Typically, ten passengers and two crew. There's a belly extension I don't recognize. It isn't an antenna."

She didn't like this.

"Perhaps it's lost. Or going walkabout. Forty-five seconds out." At a combined closure rate of seventeen hundred kilometers per hour, distances shrank fast.

She watched it continue its approach for five more seconds. That earlier itch turned into a burn.

"Grant. Get us away from this guy."

"Roger." He keyed his connection to the pilots. "Jackson, turn immediate heading—"

He yelped and slapped off his intercom headset.

"What the bloody hell?" He was rubbing at his ears.

"Report?" Rowena asked when he didn't speak.

"Pray I'm hallucinating." He picked up the headset, held it near one ear, then dialed down the volume before pulling it back on. "Jackson? Boller?"

The Wedgetail pilots' names.

Rowena tapped for the cockpit intercom channel.

Nothing.

Except a loud roar.

Like—

"What did you hear, Grant?"

"Screams. Like blood-curdling ones. Kind of sound you never want to hear—ever. Jackson? Boller?"

All she heard was wind.

Grant undid his seat harness.

Rowena had been wearing only her lap belt, but out of the corner of her eye she saw Nick pulling on the two shoulder straps to make it a four-point harness. She did the same for herself. When she pulled the strap from the front-edge of the seat to attach all five points, Nick looked pained before doing the same. All down the cabin, she could hear the quiet snick of five-point harnesses being latched into place.

Grant pounded on the door a few times. Then he keyed in the unlock code on the external keypad beside the cockpit's safety door.

After waiting through the long pause that gave the pilots the option to override the unlock request, the three lights turned green, indicating all three locks had opened.

He turned the handle and tugged.

Then harder.

He pulled his hand back and looked at it strangely for a moment, rubbing it. Then he ran his hand around the edge of the door.

Next, he shoved aside one earmuff of his headset, picked up the intercom phone hung beside the door, and called out the pilot's names. He listened, then hung it up very slowly and turned to face her.

"I think we just lost the pilots."

2

GRANT WAS FLIGHT QUALIFIED, BUT THAT DIDN'T DO HIM ANY good on the cabin side of the door.

He touched the door handle again. Cold, icy cold, changing even as he'd gripped it. That could happen only if the cockpit was open to the outside air at thirty-nine thousand feet—minus fifty degrees Celsius.

Around the edges of the door, gasketed against possible gas attacks, he'd felt cold metal and the slightest inward breeze at two of the corners.

If the crew had gotten their oxygen masks on, he'd be able to talk to them. Or at least hear them shouting into their masks.

No response when he tried the handset again.

Birds couldn't reach this altitude. A vulture had once struck a plane at thirty-seven thousand feet, but that had been fifty years ago over Africa, not here. Even if that's what had happened, a bird strike shouldn't have taken out both pilots.

He thought of the 1990 British Airways flight when the front windshield had blown out due to being fitted with the wrong screws. It had dragged the pilot out the windshield. He was only saved by a cabin crewman who happened to be in the cabin, delivering tea. He'd hung onto the captain's feet for the entire descent and landing, saving the captain's life while the copilot landed the plane. And that had been from seventeen thousand feet, not thirty-nine.

The screams. He'd definitely heard two screams—one male, one female.

Flight Lieutenant Mathilda Jackson. Please let her be okay. After six months together, they'd started talking about getting engaged. Maybe get an off-base house in Katherine, or at least a flat to call home. If she was gone, he'd—

"Systems, this is comms. We also lost topside TCAS and GPS." It was his communications tech reporting over the intercom.

The Traffic Collision Avoidance System had two antennas, one above the cockpit and one below. The GPS antenna perched directly aft of the topside TCAS; they were the first two of the many mounted along the plane's spine.

"Cause?" He asked his tech.

"Unclear. Still have signal from the lower TCAS."

"Roger, keep troubleshooting. Report when you have more."

He glanced at Rowena. She'd been watching him, but he barely knew where to begin. Mathilda was—

Focus.

Focus on duty.

Report even though Rowena would have heard everything.

"Pilots apparently incapacitated. Cockpit open to atmosphere at altitude. We've lost topside TCAS and GPS."

"Whatever took out the pilots probably took out the first two antennas." Of course. That sharp mind of hers jumped to the obvious conclusion far faster than his ever could. She was absolutely right.

Which meant—

Grant keyed his mike. "Comms, this is Systems. Do we still have SATCOM? And if not, how about VHF?"

"Five-by-five on SATCOM and VHF. Both still show stable signals."

"Roger." He turned back to Rowena. "Forward-most two antennas gone. But we have the others."

"With our pilots incapacitated, how do we get back control of the cockpit?" In other words, how was *he* going to get them flying rather than lofting along on autopilot until they ran out of fuel and crashed into the ocean beside MH370—wherever the hell they had gone to die.

Grant wanted to wrap himself around all that cool control of Rowena McCain. Not the woman herself, a damned prickly sheila. She'd made sure that he'd heard that message loud and clear from the first time they'd met. But he couldn't resist poking at that *perfect officer* material because, damn, was she a major improvement over the last guy.

She reminded him so much of his best mate in secondary school. They'd been right and left wings on the most mediocre soccer team in Melbourne—never great nor terrible, all right up the middle, despite their best efforts. He'd had a lot of fun but, like Rowena, Bobby took it all so seriously.

Unlike him and Bobby, she was the most competent officer he'd ever served with. And right now, having Group Captain Rowena McCain sitting beside him forced him to think they might find some way out of this.

"Uh...we have to balance the pressure between the main cabin and the cockpit. Right now, the door is being held shut by the difference in air pressure. Two-tenths of an atmosphere in the cockpit is about three pounds per square inch; cabin set for standard in-flight lowered pressure, say eleven psi on this side, giving a differential of eight psi holding that door shut." Some numbers simply didn't work as well in metric, a hundred kilopascals?

"Get on it." Then she turned to Nick on her left. "Get me everything you can on that Falcon jet. I need information to send to Command."

"Could it be coincidence?" Nick asked.

Grant wondered about that himself. The Falcon hadn't fired at them—the Wedgetail was equipped to identify and avoid a missile, including automatic evasive maneuvers and chaff boxes. Neither of which had happened. The Falcon had still been six miles out when they'd lost the pilots.

Rowenna tipped her head in consideration. "Just don't lose track of it, Nick." Then she was on the radio, reporting the loss of the pilots.

Focus, Grant.

He was out in the wind on his own.

How to break into a cockpit fortified to stop precisely that?

There would be no lowering the cabin pressure from back here; those controls were in the inaccessible cockpit on the wrong side of the pressure barrier. And that air pressure, so much higher in the cabin than outside at thirty-nine thousand feet, held the various cabin doors shut with...five tonnes per square meter. That's if they weren't already locked in place by flight-lock plungers as long as the throttles were advanced. No physical way to open the main or wing doors in flight. He could smash out a window, but he'd save that idea for a last resort.

Where the hell was Bobby when he needed him? Bobby was the one who could cobble together a working ute out of the parts from three wrecked pickup trucks. Grant's skills were that he'd been a better driver *and* could always scare up a couple sheilas to ride with them.

He'd become an RAAF pilot, and Bobby still worked in his pop's car shop. How the hell was he supposed to get through that door—fast? Especially if he lied to himself that Mathilda might still be alive on the other side. It had been two minutes since those screams. Brain death from oxygen deprivation at this altitude started at four minutes.

No sledgehammer would get through that door in time, even if he had one.

No crowbar.

How about—

He dumped his headset and raced down the aisle between the backs of the techs staying focused on their consoles. No one in the crew rest area. He keyed his way through the door at the aft end of the Wedgetail's cabin.

Under the Top Hat radar antenna, Grant could feel the power humming from the massive equipment cabinets that lined both sides within the back half of the fuselage. Should he have had them shut down the radar before he came back here? Too late now. If microwaves or something were going to cook him, it simply gave him all the more reason to hustle.

The MESA radar seemed to loom in the ceiling above his head, as likely to kill him as not. Only a narrow maintenance aisle stretched between the cabinets of electronics necessary to run the beast.

During his preflight inspection, he'd spotted a toolbox back here, left by a service tech. Grant had figured to teach him a lesson about cleaning up by not returning the kit until after the flight. Now he blessed the man. Twice over, too, after Grant dug out the battery-operated drill and it gave a bright *whirr* of a full charge when he pulled the trigger.

Biggest steel bit he could find. Spare battery.

Then he pictured all the small holes it would take to relieve the air pressure differential enough to open the door. Too long.

He might have to resort to busting out a window after all. Then he spotted a hank of half-inch rope.

He remembered the last time he'd ever let Bobby drive. Bobby had dropped two wheels into a ditch a kilometer after they'd picked up the Larkin twins for a seriously hot date.

Bobby had made some excuse about not expecting where Betsy had slid her hand while he was shifting gears.

Grant had been so furious as he watched those two fine girls start walking home in a huff that he'd almost missed what Bobby did. A hank of rope just this size run between the rear hitch and a ghost gum tree. He'd had them out of the ditch in five minutes—five minutes too late in the twin's eyes when they'd caught up with them halfway to home. They wouldn't even accept a ride for the last of the hot, dusty stretch.

Hurrying forward with the drill and rope, Grant closed the heavy door, isolating the radar controls in the back half of the plane.

"Oxygen masks!" he shouted as he passed the operator stations. "Everyone, masks!"

Once he reached the door, he tossed the drill and battery onto his seat. Then he prayed that the door handle had been built as stoutly as the door.

Looping one end of the rope around the handle, he tied the other to the base of Rowena's chair. His own chair was too close to the door to get the right angle. Then he thought better of it and doubled it around and back to the handle. He had no idea what would happen if the rope broke.

"Hey! What are you up to, Grant?" Rowena's voice was barely understandable through the oxygen mask she'd pulled down from the overhead cubby.

He ignored her. If she wanted to think he was flirting with her legs, she was welcome to. Whatever rang her chimes. Three minutes was coming up fast, and Mathilda would start some serious dying by four.

Grant stepped to the middle of the tautly strung rope. A glance showed that everyone had their masks on—except him. He yanked on the portable system that hung on the back of the comms cabinet.

Grabbing the middle of the rope, he pulled it sideways. The

power of triangles. A small pull sideways applied a massive amount of force at either end. One end pinned to Rowena's seat, the other to the door handle. That's how Bobby had freed the truck from the ditch. Triangles.

He applied a steady pull sideways. The handle didn't rip off. That was a good start.

He keyed the unlock code again, which had automatically reset. The infinite seconds of the entry alarm sounding in the cockpit stretched on and on but elicited no override. Please let her be alive. The lights went green.

"Shit! Nick!" he shouted through the mask. "I need you to turn the handle while I pull."

Rowena was first out of her chair though, shifting to another portable breathing kit. She also grabbed a fire extinguisher, which made little sense. The door was cold with altitude, not hot with fire.

Stepping past him, she knelt below the line of the rope and twisted the handle.

Once again, Grant pulled on the rope.

Slowly.

Slowly.

Would the metal in the handle be significantly more brittle for being another seventy degrees Celsius colder than normal? Bobby wasn't around to ask. It didn't matter. It would either work or not.

The scream was different this time. Definitely non-human —wind shriek.

As he leaned harder and harder against the line, the door cracked open just enough. Cabin air blasted into the cockpit and was ripped away by the low pressure at this high altitude.

The moment the pressure dropped, additional oxygen masks dropped out of the ceiling. Then the pressurization system kicked into overdrive, pumping even more air into the cabin.

His ears banged one way when he got the door cracked and the cabin pressure plummeted. They banged the other when it slammed closed again and the air system strained to drive the cabin pressure back up toward normal levels.

Grant leaned into the rope again, Rowena swung the handle.

The air's shrill cry turned into a roar once the door swung open by a hand's breadth.

Rowena's tight hair bun let go and her face disappeared in curls of long black hair whipping forward.

The wind from cabin to open cockpit slammed her brutally into the gap. She managed to brace herself by squaring her shoulders and hitting one on the door and the other on the door jamb. If the handle broke now, it would chop off her face and most of one arm. Yet he could open it no wider. He already had the rope pulled until his back lay against the closed main passenger-entry door. He'd have gotten another thirty centimeters of pull if he'd stood on the other side of the rope.

Next time.

If there was a next time.

Despite her desperate position, Rowena managed to slide the fire extinguisher into the gap. Damn but she was sharp.

She waved a hand for him to slacken the rope and dragged her head clear.

He eased it down until the fire extinguisher took the load. Then he stepped forward to help her out of the door's maw.

Rowena's eyes were rolling back in her head by the time he managed it. Her mask had been ripped off by the maelstrom of air exiting the cabin and rushing into the cockpit. Her forehead had a nasty gash from where she'd smacked it into the edge of the door. Possible concussion too by the way she was behaving.

He dragged her back to her seat and Nick helped him strap her in and get a fresh mask on. Someone from down-cabin found a first aid kit. Nick wrapped a bandage around her head several times to staunch the bleeding. All they could do for her at the moment.

Nick donned another portable kit while Grant tightened the rope. Together they finally managed to fully open the door, careful not to get tossed about by the mass of air exiting the main cabin and heading out the missing cockpit windows.

Grant braced himself against the pull as he eased into the cockpit with Nick close behind him.

3

Both front windows were gone.

Nick more surged than stepped into the cockpit behind Grant. He managed to dodge sideways out of the wind racing through the door. It died quickly as the cabin pressure equalized enough that the air currents did *not* drag him straight out the missing windshield. The last of the warm air brushed against his back as the frigid cockpit air washed over his front. He felt like Han Solo caught half buried in carbonite and half sticking out into the world.

The sound was horrific. Eight hundred kilometers-per-hour of too-thin atmosphere hammered into the plane with an unholy wail. He assumed it would be a full-on roar at lower altitudes where there was more air to tear at them. The windows weren't shattered. The heavy acrylic had been melted and flowed in uneven gaps until little remained.

From the relatively stable air pocket behind the pilot's seat, he could see the entire vista of the Strait of Malacca. The broad, forested plains of Sumatra backed by the Barisan Mountains and its forty volcanoes, though none were erupting at the moment. To the right, the quieter rolls of the worn mountains of the Malay Peninsula reaching above the tree line only here and there.

In a great stripe before them, like a blue highway fifty kilometers wide, lay the strait itself. Thirty percent of the world's annual trade, carried by ninety-five thousand ships—one every six minutes, night and day—dotted the waters below.

Grant turned toward the copilot's right-hand seat first...

Nick followed his stare.

By her long blonde hair, it was Mathilda Jackson. Except there was something odd about its length and coloring, as if parts had been burned away. Grant turned aside and lifted his mask barely in time to barf behind the copilot's seat. The swirling air plastered half of it on Grant's clothes and some on Nick's own.

Nick fought past Grant as the man struggled for air to heave again, and looked at the pilot in the left-hand seat.

He had no face. In its place, blackened and shrunken skin stretched tight over the skull. His mouth wide open and his eye sockets empty.

Now Nick knew what the extension under the Falcon's belly had been. A laser. Big enough to melt the windshield as it passed close and scorch the pilots' faces. Fifty, possibly a hundred kilowatts—military grade.

Definitely not a coincidence. The Falcon 2000 had attacked them.

Nick checked Mathilda for a pulse.

It was there, fluttering. Though not as badly burned, Mathilda looked long past caring.

Nick undid her harness and pulled her out of the chair.

He dragged her as gently as he could out of the battering wind and toward the cabin.

Grant weaved on his feet in the small space behind the copilot's seat.

Nick lay Mathilda down in the aisle, then reset Grant's

oxygen mask over his face. Rather than trying to shout through the thin air loudly enough to be audible over the shrieking wind, he pushed Grant toward the copilot's seat. He flopped down like such a rag doll that Nick was half afraid he'd be sucked out the missing windshield to tumble down into the blue waters below.

But the air pressure had balanced and no wind pushed through from the cabin. Instead it battered and swirled about the cockpit space. Bracing his feet wide against the bitterly cold torrent, Nick clipped Grant into the harness.

Putting his mouth close by Grant's ear, he shouted, "Time to save our asses!" Grant was the only other flight-qualified officer aboard.

Grant nodded once, a second time as if gathering himself together, then reached for the flight controls.

Nick thumped him on the shoulder, the only kind of recognition that could be felt in the hammering gusts, then dragged Mathilda aft.

Past the slumped Rowena, his own empty workstation, and the other staff—several bleeding from their ears or eyes at the sudden pressure change, probably desperate for someone to tell them what to do. Several of them were doubled over in obvious agony. The sudden decompression from the normal seven-thousand-foot cabin pressure to thirty-nine-thousand, under twenty percent of what they'd experienced at sea level a few short hours ago, had bubbles of nitrogen forming in their joints. The comms operator lay unmoving on her console with her eyes wide open—something had blown out in her brain.

Nick tugged Mathilda aft to the crew rest area.

He should go and check on his commander. He'd never served under anyone like her and knew he'd never again have the chance.

He should go forward and get the pilot; Nick hadn't thought to check Boller's pulse.

Rowena's report to Command had only the barest information: location and loss of pilots, a crossing aircraft. Nothing about the Falcon or its laser. He knew far more now and should call it in.

Yet none of those things seemed more important than sitting beside Mathilda Jackson. He put a ceiling-dropped oxygen mask loosely over her face—but didn't give it the tug that would start oxygen flowing and prolong the inevitable.

Nick felt the shift when Grant finally nosed the plane down.

Not too fast, mate. Not too fast. Get back into the oxygen too soon and her body might survive. Her brain would have already suffered permanent debilitation from oxygen deprivation.

Nick held Mathilda's fine hand between both of his, one finger slid onto her wrist pulse.

An absolute head-turner, he'd skipped lust and jumped straight to gone on her the first day they'd met. That charming lilt leftover from her German immigrant heritage distilled by a generation in Oz. Her amiable smile and trusting ways. She was one of those people glad to share her deepest thoughts if asked. Inviting him to do the same.

They'd had a couple of *friendly lunches* together and he'd been gearing up to ask her on a date when Grant had crashed onto the scene. She'd fallen for his charm before Nick realized what was happening.

He couldn't begrudge Grant his good fortune; he was Mathilda's choice. But—

The small cold hand in his warmed slowly, too slowly. That was good. Little or no heat came from inside her—incongruous with all the warmth that had come from her heart. She'd treated him as if he weren't some beast of an overgrown water buffalo. But the only joules of energy seeping into her hands came from his two clumsy meat hooks.

He squeezed her fingers and tried to imagine her squeezing his back, but even pretending didn't make it so.

By the time Grant leveled out the plane at a lower altitude, her pulse still beat. The rhythm faltered worse than a child's attempt to play *Für Elise* on the piano, but it continued.

Please, don't survive this, Mathilda. He spoke to her body, knowing the woman inside was already gone.

He didn't know what made him look out the window. It wasn't a typical habit as there were very few windows on an E-7A Wedgetail: the cockpit, the small circular window on the main passenger door, and the ones here in the crew rest area. Rowena never came back here during a flight except to grab some tucker to take back to her desk, so he did the same.

The Falcon 2000 flew alongside. Outlined perfectly against the rich blue of the sky at altitude.

Now he knew why Rowena McCain had ordered the pilots to get away from the Falcon, only to be answered by their screams. The flight pattern of the Falcon had made no sense in altitude or direction unless—unless they were there specifically to kill the E-7A Wedgetail. This plane.

He saw the beam that would finish the deed. Deep-red flashes pulsed from the fixture under the fuselage of the Falcon; so dark that he knew most of the energy was actually infrared and only a little of it spilled into the visible spectrum. The target looked to be forward. The Wedgetail's cockpit —again.

Nick knew of only three countries with military lasers powerful enough to melt the windows with their heat while burning the pilots so badly.

China, the US, and Israel.

Nick couldn't hear Grant's scream all the way back here, but he could feel it.

The plane felt as if it had stumbled in midair, then began an uncontrolled plunge.

Nick fastened his seatbelt one-handed. He clipped the one around Mathilda's waist, though she was past caring. He wasn't.

Her heartbeats were slowing, each farther apart than the prior one, until he could count the seconds between them.

Two seconds between beats as the plane began a spiraling roll.

He should say something to ease her passage.

Now three.

As always, with women who attracted him...

Three again.

...he had no idea what words to offer.

He kept her hand clasped in both of his through the 737's sickening gyrations. Rolling left. Right. Leveling out. Rolling again.

He ignored the flashes through the window of land, sky, sea, and again the sky.

Three.

Nick Nelson managed to count to four before the jet plowed into the ground.

His last thought—before he never had the chance to count *five*—was about that fitting under the belly of the Falcon 2000 jet.

What was an Israeli Iron Beam military laser doing over the Strait of Malacca?

4

____

Cawangan Khas
Royal Malaysia Police, Special Branch
Complex 3, Kuala Lumpur, Malaysia

HER BELT VIBRATED, ONCE.

Rachel Yung waited until the end of the meeting. Despite the importance of that single vibration, no one must ever suspect that phone's existence. Neither Lee, her most trusted assistant seated to her left, nor the assistant chief to her right reacted. As it should be. Especially not the assistant chief—an appointee forced upon her by the Minister of Home Affairs and bound to be a spy for him.

Twenty-seven long minutes passed before the others filed out of her office. This week's content had been mundane. No new or immediate threats, but it remained necessary to review existing ones in detail—if only to lock them into her department heads' brains. The eight of them sat around the table in her office. She'd chosen an uninviting white table with only enough seats for each department head and kept it narrow. It forced them together, less able to set up the mental space of their own camp.

Close enough that a photo could be held out without having to be passed around except for the finest details. In the open center of the table, she'd taped down a map of the region. Not just from the Peninsula to Borneo, but from India to Papua New Guinea and from northern Australia to Taiwan. *That* was their threat region, not just the six they shared borders with.

Yet the news wasn't all bad.

Malaysia was buffered from the rapidly decaying military coup in Myanmar by Thailand stretching between them, but it couldn't be wholly ignored. There existed the necessity to plan for what happened if the pro-democracy forces managed to put down the military—again. Military personnel, along with all the gold and other negotiables they could convert, would come flooding out of the country looking for a safe haven. Should Malaysia act as a sanctuary for Myanmar's junta? Or bury their bonesdeep? Which was no more than they deserved. The debate hadn't settled yet, but she was favoring the latter.

As only her vote counted, there existed no doubt about the outcome of that scenario. But she let them quibble and seek allies for their point of view. First, she didn't wish to disillusion her staff unnecessarily. Second, it would be convenient if they eventually decided on her chosen course of action without her having to trump their play.

Of all unlikely people, it was the head of logistics who tipped the group consensus in the proper direction. Rachel made a mental note to watch him carefully—worth grooming or potential threat?

Overly liberal Indonesia, and especially their media exacerbating every minor international disagreement with Malaysia, continued to be irritating but, also as usual, of little consequence.

Singapore represented a thorn of such pain as to verge

upon the intolerable. For over a hundred years they'd been bleeding Malaysia's Johor River for their water supply. Every attempt to renegotiate the deal had impossibly been twisted. Past leaders had entered meetings with strict agendas—then returned with extended leases and the requirement to build new reservoirs at Malaysia's expense to bleed Johor State drier than it already had been. All for Singapore's benefit.

But Rachel understood; they weren't to be denied. Along with Indonesia, Singapore controlled the narrow southern mouth of the Strait of Malacca. That made them unassailable unless conquered outright, which no power in the world would tolerate. Also, the tiny pinprick of a nation had the most sophisticated and well-equipped military in the region. Most annoying.

The West, China, and India all had agendas that would make the eighteenth-century divisions of Japan and China look civilized—if they were given half the chance to implement them. These were reviewed quickly, as their impact upon Malaysia would be difficult to spot ahead of time or prepare for in advance as the impact would range somewhere between massive and catastrophic.

Special Branch had put down hundreds of terrorists' plots since its founding, though the Islamic State was being the most troublesome since the decades-long effort necessary to put down the Communist Insurgency after World War II. Given the chance, she'd drop a nuke on the Chinese personally. One in Laos wouldn't hurt her feelings either. And Saudi Arabia and Iran both deserved them for their creation and support of the IS. It was fortunate for them all that Malaysia was *not* a nuclear power or she'd be sorely tempted.

Special Branch wasn't the military. Technically they were the counterterrorism intelligence arm of the Royal Malaysia Police. Of course, the last time she'd kept the RMP in the loop on anything important had been the day she became SB's Chief of Police. No mandate in the country's laws mentioned Special Branch, but she made sure to keep all the...*information* handy on those who created their budgets to ensure that SB's only ever increased. Enemies of the state—foreign or domestic, as defined by her department alone—experienced severely foreshortened lifespans.

As the meeting broke up, she waved off her assistant, who would hover constantly if Rachel let him. It was Lee's job to hover and be of service, but not now. Not with this. Nothing announced by that vibration in her belt could possibly fall under his purview. This had nothing to do with Special Branch operations—though she certainly borrowed their task forces when necessary.

Once he'd departed, she crossed from the conference table to her desk and hit the lock switch. Now it would require a significant breaching charge to enter her office on the top floor of Complex 3's headquarters. The room had been scanned for bugs, of course—every morning—but she turned on an EM masker just in case.

Only then did she open the inside clasp on her belt and extract the credit-card-sized cell phone from its custom pocket. She'd made the wide belt a personal style ever since the days it had contained a stiletto blade when she'd first been a field operative. The greatest weapon of the *modern* age could now fit in the palm of her closed hand.

The text message was short and to the point: *Wedgetail down.*

A chill ran down her spine. Her contact had warned her something big was coming and to be ready. But this?

Three billion Malaysian Ringgits worth of airplane and twelve highly trained people...down. No news had reached her of it, though it certainly would soon enough. Or perhaps it would be lost at sea without a trace like Malaysian flight MH370. Either way, within twenty-four hours the news of its disappearance would have spread far and wide. But, for the moment, she had the reins of the steed.

Her contact had refused any meeting—she was still old-school enough to want to see him face-to-face before agreeing to anything. Despite his attempts at anonymity, she'd managed to track down his details. Hiding in this modern age grew more difficult by the hour. On him? She'd built a sufficient profile to reach out and *touch* him or his family anytime she needed to.

She'd also made sure that it would be much harder for him to do the same. After decades of surviving the communists, IS, and Malaysian politics, if he came after her, he'd be fencing with shadows until she decided to eradicate him.

Even the go-between who had connected them was no longer connected to anything except the ocean floor. That hadn't even been her doing—technically. A broken helicopter had plunged him and his mistress into the strait's depths while en route to the Pangkor Laut island resort. All evidence pointed to the mistress' angry husband, who Rachel had anonymously tipped off about the affair.

She'd done all she could, preparing to fight the man for her share. After all, she was the one on the front lines taking the risks.

Yet he'd demanded nothing. *I give you the information, you use it however you see fit. Sometimes I ask a question. End of deal.* Definitely her kind of deal, except it raised every red flag of caution from decades of work along the clandestine edges of Special Branch. But his information had always proven to be solid, though so far only in small ways as they tested each other out. A few million here, another five there. His tips had never failed her, and he'd still never asked for a thing in return beyond the occasional update on Malaysian security assets at the time.

Yesterday he'd asked what security would be aloft today.

The Australian E-7A Wedgetail.

No Malaysian assets?

None. The Wedgetail had proven so effective that the RMAF had decided to save money by not overlapping with the Aussie's patrols.

And now she knew why he'd asked.

Yes, it was awful. Yes, she'd mourn for them later. But she'd already wasted twenty-seven, now twenty-eight minutes of this opportunity. That couldn't have been helped; any interruption to the weekly meeting of all department heads would raise suspicions among her subordinates. She wasn't foolish enough to think she could do everything herself, so she'd placed the best people she could find in each position. However, along with brains and skill came ambition.

The weekly meeting was her hammer to remind them of the danger should they test her defenses.

Before her long hair had gone silver, people had often mistaken her for the actress Michelle Yeoh. Born less than three hundred kilometers apart on opposite sides of the capital of Kuala Lumpur, they were both underestimated for their slim figures. Except while Yeoh was being crowned Miss Malaysia, Rachel had been killing communist insurgents in the jungle. Fifty years she'd been a fighter—she'd started young—first in the jungle of trees, then in the jungle of politics. It had honed her like the fine blade. She now kept her stiletto on her desk as a letter opener to remind others not to underestimate her. She kept it razor sharp.

But now the question waited. How long until the Australians or some other busybody once more flew security over the Strait of Malacca? Hours, yes. But days? After such an incident, there would be time, investigations, and debates. Perhaps *weeks* as these investigations always seemed to take forever to unravel causes. And the Australians were unlikely to risk another of their oh-so-precious planes until they had answers.

If it had gone down at sea…months?

A day, a week, or a month, she was the very best placed to take advantage of the situation.

Rachel turned her chair to look over the wide view of Kuala Lumpur. The city might barely make the world's top fifty for size, but it boasted four of the twenty tallest buildings anywhere: the Exchange 106, Merdeka 118, and the PETRONAS Twin Towers. No one, but no one was as insecure as a Malaysian male, except perhaps those two idiots running China and Russia into ruin.

She shouldn't complain. When The Exchange building had surpassed the PETRONAS Twin Towers by less than two meters, it had made little difference. It was an unimaginative and lifeless slab when compared with the two penile conical towers of the PETRONAS building.

But, when the hundred and eighteen floors of Merdeka 118 had been finished last year—second tallest in the world after the UAE's Burj Khalifa (an entire *nation* with a severe inferiority complex)—it had surpassed both the PETRONAS Towers and The Exchange by over two hundred meters. The business migration out of PETRONAS into Merdeka, now the luxury address of all Southeast Asia, had vacated vast swathes of the PETRONAS Tower Two. Tower One still belonged to the national gas and oil giant who had named the building after themselves.

Rachel had taken the opportunity to acquire the top office floor of Tower Two for a song. Even better, it had been paid for by Special Branch, not her own funds, though they'd never know it.

She had considered shifting her office there but decided it was better maintained as a private enterprise. Instead, she'd renovated half of the floor as her home and given over the other half to her Chief of Operations.

After double-checking the office signal jammers, she selected a secure outside line and dialed.

"Yes, ma'am." No need for more, this line was unused except by her. Across the three kilometers separating them, she felt she could see her personal Chief of Operations looking back at her.

"Tell the captain that it's time to go to work."

"Yes, *ma'am!*" His enthusiasm, she knew, was genuine. He'd worked ships along the Malacca for three decades before it cost him a hand, a loss that dumped him ashore.

"And give a heads-up to our friends over in Tower One." Yet another reason to maintain a space in PETRONAS Tower Two. It placed her people a mere sixty-meter skybridge from the national gas and oil company—a Fortune 250 operation.

"Yes, ma'am."

They both hung up their phones. Over time, a great deal of information had flowed across that bridge in both directions. PETRONAS' shipping director had learned it was to his advantage to keep her and her people well informed.

It was high time a fresh slice of that particular five percent of the nation's GDP flowed into her private accounts.

Royal blood ran in her veins, as it did so many in Malaysia, but it felt as if it had concentrated in her family rather than dissipated as it had in so many. The class of the Malaysian elite was decidedly lacking of late.

Rachel had *earned* the title of Queen of Special Branch; she'd heard the whispers, though not acknowledged them. The fear she could strike into other's hearts with the slightest gesture was all the satisfaction she needed. But she also reigned as Queen of the family enterprise, and none contested her there.

She turned off the jammers and called her assistant. "An Australian patrol plane has gone down. Find out where. If it's on our soil send…" Who were the least likely to handle it well?

"…a standard security team from the Royal Air Force."

5

———

Changi Airport, Singapore

"Look, I agreed to Australia. I never, *ever* agreed to visiting Tennant Creek." Holly hadn't won the argument in Seattle. Or on the flight across the Pacific to Singapore. In an hour, they'd be in the air to Darwin, and she'd probably lose the argument there again as well. Why was she doomed to keep revisiting her childhood home deep in the Outback, a place she'd never intended to see again after Mother had thrown her out at sixteen? And for some incomprehensible reason, this time the other three members of Miranda's NTSB air-crash investigation team were along for the ride.

"Not my doing, Hol. That was all Miranda."

"Mike, seriously. I keep making the same points and it keeps getting me the same result. The definition of dumb-ass stupid. You're the smart one here. Think up something new. Get me out of this!"

"Out of this, here? But it's lovely." He waved an expansive hand. Then he looked at her as if she'd committed some crime. "Hold it there, Harper. Did you just pay me a compliment?"

41

"You goofball." She poked her finger into his ribs, not sharply, but enough to let him know she was serious.

He was right, though, it *was* lovely. They stood in a giant butterfly garden built inside Singapore's Changi Airport. Fifty meters long, half that high and wide, and roofed with a great curved glass ceiling like a crystalline Quonset hut. Inside grew a flowering tropical forest, complete with an actual two-story waterfall, viewing platforms high and low, and a thousand or so butterflies in every color imaginable.

Mike had taken her to a much smaller butterfly garden set up in a tent among the trees and gardens of the Seattle Arboretum. An actual date, which had been oddly sweet. Dating was a new aspect in their four years of sleeping together.

Strangest of all, she'd been charmed. *Her. Charmed.* Mike deserved another sharp poke for that, but she forced herself to behave. Had she caught terminal soft-in-the-head disease during that Swedish investigation?

The Arboretum's large butterfly tent, with a double-screened entrance, had been raised on a field of lush green grass. Outside the tent, the gardens had smelled of springtime. Inside, pots of tropical flowers were set about to entice the hundred or so butterflies released within. In retrospect, she could see that most of the creatures had clung mournfully to the screen, dreaming of flapping about in the wider world beyond.

Not here.

Amidst Singapore Airport's captive jungle, they hid in trees, rested on flowers, fed on pineapple slices left out for them. The sweet air rippled with the scent of flowers stirred by butterfly wings, making it even harder *not* to be charmed. In here, safe from predators and weather, they lived out their lives in perfect security. More comfortable, but still a gilded cage?

She sure as hell didn't want to crawl back into the dog-kennel-sized cage of her childhood in Tennant Creek—definitely not gilded, not even in hindsight.

"Seriously, Holly?" Mike slid an arm around her waist. "I think you're fighting a lost cause. How many people do you know who can change Miranda's mind once she gets an idea?"

"You?"

"I honestly tried, Holly. I mean, I'm curious to see where you grew up, too, but I tried for your sake. It didn't work."

"Damn you for being decent. It makes it that much harder to complain." She stared at a white, yellow, orange, and black-trimmed butterfly that a nearby sign identified as a Painted Jezebel. Perfect. Just perfect.

A painted, immoral lady who always got what she wanted. *Stupid butterfly.* She'd gladly be immoral if it would get her out of the inevitable. After all, doing her best to be a good and moral member of the team had earned her what? A trip to Tennant Creek, Northern Territory, Australia. And once Mike or Miranda saw where she came from, they'd never think decently of her again.

"Why the hell can't my past stay where it belongs?" Because once *she* saw it, Holly couldn't imagine thinking decently of *herself* ever again.

"Like in the past?"

"Like in the past."

"You figure out that one, let me know."

Yet Mike moved through the present while his past never touched him. Mr. Smooth-and-Together. "How the hell did we end up together?"

"Just lucky, I guess."

That didn't sound right, but she had no better answer.

It had all begun over dinner a few months ago.

The four of them hadn't talked once about Andi's betrayal or her recent return to the team—not even tangentially. But the topic of a vacation came up. Their first attempt at a team vacation, hiking the Herriot Way around the Yorkshire Dales, had been the prelude to the unmitigated disaster of Captain Andi Wu being thrown off the team for eight months.

Go somewhere different? Andi had suggested.

The antipodes of the UK, Miranda had declared. That turned out to be in the Pacific Ocean south of New Zealand. Which had brought up the topic of Holly's homeland in Australia. Miranda had declared that as sufficiently *antipodal* and noted that she had an interest in the Australian Outback, based on Holly's stories of her survival adventures there. *You grew up there. You can be our guide.*

Somehow a trip into the Barkly Tablelands had decided everything—leaving Holly to fight the line with all the effectiveness of a dying fish dragged onto the parched sands of her past. Shit! When had she started thinking in poetic garbage?

And her adventures? Like some pathetic Victorian explorer hell-bent on dying on camelback out in the Never Never of Central Australia? Not even that glamorous. More like her *escape* from Tennant Creek into the Barkly to get *away* from her then-life. Not that the region was such a charmer. The arid grasslands were known mostly for its bountiful species of venomous snakes.

"Andi? Should I ask Andi to try?"

Mike kissed her on the nose and almost earned a fist on his own. "Andi is still on pins and needles around Miranda. She's not going to risk rocking that boat for a single second."

Holly sighed. It was too true. Andi had only been back half a year. Everyone was much happier—even Holly herself, which she hadn't expected—but Andi was playing it very cool. And Andi was typically plenty chill to start with. It made her suspicious side wonder what Andi was hiding this time, as if she'd dare.

Even now, neither Miranda nor Andi joined them inside the

butterfly garden to help kill the time between connecting flights. Meg wasn't permitted in the garden despite her status as an autism therapy dog. *If my dog can't go because she might eat a butterfly, then I won't go.* To which Andi had added, *If you don't go, then I don't.*

Instead, they sat out by the blue tile pool in the middle of the concourse, with Meg perched on the wide ledge to watch koi as big as she was swimming lazily by.

"If I pray for a miracle and actually receive a dispensation from this abuse, does it mean that I need to believe in your Catholic God?"

"Hey! Not my God!" Mike held up his hands defensively. "He and I had a permanent falling out a couple decades ago. If I had to pick one, I'd probably go with worshipping Diana the Huntress. A scantily clad Holly Harper look-alike, bearing a bow and arrow, running through the woods with her long hair streaming in the wind. Speaks Greek instead of Strine, but that can't be any harder to understand. Yes, there's a definite image to improve my mood." He scooped his fingers through her gold-blonde hair and brushed it out behind her.

He played with it more than ever since she'd started growing it out for him—mostly. Down to the middle of her shoulder blades and he was a goner. She also might be having a grudge match with the D/CIA Clarissa Reese, so proud of her perfectly coifed ponytail. By the next time the woman trimmed it, Holly would pull ahead.

"Guys are the strangest critters anywhere." And *she* was the one pointing a finger? Competing with the waste of space Clarissa? Maybe she'd hack off a foot or two the next time she had her knife. A butterfly no bigger than George Washington's head on a dollar bill landed on the fingertip she'd raised to make her point. Its wings sported black-on-white concentric circles, which outlined an 88 in the center.

"Stranger than that?" Mike's tease didn't sit any better than the guillotine of her near future.

"Shut up." She didn't like the butterfly arguing in Mike's favor.

Having proven its point, it fluttered away seeking someone else to humiliate.

"Isn't Diana also the virgin goddess and the protector of childbirth?" Holly wondered where she'd picked up that tidbit as a bright orange something fluttered inches past her nose with wings as big as her palm. "So, are you saying you never want to have sex again or that you want to have a child with me? How do those two go together in one goddess, anyway?"

When Mike didn't answer, she looked over at him. He was studying a blue-and-black butterfly no bigger than the end of his thumb it perched on—too intently.

"No way, Mike Munroe. Tell me you did *not* just go there."

He grimaced. "Only for a second, and I assure you that it wasn't intentional."

"I should've stopped at the scantily clad image of me running through the woods."

"Don't forget the streaming hair." He waved a hand to send the butterfly aloft, then wiped his forehead and didn't quite meet her gaze. "Uh, yeah. Let's stick with that."

Their relationship, since the mess in Sweden, had been better than ever. But there was this growing...*thing* now about taking The Next Step. Or not. Whatever that meant anyway.

Neither of them had mentioned it, of course. So far, they'd both remained careful *not* to go there, *until* she'd stomped her Army boot in it.

Real smooth, Harper.

6

———————

"Hey, you two." Andi stepped up. "Oh, I know those looks."

Holly winced, inside. "Go to hell, Wu. You do not. And if you say them aloud, just remember that I'm like a foot taller than you." Though she didn't forget how fast Andi was. Andi's nervous system had been wired whole levels higher than even her own former Special Operations one.

"Eight and a quarter inches, but I'm not keeping track."

"I thought you weren't coming in here. Thought we were finally safe from you here with the butterflies." Because for all of Andi's caution, seeing how happy Miranda and Andi were together made her feel like even more of a shit for blowing them apart last year over something as trivial as a life-threatening betrayal. Not that she'd been wrong. But, weirdly, that hadn't made her right either.

"You wish. Besides, Miranda got a call."

"From?"

"Drake. I didn't wait around to hear why, but I bet we're on the move."

Holly shivered despite the tropical warmth maintained for the butterflies.

Mike's comforting hand sliding up and down her spine emphasized the shiver, which defeated his purpose.

General Drake Nason was the Chairman of the Joint Chiefs of Staff. When he called, there was always a disaster in the offing.

"It seems that your prayer got answered, Holly." Mike whispered into her ear.

"Yeah," she'd asked for a distraction, but...bloody hell! Somewhere a major plane had gone down ugly. "Now we're wrestling with brown snakes."

"Is that bad?"

"The Eastern Brown is so mean that they make me look as nice as Andi. By the way, there's plenty of them in the Barkly. Just so you know."

Mike and Andi both laughed, but thankfully it was Mike who managed to speak first. "Come on, no one is that mean."

"Most poisonous in the world too." She offered an implied glare at Andi, which the little American-born Chinese woman blithely ignored.

"Direct-line relative of yours?" Mike asked.

7

———————

BY THE TIME THEY REACHED MIRANDA, SHE STOOD AT THE CENTER of three uniformed soldiers, clutching a growling Meg to her chest and staring at the terminal's flooring.

"Crap!" Andi raced toward them.

The three-man well-armed strike team, Holly knew their type on sight, had formed a cordon about Miranda. People along the concourse were scuttling aside to steer clear of the corralled *terrorist* clutching her Glen of Imaal Terrier. People simply didn't come more meek than the slender, five-foot-four, genius air-crash investigator.

Holly raced on Andi's heels but needn't have bothered. The guard who tried to stop Andi would have been flattened if his companion hadn't been quick to grab him. Andi ricocheted off the body check—worthy of the *Mighty Jills* national hockey team—and went nose-to-nose with the third one, an officer. Which was a good trick as he was unusually tall for a Chinese man, even taller than Mike.

"Back. The. Fuck. Off." Andi's tone was dead flat and *did* sound as dangerous as an over-poked brown snake.

Despite his training and the double-bar rank of lieutenant

on his chest strap, he stumbled back a step. Initial shock, Holly had seen it before. And the measure of him? He took the step forward again forcing each of them to crane their necks to face each other.

When the other two had recovered their balance, Holly stepped in to intercept them. "Oi. I wouldn't be doing anything silly, mates. Just stand fast unless you want to go for a swim with the fishes."

One made a grab for her. Classic two-chevron corporal move.

Snagging his thumb, she leveraged him face first into the koi pool before he had a chance to yelp in pain. That noise surfaced as big underwater bubbles. All the koi shot to the far end of the pool.

She also had his sidearm out of its holster and pointed at his sergeant's face. He was only a meter away, in range of an easy disarming grab—if she hadn't been trained by Australia's best. Instead, he froze as his companion began struggling.

"Aw, mate. You're not even going to try?"

He made no move.

"You okay, Wu?" Holly was turned the wrong way. Her overlong hair wouldn't flip out of the way to see what was going on there. That would teach her to try to please a man.

"Haven't killed him—yet!" Andi's snarl was all the answer Holly needed.

The corporal with his head in the pool was starting to struggle in earnest. Holly released him and he collapsed onto the airport's floor, hacking and spitting out fish-flavored water. She jammed his weapon back into his holster, never looking away from the sergeant.

"Sit," she nodded toward the wide tile bench around the pool. "Don't even so much as think of moving. We clear, mate?"

He hesitated.

"You don't want to be messing with a Snake Eater, do you?"

One of the many nicknames SASR had earned over the years. The Special Air Service Regiment was Australia's answer to the UK's SAS and the US Army's Delta Force. Holly had served for nine glorious years—until they weren't so glorious all of a sudden.

The sergeant's eyes widened before he nodded and sat down so fast he almost went into the pool himself. Only after she nodded permission did he lean down to check over his buddy, keeping his butt firmly planted as he did.

Other airport security were rushing over, but the lieutenant in front of Andi raised a hand to stop them. She, Miranda, and Andi were soon inside a circle of armed guards. Mike too! He always stood back and observed when things went dynamic, at least until it was time for him to step in and do his *calm-everyone-down* thing. Not this time. He stood directly in front of the still-frozen Miranda. Facing outward.

In the sudden silence, Miranda very slowly leaned forward until both her and Meg's foreheads rested against Mike's back. Meg snuggled her head under Miranda's chin. Mike stood solid. Holly supposed it was a good thing she was already gone on the man or she might go weak in the knees.

Andi appeared far too angry to speak, so Holly took a lesson from Mike and stepped to the fore.

"So, Lieutenant. What fuck knuckle issued a horseshit order for you to arrest Miranda?"

"We were sent to *escort* Ms. Chase to an emergency flight. There's a helo inbound to take her somewhere. That's all I know. And who the hell are you?"

She held out a hand. "Sergeant Holly Harper of the Australian Army—released."

He looked very nonplussed and certainly didn't shake it.

"Said she was a Snake Eater," the sergeant called out.

"Might have."

That got a reaction, though still no handshake. He looked

down at Andi. "Which makes you what?" Probably not his smoothest move.

Holly answered before Andi could kill the guy. "She's the one even I wouldn't mess with."

Andi slanted a surprised glance her direction.

Holly shrugged. "Hey, I may be only a stupid grunt, but I do learn eventually." She turned to the Lieutenant. "She's Spec Ops but an officer-type. Also released, but very, very awkward to tangle with."

Still angry as a cut snake, Andi managed the barest nod before turning to the lieutenant.

Holly addressed him. "You spook Miranda again, mate, I can't be accountable for *her* actions." She patted Andi atop the head like she'd pet Miranda's small terrier—no reaction said *angrier* than a cut snake—then glared at him. "Or mine."

"But all we did was ask her to come with us." Not quite a whine, but he knew he was out of his depth. The circle of airport security were slow standing down. The sergeant had risen carefully to his feet once his corporal sat upright, though he still leaned heavily against the side of the pool massaging his hand. The sergeant circled around dismissing the general airport security folks.

Mike stepped forward, Miranda followed close behind, staying safe in his shadow. So cliché that Holly almost laughed, woman staying in a man's shadow. Not her!

"You were well inside her personal space, Lieutenant," Mike's voice sounded terribly reasonable. "Did you touch her?"

"She wouldn't look up. Just my hand on her arm to get her attention. Nothing more, I promise you. But she went all...weird."

Mike was shaking his head. "Don't they give you guys any diversity training? She's autistic. Meg's vest, which is labeled Therapy Dog, is another hint to watch for next time. She hates being touched unexpectedly. And if you gave her an *order* to go with you…"

The lieutenant's grimace answered that. His belt radio squawked, "Lieutenant Noor, where's my package? The helo is only five minutes out."

"Oh, this is going to be so much fun. May I borrow that?"

The guy eyed him carefully.

Holly unclipped the radio hanging on the lieutenant's shoulder harness before he could respond and handed it to Mike. They traded smiles as he keyed the Talk button. Better him than her, because she'd cut the guy a new—

"Give me one good reason to not put your *package* on a plane back to the US of A."

She and Andi both shot him a double thumbs-up. Even Miranda peeked around Mike's shoulder to see Mike acting so out of character.

"Who is this?" the radio voice demanded.

"This is the guy with a direct line to President Roy Cole of the aforementioned country and isn't afraid to use it. Now just chill and make damned sure we do *not* meet you at the gate."

Andi's smile went feral, and probably would have matched Holly's own if she hadn't been so surprised at Mike stepping up like that.

When there was no reply, he handed the radio to the lieutenant.

"Thank you, Lieutenant Noor." He glanced over his shoulder. "You good to go, Miranda?"

Holly spotted the top of a careful nod, double-checked it with Andi, who had the best read of all of them on Miranda's emotional state, then faced the lieutenant. "That's your cue, mate. Lead the way."

The sergeant helped the corporal, still soaking wet from the chest up, to his feet. He very carefully didn't look her way.

8

MIKE HAD BEEN, AS USUAL, LOOKING THE WRONG WAY AS THEY
were whisked out of the terminal through a security door and
into a waiting service vehicle.

In Antarctica, he'd kept a careful eye on the Chinese agent
—based on past experience, that was the major threat. Yet the
Russian had been the one who almost killed all of them,
ultimately only managing to kill himself and a fifty-million
dollar airplane.

Mike had been watching over Miranda in the UK while
Holly threw Andi off the team without even asking his opinion.
Then, he'd been so worried about Miranda on her own that
he'd completely missed Holly drifting away from him until it
was almost too late.

Serving on Miranda's team might have changed his life, but
he was coming to think that keeping Holly in that life might be
even more important. Four years they'd been together. Four
years. He still couldn't equate that with any past version of
himself that he recognized.

Future versions of Mike Monroe? He'd always focused on
the here and now, happy enough when a pretty woman passed

his way. Holly wasn't the most beautiful woman he'd ever been with, though not far off the mark. She was too...*alive* to be rated by her beauty alone. He hadn't seen any of that coming.

And today he'd been watching how magical the woman looked while surrounded by butterflies. What had slipped past his guard was Holly's honest distress. When she and Andi had taken on a trio of armed soldiers minutes later, he hadn't thought once about himself. Instead he stepped straight into the fray to protect her.

He'd frozen once there. Had Miranda hiding her face against his back been a bulldozer, he still wouldn't have moved. What had finally broken him loose was not wanting some stupid commander to overreact and order an attack on Holly.

Not on *the team.*

Not on *him.*

On Holly Harper! That's how far she'd slithered about him, like one of her brown snakes. Far enough to make him stupid. He was never stupid about people. Well, other than the one notable exception that had destroyed the latest version of his old life. His closest brush with death had been his last day as an FBI mole—at least his closest before he met Holly and Miranda. An old life, which he'd been wearing like a re-used Halloween costume, worn to ill-fitting tatters.

No costume here. Even using his real name, which he hadn't done much since escaping the orphanage.

And now? He *still* hadn't learned his lesson.

This time he'd kept a close eye on the Singaporean soldiers. They were hustled out of Terminal 3 and into the blazing midmorning tropical heat. The light sweat he'd acquired from the warm butterfly jungle and cold sweat from dealing with the armed soldiers had evaporated in a single flash of steam—to be immediately replaced by the thick humidity that insisted humans should never have settled here to begin with.

Their van had stopped briefly at Gate A9 to gather their

baggage from the loading Darwin flight. Rather than racing down the runway's perimeter road, they were cleared to weave through the massive jets all sidling up to the terminals, and straight across multiple taxi and runways. Complete with a pair of escort police and their flashing blue lights.

At the far side of Changi Airport, they raced up to a massive Chinook helicopter. He remembered only too well the investigation of the one utterly shattered in a wildfire. The size of a Greyhound bus with an enormous three-blade rotor mounted atop either end, this one looked solid enough—as he was sure the other one had before it had been shattered into a thousand pieces and scattered over the Washington State wilderness.

He flew and understood fixed-wing aircraft. Helicopters, even with an expert like Andi Wu at the controls, simply felt wrong. That they worked at all was as strange as...being in a relationship with the same woman for four years.

That's when he turned and saw what he should have been watching—not the now obsequiously polite airport security team.

An F/A-18F Super Hornet jet fighter had rolled up close behind them, its engine noise masked by the Chinook's beating rotors and idling turbines. A man climbed down out of the rear seat and was greeted with an enthusiastic hug by Holly. At least the guy had the decency to look uncomfortable, thumping her a couple times on the back.

Holly hooked an arm through his and dragged him over to Miranda. Mike moved close so that he didn't miss even more than he already had.

A few inches shorter than Holly, he was as dark as she was light, all the way from his hair to his skin to his frown.

"Miranda, this is Barty Kirwan. He's the jerk Chief Commissioner of the ATSB who sent us to Antarctica and almost got us all killed." An introduction she made in the most cheerful tones as if he'd sent them a humorous Get Well card. "Barty, this is Miranda Chase, miracle worker at the NTSB in a small package."

He held out a hand. Miranda responded with her standard stare and no shake. Most autistics hated to be touched, especially by strangers. Andi followed through with no discernible pause, taking his hand and making her own introduction. They were becoming a two-woman comedy routine. How many times had this exact scene played out?

"And this is Mike Munroe. Don't worry, no one understands what he does, least of all him."

Mike knew *exactly* what he did for the team. "Except for when you're getting missiles shot at us, Hol, I'm the one who keeps the team alive."

Again Holly's blink of surprise, just like when he'd stepped up to face Lieutenant Noor's boss on the radio. She, the one who needed his skills most, was predictably the one who understood them the least.

Holly turned to the *jerk* Chief Commissioner. "What are you doing here, boss? We're on the hop, you know."

Barty waved at the Super Hornet fighter jet now being refueled from a roaring tanker truck, adding to the cacophony. He shouted to be heard, "Two hours ago, I was sitting down to breakfast with the wife and m'folks in Katherine."

Mike looked down. No ring. But he'd said *wife*. He beat his own stupid jealousy into submission, then had to wonder: since when had he been jealous of anything Holly ever did? More often than he'd like to admit, though not once had it had any real basis.

"Now I'm here," Barty continued. "The closest Royal Australian Air Force Accident Investigation Team is down the Alice, tied up in some other kinda brouhaha. They seconded me to the RAAF and shoved me aboard that thing." He held out his hands to show he didn't have so much as a toothbrush. "This your fault, Harper?"

"Hey, Barty. That hurts. You know I don't blow up planes unless I'm told to."

"No one should blow up planes!" Miranda shouted. Which was good in one way, her voice was typically so soft she'd never be heard over the idling Chinook or the truck pumping the Hornet's tanks full of JP-5. But it was bad in that almost nothing caused Miranda to shout unless she was barely hanging onto the edge of her sanity.

"First, it's not very nice. And second, it destroys something so lovely."

"And it gives us more work," Andi added.

"It does," Miranda confirmed. "But that doesn't make it a good thing."

Barty looked over at him.

"Hard to argue when they're right." Mike pointed out in case Barty was thinking of confronting Miranda on her odd words.

He answered with a grunt. Then asked, "So, what went down?"

They all looked at each other.

Mike would laugh if it wasn't so sad. "Miranda, what exactly did General Nason say when he called you?"

"First he said *Hello, Miranda.* To which I answered—"

"Sorry to cut you off," Mike had been testing different ways to interrupt her while causing minimal upset when she went off the needed track. Miranda hated incomplete thoughts even more than she hated being touched unexpectedly. This time he only elicited a blink of surprise. "I meant what did he say about the crash?"

"He said, *We have a high-priority situation. I need you and your team in the air immediately, Miranda. Call when you're aloft.* I tried to get the intonation and timing as precise as I could, but my voice isn't as deep as his so imitating it is difficult. That's all I remember because that's when the lieutenant found me and started asking all of his questions and..." she began but didn't complete a touching gesture on her arm.

"Well, then, let's get aloft."

"Oh good. Then we can call him back. I've been worrying that I'd forget to do that. Very good, Mike. Yes, I like doing things in order."

As she said the last mostly to herself, he led her aboard the Chinook. He did it by the simple expedient of taking both her luggage and his own from the back of the van that had raced them here and walking up the helo's rear ramp. Miranda followed her gear with Meg trotting happily alongside.

The thirty-foot-long cargo bay was empty except for two loadmasters in green onesie flightsuits with multiple patches. They were handing out packets of earplugs.

"Do you know where we're going?" he asked a helmeted crewmember, which would afford some clue as to what was happening.

"No, sir." The woman responded cheerfully in excellent English. "Hopefully the pilots do."

"I hope so too."

The engines, which had been spun down to an idle, were climbing back up in pitch and noise level as they dropped their bags in a pile and moved to cluster together in the fold-down side seats.

Mike looked up in surprise as the ramp began closing. The sergeant and corporal who'd been part of their escort had stayed behind, but Lieutenant Noor had come aboard.

"You're with us?"

"The whole way," he tapped the face of his radio. "The Old Man wants me to ensure your safety as guests of Singapore."

"What's your clearance, Noor?"

"Clearance? Like passports?"

Which answered Mike's question.

"Oh, you mean security. As an officer I have a Confidential clearance."

The ramp clanked fully shut as the queasy slide of the helo's wheels leaving the ground signaled the hurry of their departure. Mike grabbed onto a handhold as did Noor.

"What's your first name, Lieutenant Noor?"

"Adiputera. It means first son or first prince. But everyone calls me Noor, and that is okay to do."

Mike tried to find a way to say it tactfully...but all he could come up with was, "Noor, uh, perhaps you could go sit forward with the loadmasters while we place a phone call."

He looked hurt but, after checking Mike's face, he finally staggered away, balancing against the bouncing of the flight. He said something to the man and woman up forward. They all three stared back at the team. So much for friendly beginnings.

"So, let's see what you got me into this time, Harper." Barty nodded to Miranda, "Time to place your call, I be thinking."

Miranda dialed and placed the phone on speaker, which was going to be a challenge. The two massive turboshaft engines capable of generating over nine thousand horsepower were mounted about two meters above their heads. The sound insulation consisted of a few thin sheets of hull metal and a containment shield in case the engine shattered. If it did, no amount of metal would save them, the Chinook would plummet to the ground in ever-so-many pieces. Sometimes Mike wished he knew far less about aircraft and could blithely enjoy the ride as he used to.

The five of them, including Barty, huddled around the phone and took out one earplug each.

"Hi, Miranda. Are you aloft? Yes, I can hear that you are. Can you hear me?"

"Barely," Mike shouted. "Please be sure to speak clearly, General."

"Roger that. Two hours and thirty-nine minutes ago, while on routine patrol over the Strait of Malacca, an E-7A Wedgetail belonging to the RAAF went down in Malaysian territory."

That had them all looking up at each other. The newest and best AEW&C—Airborne Early Warning & Control—platform ever lofted. Australia had been the first to adopt the new aircraft because of all the threats coming into the South China Sea and even Australian territorial waters from China. Now South Korea, Turkey, the UK, and the US were all ordering them as fast as they could be built. Per Miranda's standard practice, the team had made a study of them when the USAF had selected the platform for their future patrol aircraft.

After giving them a moment to absorb that, Drake continued, "We know very little. They reported an *irregular* aircraft in the area, then the loss of the pilots. There was no further communication."

That was definitely bad news.

"Some five minutes later, it descended in a regular fashion to a lower altitude. After briefly regaining level flight, it then plunged down and impacted the ground in the vicinity of Mount Ledang near the city of Malacca on the Malaysian Peninsula. There were no further transmissions. We do have a signal from the emergency locator transmitter and the Royal Malaysian Air Force has dispatched a security team. They've been told to search for survivors only and not to do anything else. A full Australian investigation team is being assembled but will probably be a full day for preparation and diplomatic clearances, so you're the team on site. This is a highly sensitive airframe and its key components and data must be secured, even if it means destroying the aircraft. You are our closest asset."

Drake stopped so abruptly that they all leaned forward quickly as if stumbling. It was a wonder that they didn't bang heads.

Except Miranda, of course. "The *first* priority is to understand why it went down."

The general paused for a long moment before agreeing.

Which told Mike that security of the technology came *before* anything as trivial as the crash. Not security but national security. And they were the point team? None of them were trained in something like that. Then he looked around. Except Holly and Andi. And probably Barty. Okay. And the general would know that those three would get the message despite his agreeing with Miranda—*for* Miranda.

"We lost a Wedgetail?" Barty's whisper couldn't have carried to the phone.

"Three-quarters of a billion dollars," Mike would wager his own voice wasn't much louder.

"A billion Australian," Holly noted.

Outside of Air Force One and the Nightwatch doomsday planes, it was probably the most expensive plane ever built— ten times the cost of a standard Boeing 737.

"Miranda, I know I say this every time," Drake continued with a low shout, "but we need answers fast. If this is some move for control of the Strait of Malacca, that's a third of the world's trade at ten billion dollars a day."

"China," Barty's snarl carried easily to the phone this time.

"Right. Our worst fear is that they're intending to revise the nine-dash line they used to justify grabbing much of the South China Sea and are now extending that reach. We're hoping for a more mundane cause."

"What does that have to do with why the plane crashed?" Miranda asked.

Barty twisted to look at her. Mike waved him off but not before he'd made Miranda gather Meg close and stare down into her fur.

Drake, at least, was used to such questions from her and left the space for one of the team to explain it.

Andi took it on this time. "Miranda, you worry about finding out why the plane went down. It will be up to people like Drake to figure out what to do about it once we know."

"Right," she nodded fiercely to Meg, "I keep forgetting when Drake talks like that. All we care about is the plane," she continued reminding her dog.

Mike leaned back and tapped Barty's shoulder to do the same. In the swamping noise, it was as good as moving to another room. "All she sees or cares about is the plane. Geopolitical ramifications simply don't compute in her brain."

"And you guys work with that every day?"

"Yes."

Barty stared at the top of Miranda's head for a long moment as she conversed with her dog and Andi. Holly had taken the phone, dropped it off speaker, and was hounding Drake for every detail he had. Finally Barty grunted. "You guys have an interesting dynamic."

"Just one step this side of psychotic…"

Barty came as close to a smile as Mike suspected he ever did.

"…at least on our good days."

That actually earned him a bark of laughter. "Okay, mate. You got me. Can't wait to see what the woman does." Then he grew serious. "China taking out a Wedgetail?"

Mike tried to relieve the tension by cricking his neck to the side, but it didn't work.

That was World War material—or at least one that would engage the whole Pacific Rim, from Japan to Chile and Australia to the US.

The Pacific Ring of Fire indeed.

9

———

Holly wasn't sure how she felt about Mike bonding with her old boss. Not that she could do a thing about it. Drake had kept her on the phone for the first half of the forty-minute flight from Singapore's Changi Airport to Mount Ledang, proving quite how worried he and the President were on this one.

The problem was, Barty knew more of her past than she was comfortable with Mike knowing. Or Barty for that matter. They'd both been SASR, him injuring out about the same time she'd...departed...for trying to throttle the Governor-General of Australia during her team's memorial service. It wasn't until she went for the ATSB that she learned that's where Barty Kirwan had landed.

But the two of them traced back much further than that. They were both children of the Outback's Northern Territory.

Separated by five hundred kilometers and a lone but rather fine pub partway between, they hadn't met before joining the service. But he had built a deep love of the Outback on outings with his Dagoman kin, and she might as well have been Warumungu for how much time she'd spent with the Blacks—now properly First Australians. She'd spoken the local language better than most of the mob her age of any color.

They'd finally met as grunts in the 1st Combat Engineers Regiment – Darwin. They were both comfortable working with explosives and they'd bonded over trading advanced techniques and thinking up new ideas to try. On free weekends, she and Barty, if his wife was busy, would simply wander off into the Bush. It wasn't a place of danger to either of them; it was a place of silence and beauty. Even bounty.

They'd gone SASR together, on separate teams because it was rare to embed two troopers of the same specialty together. While she wouldn't call it a friendship—Barty was too taciturn for such—they'd maintained relations, primarily in problem-solving the fine art of destroying enemy emplacements with innovative techniques. *From obvious to oblivion*, they'd always said between them. They'd both taken on a special fascination with the marrying of explosives and unwanted aircraft—like Libya's, Syria's, and more than a few of Russia's.

And now they were flying together to see what they could learn about why this Wedgetail had come apart.

After hanging up with Drake and unable to see forward, Holly moved to where the loadmasters sat at the front of the bird and indicated a navigation and shooting portal. A Chinook pilot could only see ahead and directly to the sides. Anything behind the cockpit to either side, he'd depend on his crew chiefs leaning out the side windows and keeping him apprised of obstacles and clearances.

One of the chiefs waved for her to look.

She pulled out a pair of impact-rated sunglasses, clapped a hand on her Matildas ball cap, and leaned out to face ahead.

At twelve hundred and seventy-six meters, forty-one hundred feet, Mount Ledang was no giant. But it was the southernmost notable peak in the mountain range that ran north from here for five hundred kilometers to form the Malay

Peninsula. The jungle shrouding all sides of the prominence reached a thousand meters above the surrounding plains, emphasizing its height and isolation.

A thin trail of dark smoke still bloomed from the distant peak in fitful puffs that could easily be mistaken for a small but active volcano. It wasn't enough that the plane had crashed, it had burned as well. The char from those kinds of investigations stained your skin down to your very pores and took weeks to purge. Holly hated those.

They were still ten to fifteen minutes out by her best reckoning. She'd enjoy it while she could.

When she ducked her head back inside, Lieutenant Noor was watching her carefully.

"Your conversations are done?"

At her nod, he waved politely toward a pair of fold-down seats—clear of the loadmasters but not by her team either. She wanted to head aft and break up whatever Barty was saying to make Mike laugh like that. But decided that it was better if she pretended not to notice or care. Mike would see through that, of course, but she still might fool Barty.

"Sorry about Mike giving you the boot, mate. It's just how the world works sometimes."

He nodded an easy acceptance. "There is a legend about that mountain; *the* great legend in all Malaysian folklore."

"Why does a Singaporean lieutenant know it?"

"My family's ancestral land is here in Malacca. I have come back to see relatives and climb the mountain several times."

Since he didn't appear to be hitting on her—and she couldn't decide if she wanted Mike to think he was or not— she'd indulge his desire to tell a story. "So give over."

"Puteri of Gunung Ledang, literally the Princess of Mountain Ledang, was a celestial princess."

"A romance story?"

"Romance or war are at the heart of all good legends."

She wished it was a story of war, but she wasn't betting on it.

"A great Sultan of Malacca—that's the city out the port side window…"

Holly glanced out one of the helo's round side windows. A sprawling city, with only a tight business center reaching above a few stories tall, hugged the coast to the southwest.

"…saw the princess of the mountain and fell madly in love. There were many difficulties—"

"What with him being a mortal sultan and her being a celestial princess?"

"Yes, among others. But his heart proved unrelenting despite her attempts to rebuff him."

"Jerk."

Noor shrugged. "So, she set him seven impossible tasks to win her consent. Build a bridge of gold so that she could walk from her mountain to his city. Build another of silver to walk upon for the return journey. Seven jars of virgins' tears, seven great trays filled with the hearts of fleas, seven—"

"Got the idea."

"The last was a great bowl filled with the blood of the Sultan's son."

"Nasty. Bet that stopped him cold."

"That," Noor shook his head, "is the problem. It didn't. He completed the first six impossible tasks, about which there are many more tales. It bankrupted and destroyed his sultanate, but that didn't stop him. Then he took a great blade and was headed to his only son's bedroom when the Princess appeared to him."

"Did she give in and say, *Goodonya, that'll do, mate?*"

"Oh no. A Malaysian romance story is not like a Western story where love conquers all. She stood before him and swore that she could never be with a man who would sacrifice family to satisfy his own desires. *Poof!*" He made an upward tossing motion. "She was never seen again."

"Proving he was a sucker—destroying his kingdom for a girl he could never have."

"Some say that he should have seen that the seven impossible tasks were her refusal of him, but his pride wouldn't let him see the truth. Others, who would point at the fickle ways of women, say it was because she couldn't bring herself to simply say she wouldn't have him. In the end: kingdom destroyed, the son survived, but her answer remained no."

"Too bad about the bridges. Probably worth a pretty penny."

Noor smiled broadly. "Another name for the Gunung Ledang was Golden Mountain. It is said that in the thirteenth century, great deposits of gold and silver were mined here."

Knowing when she was truly beaten, Holly could only laugh. "That'll teach me to go messing with legends. I'll definitely dodge any celestial princesses running about the mountaintop."

"I don't know," Noor looked wistful. "After all, her beauty *is* legendary."

"Probably buying a world of hurt if you pursue her, but best of luck to you, mate." A glance out the side window showed they were getting close. Leaning against the windows, she could just see the mountain's flanks. "What are we going to find down there?"

He nodded, as if creating trust had been his reason for telling the legend. And it had worked. *Full points, Noor.*

"You are familiar with tropical rainforest?"

Holly winced. "All too familiar." Almost every one of her worst experiences in SASR had been in that particular biome. Far too much of it lay close to the north from Australia. She'd seen the wrong side of Papua New Guinea, Myanmar, Vietnam... She shuddered away from several of those memories. For one thing, there was far too much sweating in the tropical forests. For another, it often teemed with critters—

and people—intent on her imminent demise. "The Malay peninsula has..." she prompted him.

"All of the usual, though up at Mount Ledang's altitude, many of them will be not bothering us. Tigers are so very rare now and the sun bears do not like all the tourists who come to climb the mountain. The elephants avoid the steep upper slopes. But what lives here is not limited like a jungle, there are many thousands of species living under the high canopy."

"Wonderful. So I won't get eaten, merely bitten, stung, and scratched."

Noor shrugged a yes.

"The people?"

"That is what I wanted to speak to you of. Malaysia is not Singapore, but it is not Vietnam or Indonesia either. In most world indexes, it is in the top third: income, longevity, lack of corruption." Singapore, like Australia, was top ten on most lists, both consistently way ahead of the US except for GDP per capita and the size of their military.

"They said a Royal Malaysian Air Force team is already on site." Holly hadn't kept up on local changes since she'd left SASR five years back.

Noor's grimace wasn't too horrid. "Not very corrupt. Most of them mean well. One from the RMAF won't think outside a very small cage."

"*Box.* Think outside the box, mate."

He nodded his thanks. "I would have expected Special Operations if a Wedgetail went down."

Holly shifted to make sure she had a good striking angle on Noor if needed. "What makes you say *that,* mate?"

"I may only be a lieutenant, Ms. Harper. But I'm not blind. A sudden call for American and Australian assets, including the one who arrived in the RAAF Super Hornet. A Singaporean helicopter, one of our big Chinooks, is immediately provided for your exclusive use—until you choose to release it. Cleared straight to the site, without customs clearance, which the Malaysians are very particular about, especially with Singaporeans. The moment you get aboard, there is a secure phone call?" Then he tapped his radio. "My boss may be abrupt, but he is thorough. He looked up Miranda Chase as her name was all we had to go on. Her credentials are impressive. And you stated you were former SASR."

Holly grimaced. "I shouldn't have done that. But you and your boys ticked me off."

"Yes, I am sorry about that."

She decided that was reasonable and eased off without showing that's what she was doing. "So, what's a smart guy like you doing as a mere lieutenant?"

"I'm only twenty-four. Give me more time."

10

MIKE WISHED HE'D MET THE YOUNGER HOLLY.

Barty had story after story about her as they flew over the Malay Peninsula. He particularly liked the one of the first time Holly was in charge of a truly large explosion.

"You've never seen anyone who understands chemistry that goes bang the way that gal does. But on her first big takedown —" Barty looked positively starry-eyed. SASR operators really were from another planet. "There was this big old warehouse up to Darwin that the Top-enders wanted dropped and they let us troopers have a go. Massive concrete thing. No way to be subtle about it, and no need, it was well clear of town."

Barty actually smiled at the memory. For a moment Mike had been afraid his face would break.

"That sheila decided to hit it full-bore: different chemistry used on each support to see what we could learn. From stick TNT to C-4, SX4 sheet explosive, even got her hands on some black powder, and where she found Russian PVV, not even the Dreamtime trickster Crow knows. We did drill-ins, surface mounts, shaped charges, had ourselves a real ripper; a chance to see what did what right proper. Harper fired that sucker off and it blew sky high. We were outside the debris zone, by about the length of a dingo's nose, but we didn't count on one thing..."

Mike made a few guesses but knew he hadn't hit the mark by the wrinkles around Barty's eyes indicating he was smiling, inside at least.

"We made one holy mother of a shock wave—so big it probably blew dust off the top of Uluru fifteen hundred kilometers away to the south. Knocked us both flat on our butts, it did. Rolled our truck too. Only thing that saved our trooper asses was our captain had been the one to sign out and park the truck. Lower story of that building wasn't broken up, it no longer be existing. The rest of the building...it hung there on the air cushion of that shock wave long enough to think about life for a while before it fell outta the sky like a drop bear."

Barty watched his face, but Holly had told him about Australian tall tales, at least that one. "Always wear a bit of vegemite behind me ears when I'm in-country, mate. Can't be too careful around them drop bears." The noxious sandwich spread and an Aussie accent were supposed to protect against them plummeting down from the trees onto some unsuspecting tourist.

They shared a laugh, though Barty's sounded like a rusty gate groaning from lack of practice.

His own tales of Holly going hyper-protective of Miranda sobered Barty somewhat. Had him glancing at Holly a long moment where she sat down the cabin with the Singaporean lieutenant. It didn't bother Mike at all that the lieutenant was handsome and a decade younger. Not a bit.

"That's a tad curious, Mike. The girl I'm knowing..." he left that unfinished.

The helo slid into a wide bank. Glancing out the window, Mike could see a swath of dark shadow through the thick green of lush trees. The debris field ran a couple soccer fields long—Holly must be rubbing off on him. He'd had season tickets to the Denver Broncos back in their heyday of the early 2010s under John Fox. But now Holly had him thinking in soccer field lengths? Truly wrong.

It wasn't a wide swath. The plane had glanced off the rounded rocky peak, leaving its entire empennage perched there like a monumental cairn. With its tail gone, it had plunged down the south ridge, losing its wings along the way. Each of those had started downslope fires as the fuel had spilled and ignited to either side. The wings were relatively undamaged, only showing minor charring of the light gray RAAF paint, more than he could say for the downslope trees being fed a constant trickle of fuel from the leaking tanks.

Tailless and wingless, the fuselage had plummeted along the stony ridgeline for several hundred meters until it had run into a television broadcast tower. Longer than the plane, the box-steel mast had folded over the cockpit and lay crumpled along the length of the plane like an exoskeletal spine.

"Oh, this is going to be so much fun."

"Scavengers," Barty gave a low shout, about equivalent to a whisper aboard the Chinook helo.

"Shit!"

He could see people were rummaging through the wreckage. And a cluster of Malaysian soldiers stood beside a line of body bags in the TV tower's service building's small parking lot—doing nothing to stop them.

Mike had only ever read about this. There'd been a crash in South America somewhere. The locals had stripped the plane most of the way down to the frames by the time the crash investigation team had arrived. They had to buy back bits and pieces, including the flight recorder. That had been damaged past usage by the scavenger—he'd tried to beat it open and see if there were any useful electronics inside. There'd been a lot of curved aluminum roofs that sprang up in the area with various sections of the airline's colorful logo jumbled among like bits of shattered glass.

He popped his seatbelt and raced by Holly up to the cockpit. "Land us on the access road, downslope of the crash."

"We have orders to—"

A hand on his shoulder moved him aside, forcing him to hunch behind the pilot's seat. He resisted at first, then recognized the touch and let himself be moved.

"Well, mates," Holly slid forward. "Man suggested you land below the wreck, I'd suggest you do that. Pronto!"

Out of her sightline, Mike could see over the shoulder of the pilot as he reached for a sidearm with his outside hand.

He glanced at Holly and tipped his head toward the problem.

"Aw, matey. Do *not* be disappointing me unless you think you have a future as a helo pilot *after* I slice off all your fingers for pulling out your peashooter." If she had retrieved her knives from their luggage, he didn't see them.

The pilot froze, glanced up to inspect her expression carefully, then eased his empty hand into clear view.

"Down. Now."

It would take a stronger man than Mike to argue with Holly when she used her command voice. Apparently neither pilot decided that they were.

He checked behind. No threat from the loadmasters, their attention was on lowering the rear ramp a soccer-goal-width away—*Crap!* A *football* field's *end zone* away.

Once he decided to cooperate, the pilot tucked them down fast and neat. Not a lot of spare room for the twin set of blades each spinning a sixty-foot-diameter circle, but he did it. Landed with his nose aimed downslope on the dirt track and only a few meters from the Malaysian Army light tactical vehicle with its eye-searing sharply geometric camouflage.

Mike turned and hustled upslope through the cargo bay as

the loadmasters completed lowering the ramp. Above, he could see the rotor blades were sweeping not ten meters from the base of the wrecked transmitter tower. Far too close for his comfort, but then he wasn't a military helo pilot.

"Come on, Lieutenant," he slapped Noor on his shoulder. "Time to earn your keep."

Together they were off the ramp before it touched the ground.

"Hands on your rifle, then translate for me."

Noor did so and nodded.

Mike began dictating. "Anyone holding a piece of the plane, put it down now. If you're still holding it in ten seconds, you'll be placed under arrest. If you're holding it in twenty seconds, you'll be shot."

Noor raised an eyebrow at the last but kept translating.

Very few reacted.

"It is the uniform and my accent," Noor explained. "They know I am not Malaysian forces."

"So fire your gun. Into the ground or something."

"I can't! I'm not authorized to discharge my weapon in a foreign-friendly country except in a life-threatening—"

Noor grunted. A blonde whirlwind spun him around once and came away with his rifle.

Holly laid three rounds into the dirt close in front of the leading scavengers.

With a yelp, several of them broke for the thick trees to either side, despite how steeply the ridge fell away into the forest. Holly dropped rounds into tree trunks right, then left, then right again, often mere inches off the noses of the scavengers. Some dropped what they had, others clutched their salvage to their chests, but more like a security blanket than a prize. They all rushed back onto the narrow dirt track, neatly corralled by Holly's threat ahead and the massive wreck behind on the only passable trail.

A trio of Malaysian soldiers came pushing through the crowd, shouting in what Mike could only assume was Malay. They broke free of the scavengers, raising their weapons. Then glanced over Mike's shoulders and went as still as the dead plane behind them.

Mike risked a glance over his shoulder.

Barty, flanked by the two Singaporean crew chiefs, stood with their rifles raised and zeroed on the Malaysian soldiers. Andi stood at the head of the ramp with her own sidearm raised, directly in front of Miranda, still lost back in the shadows. Noor, perhaps having vague hopes of not dying in an international incident between neighboring countries, didn't draw his sidearm, but he kept a hand on the butt of it ready to go.

During the Malaysians' moment of inattention, Holly stepped up to the soldier with an officer's sunbursts rather than mere stripes for rank and placed the barrel of Lieutenant Noor's rifle against the officer's forehead. His new center of attention turned him into a good imitation of a stone sculpture. Holly required only a single finger to push the officer's rifle barrel to point at the ground.

She rattled off something short and nasty in Malay.

Noor, more amused than upset at being so abruptly stripped of his weapon, translated, "She calls him *babi*, that is *pig*. Malaysians are mostly Islamic, so she names him a religiously unclean animal to someone who cares. She is amazing woman. Now she ask why he does not, did not protect the flying ship—uh, sorry, that is the literal translation—the airplane."

The man replied with his eyes crossed, trying to see where the weapon pressed against his forehead. The crowd behind him hadn't moved a centimeter.

"He says that the plane, it is but a thing. He saved the bodies."

Holly sighed. "Do you speak English?"

The man's nod moved the barrel of the gun up and down, he froze again when he noticed that.

Noor scoffed and whispered, "Please tell me I did better than that back at Changi Airport."

Noor had *not* simply caved in despite facing the impossible odds of surviving both Andi and Holly. "He looks ready to clean her boots with his tongue if she ordered it. You stood tall."

Noor looked pleased at one-upping the Malaysian officer.

"New rules," Holly announced. "First, tell them that I'll shoot anyone who tries to leave with so much as a screw. Get every scrap of salvage from these people. Find out where they picked it up and have them put it back where they found it. Better yet, tell them to stay with it until Mike interviews each of them *in situ*."

Mike knew that wouldn't work. He'd seen it often enough at the orphanage and the years before he'd conned a way out of his street-urchin teens. When there was trouble...

...the crowd melted. You couldn't spot anyone walking away —not sneaking, creeping, or sprinting. Yet fewer and fewer remained behind the soldiers. Soon, a heap of detritus from the wreck lay scattered along the dirt track, but no people remained in sight by the time the officer had finished his translation.

Holly should know that they—

"Good, that's done." She safetied the rifle and held it out behind her.

Noor took it, re-clipped the shoulder strap that Holly had undone on the fly, but kept it casually in his hand rather than slinging it onto his back. The Malaysian officer didn't miss that. Mike wondered if the officer now watching Noor understood how dangerous Holly was empty-handed.

He shook his head to himself. Of course Holly had been

trained in crowd control and when it was better to not have a crowd at all.

"Make sure no more of this plane goes astray," Holly addressed the Malaysia officer, "or I'll be adding your body to the pile and telling your bosses that the plane landed on your head. Other than that, do your best to make sure that I never see your or any of your team's faces ever again. Are we clear?"

The man turned, shouting orders, setting up a roving patrol; one that placed him as far from Holly as possible.

"Thanks, mate," Holly nodded to Noor. "Sorry to grab your kit but I was in a tad bit of a hurry."

"It is okay. I am so sorry that I was slow to react."

"Practice, mate. Lots and lots of practice."

Mike knew of the fascination that many cultures had for blonde hair color. Far more than Westerners, cultures that were genetically dark-haired—especially ones with little immigration mixing with fair-haired races—showed a rapt fascination. But Noor watched Holly with something different. It wasn't lust. It was...worship?

"Hey, Noor, buddy."

"Huh?"

"*Huh* the man says."

Noor smiled sheepishly. "I'll never grow up to be that good."

"Yeah, she's special. But you won't know unless you try."

Noor sobered at that, looking somewhere that might be his own future horizon.

"Is it safe yet?" Miranda's soft voice wouldn't have carried to them if the helo's open cargo bay hadn't acted like a cheerleader's megaphone. The rotors and engines were silent. The small crowd that had beat them to the aircraft were gone, probably hikers who had already been well up the mountain at the time of the crash. The Malaysian soldiers had now set up a patrol perimeter downslope along the service road.

"The only other access trails to the top are still on fire,"

Noor pointed to the fires where the broken wings had spilled burning fuel downslope to either side. The light breeze blew the smoke and stench away without notably fanning the flames. "The mountaintop and the wreck should now be yours and only yours."

Mike turned to the helicopter, where Miranda remained in the shadows of the cargo bay. "Yes, Miranda. It's safe now. C'mon, Noor. Let's go get the debris perimeter pinned down."

The fewer people around Miranda at the moment, probably the better.

11

MIRANDA PEEKED OVER ANDI'S SHOULDER, WAITING FOR AT LEAST a count of ten after the others had moved off. She set Meg down on all fours to lead their way down the ramp. She kept a close eye on the terrier as she sniffed the air tentatively. Miranda did the same.

Hot in the midmorning, though cooler than the Changi tarmac where they'd met the helicopter. Thick. The air was somehow thick. Humidity, combined with the scent of a thousand things growing so close together that she could barely see into the trees. And a thousand more composting into the soil.

The trees stood tall but didn't tower like the Douglas fir on her island. And nothing here was...stout. Vines and long branches drooped from above and tall trees thin as bamboo but with the wrong leaves shot up to meet them. She liked that they reached out to meet each other and hope they enjoyed it. The few heavier trees had deeply twisted branches, striving first one way then another as if not knowing what they wanted.

She didn't recognize a single plant. It was so...foreign.

Even the rocks were unfamiliar. None of the jagged shapes

and fine basalts of the Pacific Northwest. Instead, it was old coarse-grained granite worn in long sloping surfaces by two hundred million years of rain and wind.

But Meg trotted down the ramp beside Andi happily enough, so Miranda followed. At the bottom of the ramp, Meg squatted and peed on the very first patch of dark dirt.

Oh, she was being a horrible owner. She'd neglected Meg since the moment those men had surrounded her at Changi. As soon as Meg was done, she knelt, gave her a treat, and told her what a good and patient girl she was.

Good and patient.

She was getting tired of being good and patient herself. When those men had shown up, she hadn't managed to resist or even answer them. How much of that was her autism and how much her deep training in trying to be a *good girl?* Her parents had admonished her a thousand times to be that. Even Tante Daniels, her therapist and governess after her parents' deaths, had used the phrase, constantly reinforcing what a *good girl* she was.

She'd read enough literature on Meg to know the method's effectiveness in dog training. Positive reinforcement. How often had that crowded her into a box of behaving, seeking that *good girl* accolade? Even today at the airport.

She was forty-one years old, had a girlfriend, a dog, and everything. Well, not everything, she didn't have a home since her island was ravaged by a lightning strike fire. But she was *the* top investigator for the NTSB. Yet still she—

"Everything okay, Miranda?" Andi crouched beside her and tickled Meg's nose until she sneezed. It was one of their routines.

Miranda placed a finger on Andi's nose and wiggled it. She didn't sneeze, but she did smile after trying to look at her own nose.

"Hey, I like teasing your dog. It's fun."

Miranda withdrew her finger and looked at it. Fun. That was another thing she didn't have, did she? She never knew how to judge whether or not she achieved that.

"Shall we get started?" Andi nodded upslope toward the wreck.

Mike and Holly had already moved away with a fistful of marker flags. They'd taken the Australian investigator and the Singaporean lieutenant with them. The four of them had begun staking the outer edges of the debris field. The crew was tending to their helicopter.

"Are they being a good girl and boys?"

Andi glanced in their direction. "You've trained us well; we know our jobs. Even Meg." She tickled Meg behind the ears this time, eliciting a happy sigh.

"I think I'm tired of behaving."

Andi twisted to look at her with her surprised face. "Does that mean you don't want to investigate the crash?"

"No, it doesn't. It means..." Miranda thought about it but finally shook her head. "I have no idea. So, I'll be a good girl and start work."

"We can be bad girls together later."

Miranda assumed that was clever and had some hidden meaning, and answered with a nod as she usually did. Then, "No!"

"No?" Andi twisted to face her so abruptly that she tipped from her squat onto her butt in the dirt. Her face appeared to lose some of its color, but perhaps that was the bright tropical sun.

"What did you mean about being bad together?"

"I meant...sex. What did you think I meant?"

"I didn't know. I was just being agreeable, then I said *No,* perhaps more emphatically than necessary, because I'm tired of doing that. So, were you suggesting we have *bad* sex? What advantage does that have?"

"It's a joke, Miranda. One that…" Andi's face twisted up in a familiar way.

"That's hard to explain to someone like me."

She became serious. "It's dependent on a knowledge and understanding of cultural norms, something you're lucky enough to not have to deal with as much as the rest of us as you can't see them. Neurotypicals generally consider girls who want sex to be *bad*. As in misbehaving and wild."

"And boys who want sex aren't?"

"Again, cultural norms. We exist in a deeply male society, Miranda, so there are *bad* boys, but they're seen as rebellious hero figures rather than, well, sluts."

Miranda considered it all. "How is it that society is so weird?"

"You figure that one out and the women of the world will grant you their highest prize."

"Which is what?"

Andi laughed. "Not a clue. Do you know, Meg?"

Meg wagged her tail as if she did indeed have some secret information.

"Figures," Andi sighed. "Too bad you only speak dog and can't explain it all to us." Then she looked up. "No one has all the answers, Miranda. If we manage to find even a few, most of us count ourselves lucky. So, good or bad, we have a job to do here. People died."

"And a very expensive plane."

"And one *crazy* expensive airplane." Andi stood and helped her to her feet. "Where shall we begin?"

Miranda reached for a notebook and her handheld anemometer. She could see that the sky was blue and the wind light enough to scatter the smoke but not rip it aside. It made the thin trees weave back and forth, drawing figure eights across the sky. But it wasn't enough to do more than stir the understory. Even here on the open expanse of the dirt service road, the wind barely stirred the breathless air.

Her typical sphere-based pattern of analysis had been developed by her mentor to help her manage her autism during an investigation. Nested layers of analysis from outside in. Like the nested cosmic spheres the Greeks had developed, creating the *Musica Universalis* as an attempt to explain the orbits of the planets and stars.

As if she couldn't understand a plane crash when she looked at one after hundreds of investigations. Time to stop being a *good girl* and try something new? It took three slow deep breaths before she could face it, but—yes.

She tucked both the notebook and handheld weather station back into their vest pockets. "Let's go look at the wreck. We'll backtrack later if we need to."

If Andi was surprised, she didn't show it, merely falling into step beside her. Meg was never surprised by plane wrecks and this time was no different. Miranda supposed that there were far fewer other-dog scents around crashed planes for Meg to react to than a walk along a city street. To her it was simply another sunny day—a *hot* sunny day.

"Oh no!" She stopped, dug a collapsible water bowl and a bottle of water from her pack, and soon Meg was lapping it up. "I actually do try so hard to be good, but I keep messing up. I *am* a bad girl."

"You're a great *woman*, Miranda," Andi assured her. "No one would take better care of a dog, especially with all that's happened in the last few hours."

As a good sign, Meg didn't quite finish the water, happily accepted a treat, and then moved ahead to the limit of her leash to sniff at the first of the debris left by the scavengers. Miranda poured out the last bits of the water, wiped the bowl dry with its dedicated cloth, wrapped the cloth around the bowl, and slipped them into the proper corner of her pack.

"Okay," she took a steadying breath, "let's do this."

They walked through the scavenger area first. The collection was so eclectic that she struggled to categorize it. A pile of food packets, several small computers and tablets (all badly broken), three jackets, two fire extinguishers, a stack of six airline-style blankets still wrapped in plastic, an over-wing emergency exit door (complete with a broken window), and an airline seat with a simple lap belt (which must have come from the crew rest area, as a console operator's seat would have the full five-point harness).

"Is it me or doesn't this make any sense?"

"It's not you," Andi assured her. "People grabbed whatever caught their eye. Maybe this one," she pointed at the double-armful of pre-packaged food, "hadn't had lunch yet. The headset might have been selected by a teenager tired of his parents telling him to turn down his stereo. Perhaps the chair guy has a son grown too big to sit on Mama's lap anymore. Someone strong if he was going to carry it down the mountain." She gave it a kick, and it barely moved. It wasn't one of the newly developed super-light seats in the ten-kilo range, but neither was it eighty kilos of business class laydown seat complete with a shell and entertainment center. The bending at the base stated the amount of force that had been necessary to shear the bolts securing the seat to the decking framework.

In the small parking lot beside the base of the broken radio mast that lay atop the plane, the Malaysians had created an impromptu morgue. Ten body bags lined up in two neat rows. They were in the shade of the forest's verge, safe from the high equatorial sun. A lone soldier stood over them, not a part of the circling patrol.

People last. They belonged to the innermost and final sphere of her analysis. The plane was the most important part of the investigation.

Wasn't it?

But what if being at the center of her methodology model made people the *most* important element? She tried to remember what Terrence Graham, the head trainer at the National Transportation Safety Board Academy, had told her as they'd developed her sphere system.

You need to concentrate on one aspect at a time, Mirrie, to avoid being overwhelmed.

But there'd been more…

Work your way in from the outside to the core. The core?

"People are at the *core?*" She barely recognized the wreck before her. Or any of the prior ones. Every precise conceptual arrangement she'd ever formed and stored so carefully in her mind couldn't be…*inside out.* Could it?

Meg whined and placed her paws upon Miranda's calf.

In an instant, she was wrapped tight in Andi's arms. "Whoa, Miranda. Where did you just go?"

Miranda buried her face against Andi's shoulder and breathed her in. And again. At least this was familiar. She wanted to bend down to reassure Meg, but she didn't want to leave Andi's arms. Meg leaned firmly against Miranda's calf. The solid contact was a comfort to them both.

Andi knew to wait her out. Asking again a second time or a third simply piled up the queue of unanswered questions, even if it was the same one repeated. That increased the mental pressure as well.

Another whine from Meg. Miranda released Andi, who hesitated several times before letting her go. She scooped Meg up and against her chest to calm them both. Meg rested her head on Miranda's right shoulder. Andi's head typically ended up on her left. Perhaps because that was her side of the bed and it had built into a habit. Miranda liked knowing without thinking which of them comforted her by where they pressed against her.

"I *hate* being so fragile. And don't say I'm not, because I won't believe you."

"I'd counter with you being crazy resilient against a society designed to make you nuts—and, no, I don't mean the *designed* part literally. So, what's up Miranda?"

"Are people really so important?"

Andi hesitated. "I'm guessing that I shouldn't be taking that question personally?"

"What? I don't get..." she managed to stop herself. "Oh, you're talking about something other than investigations. Specifically, I'm talking about air-crash investigations. Unless you're an air crash, I wasn't talking about you."

Andi smiled at something with her *funny joke* face...but didn't explain.

Which was good, Miranda didn't know if she could deal with another level of distraction at the moment—or would it be abstraction? No, she pushed that question aside before it could take hold.

"I thought that's why you always left them *until* last. They're absolutely the most important. How many of your investigations trace back to human factors?"

Miranda reconsidered her investigations over the last twenty-one years in that light. "I suppose, ultimately, everything except for extreme weather events, though most of those could have been avoided, and bird strikes. Everything else is operator error, mechanic misjudgments, poor design, poor inspection and maintenance, inaccurate—"

"You don't have to list them all. So, what's the problem?"

"I always left people until last as the *least* important to understanding what happened. My whole career I've been wrong. I don't know anything." She waved at the plane wreckage. "I can't understand people. How can I ever understand something like this?"

"A Wedgetail doesn't fall from the sky on its own, without any warning."

"Exactly! How am I supposed to know what's happening here? It's people. I never understand people. Not even you."

Andi's made a *shocked-and-hurt* face, Miranda was mostly sure she'd memorized that one correctly: a sharp gasp for breath, a quick closing of eyes, and a drawing away. When she managed to open her eyes, they looked watery.

"I love you, Andi, but I don't understand you. Not even why what I just said hurt you. I'm hopeless."

12

———

After encircling the scavengers' leavings with white marker flags, Holly led the team upslope toward the plane.

Barty waved his hands in a sweeping motion. "Why not just push all this junk together?"

"Not the way Miranda would want it done." Holly knew that *want* was a huge understatement; it could scramble her ability to function.

Barty harrumphed.

"You want to argue with the queen of air-crash methodology?"

He offered another noncommittal grunt.

"Yeah, not me either." Which earned her an almost smile. She'd forgotten what it was like to work with a taciturn male. She always knew what Mike was thinking, maybe not what he felt, but his thoughts were always clear. Jeremy Trahn was an open book. He'd left the team for a new role at NTSB headquarters in Washington, DC. That had been two years ago, yet she still knew so many details of what he was working on, his excitement and struggles with their new baby, and every other event in his life. Barty lived by the Spec Ops guy-speak that they'd both learned way before the military—in the silence of the Bush.

She heard the grinding of gears as a truck climbed the road toward the helo, a firetruck. Mike and Noor headed down to them. The new arrivals were soon deploying long hoses past either side of the helo and the fuselage to knock down the last remnants of the fire that had been burning along the slopes since their arrival. It had already died significantly since the landing. They'd be done and gone pretty quickly, even though the crash was now over three hours old.

Holly watched Noor as he approached with Mike. The lieutenant left her at something of a loss. Lust directed her way she knew what to do with. Enjoy the ride while it lasted. At least until Mike, who she genuinely liked...and maybe more than. He must feel much the same as he put up with all of her shit. Well, most of it, and he called her on the rest of it, which felt unfair but was probably a greater kindness than anyone else would afford her when she was in a mood.

When he and Mike caught up with her and Barty, she put Noor to the inside of the search line where he could do the least harm and took the outer edge herself. That set up Barty and Mike as buffers.

"Noor will walk the edge of the obvious perimeter. Everyone stay close enough that you can touch fingertips if you reach out. Maintain that spacing. We'll stop every five steps and look behind us. Here in the forest, especially look under bushes and the like." She didn't need to tell Mike or Barty but included them so that Noor wouldn't feel singled out.

She felt like a mama dingo with a young pup just *sooo* very happy to be following her. That was a definite first. The guy had potential, smart—but so young! Had she ever been that young? By the time she was his age, she'd been in the Army for six years and Spec Ops for three. He was an academy fresh lieutenant, an officer. She'd never understood officers. Mostly it seemed their job was screwing up a grunt's life. Give her a good master sergeant to follow and ship everyone else off to the looney bin, or off to the capital in Canberra where they could do only minimal harm.

They set off. She counted five steps aloud and called a stop. "Remember to look all around."

Barty, next to Noor, had the farthest scattered bit of debris and staked it with a small flag from the fistfuls Mike had handed around.

Five more paces, and they all had to shift toward the fuselage for Noor to get to the closest piece.

They quickly settled into the pattern. Five steps at a slow walk, stop, look around, everyone pointing at the closest piece of crap that was once part of an airplane, and the person farthest out staking it. Within minutes they were moving at a solid pace. For now, Holly decided to skip the wings. Partly because she'd need a safety line to clamber around their length and partly because the burnout had included the wings' tips. Tracking bits and pieces through char on a forty-five-degree-plus slope was not her idea of a good time.

Wondering if there were any tigers that hadn't been scared away by the crash of sixty metric tons of aircraft and a pair of small forest fires, or any of the myriad of snakes that populated the region, brought it all slamming back and threatened to choke her.

She'd operated too many times in biomes just like this one. Including that final operation, in another country but it smelled the same, where her entire team had died. Holly knew she'd lost everything that day: her team, her place in the Special Air Service Regiment, what little self-esteem she'd managed to salvage from her youth.

But escaping hadn't stuck. Here she stood again, under the soughing of the wind through the high canopy and the choking stagnation of the air down here at the forest floor.

Focus, Harper! Just, god, damn, focus!

She'd never been to the top of Mount Ledang. As they approached, she took a page from Noor's book to distract herself. She sought a glimpse of the celestial princess so that she could urge her to approach Noor as they clambered along the steep slopes. The only line to the top that didn't require a steel extension ladder tied into the rocks—of which there were several off to the sides—was the path upward from the television tower. And most of that line was filled with fuselage and radio mast.

The smell. She couldn't get away from that. The Malaysian rainforest smelled like nothing in her recent past. Where the team was based in the Pacific Northwest was all about conifer above and impenetrable bramble below. Tramping through Colorado mountains, California oaks, and Arizona deserts had nothing like this.

Hibiscus, bougainvillea, and stinking rafflesia below. Long vines of liana and big-leafed creepers drooping and twisting about any tree above shifted lazily in the breeze but provided shade from the equatorial sun. Orchids, fungi, giant ferns, and more all crowded together as if ready to squeeze the life out of her.

It was almost a blessing that, in the process of crashing and skidding down from the peak especially before its wings broke free, the Wedgetail had mowed down a fair swath of the forest. She walked mostly under the verge without being consumed. And it did spare her the sun pounding down on Noor and Barty though they were a mere five meters away.

Mount Ledang's prominence stood mostly alone, as the winds hadn't tolerated the survival of taller trees, but even the smaller ones were now an annoying tangle flattened by the plane's passage. That problem was offset by how clean the crash itself was. A single line. Talk about luck!

After four years on Miranda's team, Holly had learned that

there was one absolute truth about all assumptions—Miranda proved they were invariably wrong. Which meant...someone had flown this thing all the way into the ground?

Just track the debris field, Holly.

That's what Miranda would say.

She wasn't some entitled officer. Master Sergeant Miranda Chase would be the proper rank for her—leading through raw competence, not some government-given authority that most officers reinterpreted as *God*-given. Master Sergeant Chase had a certain ring to it as well. Yeah, the blind following the crazy. Someday Holly was going to sit Miranda down with a full slab of high-octane Coopers Best Extra Stout, get her pissed as a parrot, and find out just what was going on in that head of hers.

What was going on in Noor's head? Who could tell. Perky and eager as a puppy dog. Had he really been ordered to protect them? Or had his caustic boss or perhaps his government ordered him along for some other reason? What if it was all a cover and merely heralded an action by Singapore or Malaysia against Australia for some unknown reason? An action that Noor was here to make sure remained covered up?

She tossed the idea aside.

First, no one was that good an actor.

Second, how paranoid was she? Nobody had tried to kill her, at least not seriously, in over a year and not as a personal vendetta in three. That was a record on both fronts.

The entire empennage perched atop the mountain as if the entire mountain had driven down from the sky, guided by this lonely, left-behind tail section. Perhaps the empennage wondered what had happened to the rest of the plane and it was just waiting for its parts to come back. It hadn't skidded or tumbled. It had smacked down on the rocky bluff and been snapped off clean. Perhaps the flight hadn't been so well guided.

While they were there, they recovered the Black Box recorders. Then they swept back along the far side of the plane.

On the starboard side of the fuselage this time, she couldn't resist peeking in through the missing emergency exit that had once been over the wing.

"You lot go ahead, I'll catch up in a second." Then she climbed aboard before they could argue.

13

―――――

Noor liked the methodical way the team circled the plane. When he'd first seen the wreck, he'd been staggered by the expanse of the destruction. He'd been assigned to Changi Airport security for the last six months. Changi maintained the best technology, both on the field and in the terminal. And all the planes were intact, except the few in the service sheds and even that was always neat and orderly.

The brief altercation with Miranda's team by the koi pond was the worst he'd heard of happening in Changi in a long time. More typically, the prior pinnacle of his team's dealings had been extracting a drunk-and-disorderly American or German from a flight. When in the terminal, they usually worked as crowd control during a medical emergency.

Out on patrol of the airport in general, they had even less to do. Changi was a smooth, tight operation. Corruption wasn't a capital crime in Singapore, but it was a fast road to a lifetime sentence as well as sparking a major investigation of your immediate and extended families. Changi ranked among the best airports in the world, making him proud to serve there.

Airplanes were supposed to be neatly lined up at jetways, parked over at SIA for service, or going about the business of departing and arriving.

They were *not* supposed to be scattered over acres and acres of mountaintop tropical rainforest. Yet once they'd bounded the wreck with a wavering line of small white flags, like polka dots in the forest, it took on definition and boundaries once again. It also helped that in the time it took them to circle the plane, the fire crews had extinguished the last of the spilled-fuel fires and were already rolling up their hoses.

As they neared the end of the circumnavigation, he could see that Miranda and Andi hadn't moved more than a dozen meters from the helo. Was she too self-important to walk the debris field? Was she like his commander who believed that authority came from sitting behind a desk rather than leading the way?

"What's the holdup, mate?" Barty led him and Mike up to the women. "We've got the perimeter staked out. Pretty clean hit, not much breakup. You solve it yet?"

"No!" Miranda's scream rocked Noor back on his heels.

All at once, he barely recognized her. If her clothes hadn't been the same, he wouldn't have.

Miranda Chase had been so consistently still and quiet that he'd come to wonder if she was some advanced robot who switched on only when necessary. Now, the flailing of her gestures clipped her companion on the chin and dropped her to the ground with a grunt.

Holly arrived and barked out a laugh, "Finally someone fast enough to get past Ms. Andi Wu's defenses. So glad I didn't miss that bit of the show."

"Eat shit, Harper. Surprised me is all." Though the way that the small Chinese woman was shaking her head to clear it, it had been a solid hit.

Ms. Chase appeared not to have noticed what she'd done. "I'm no good. I'm a fake. A fraud. A charlatan! People? It *can't* be about people. I can't *do* people."

Her little dog sat by her feet.

Noor had been trained on therapy dogs as they often flew in the cabin with their owners. A fact he *knew* he should have recognized at the airport; he wouldn't miss that again. This time the dog was looking plenty surprised, but was not taking any action, no worried whining or leaning into her like before. Ms. Chase's suddenly wild behavior wasn't triggering whatever this animal had been trained to counteract.

Mike ducked under one of Ms. Chase's wild gesticulations and pulled Andi to her feet.

The next blow headed for Holly's nose.

Holly grabbed the fist in midair and managed to keep it at bay.

"Shh. Easy, Miranda. Easy."

"I'm not a dog. I'm a... a... a very upset woman!" Her other fist came around, pounding the side of it into Holly's shoulder.

Holly staggered backward, landed against Mike's back, knocking him and Andi to the ground before landing on top of them. Her grip on Miranda's fist pulled her down on top of the pile. Meg the dog rushed over, jumped onto Holly's chest, and licked Miranda's face.

Noor was glad his training had him stationing himself to one side to keep an open angle if events got out of hand. It had saved him from getting caught up in the tangle.

"Oof. Get off, you," Holly tried to push the dog aside, but she apparently enjoyed being on the top of the puppy pile and resisted. "We're definitely putting you on a weight loss program."

"She's exactly the right weight for her age and frame size," Miranda answered, again in that perfectly rational voice, despite lying half on Holly and half on the others' legs. "At least within eight ounces. It's hard to get accurate data on the exact proper weight for a Glen of Imaal Terrier. Several times I've sent very precise skeletal measurements as well as dry and hydrostatic weights for determining muscle/fat ratios to both the AKC and The Kennel Club in Britain." Miranda pushed to her feet and Meg climbed down to stand beside her.

"What did they have to say to that?" Holly asked without attempting to get up off the other two. She actually lounged back and interlaced her fingers behind her head as they struggled beneath her.

Noor had thought this team was something odd, but this? "What is going on here?"

Holly winked at him, "Sometimes best to roll with the punch, mate, as Andi just learned."

"Go to hell, Harper. And get off. You're the one who's heavy."

Once they were all standing again, it was Mike who took Miranda by both shoulders and turned her firmly to face him.

"Miranda. We *know* that you don't understand the people. Wu isn't bad at it. Harper hasn't a clue—"

Holly cursed.

"She thinks she does, but she's very, very wrong. Don't worry, when we get down to that level, we can take care of it as a team. But we can't get down to the *who* of people until we know the *when, what,* and *how.* That's your gift. You're the very best at the first three of the Five Ws. You do that and we can find the last two because, once you aim us toward the *who,* the *why* can't be far away."

Miranda was silent for some thirty seconds.

Noor watched the others, but no one looked impatient or in any hurry. Though Andi Wu continued to massage her jaw. Barty had also hung back and appeared to be watching the proceedings with intent interest.

Miranda finally spoke. "And it's okay that I don't understand the *why* even after we have the *who*?"

"Absolutely. We're an investigation team. That's our job. The *why* isn't our problem anyway."

"Okay. I guess. As long as my whole life since I was thirteen hasn't been a waste." Miranda straightened her vest.

"It hasn't," the other three managed in unison.

"Then I only have one question." She began going through her vest pockets, verifying to herself what was in each pocket.

Again everyone waited. Noor didn't know anything about autistics beyond the diversity training that he *had* been required to take despite Mike's earlier assessment at the airport. He'd simply never knowingly met one before. The reality was far different from the four minutes the trainer had spent on explaining the ASD spectrum. For now, he took his cue from the others and also settled in to wait.

When she was done, she looked up at Mike, at least part way. "Why is it called the Five *W*s? It's Four *W*s and an *H*."

Noor laughed. *That* was her one question? Perhaps he did understand this woman better than he thought; she was logical to a fault. "Because *people* do call it that, Ms. Chase. There's a *W* in *how* and people ignore the illogicalness of the title because they finding—find—it easier."

"Oh. Meaning it's one of those things I'll never understand." Instead of looking upset, she pulled out a notebook and a handheld weather station. In moments she was writing down wind, temperature, humidity, and barometric readings—so abruptly finished with the conversation that he felt off balance. Then she, Andi, and Holly stepped out to inspect the debris field.

"Still glad you came along?" Mike asked him.

"Yes. You people are very strange...but yes." He'd never seen a team like this one, but his commander had told him just what caliber they were. The Number One anything out of America meant they were probably the best in the world, and this was their best crash investigation team. He didn't understand them yet, but Holly was right. If he wanted to lead the teams of the 1st Commando Battalion Special Forces of Singapore someday, he must learn to be flexible. To stay open. He hoped there was more to experience before he returned to base.

14

———

Miranda did her best to keep her attention on the debris but her vision kept blurring out. She'd never been so...angry as the moment she'd thought her whole life had been a waste.

Not descending into some autistic meltdown, but instead outright furious at all the waste.

She'd been misguided by her parents. Convinced for years that she was mentally deficient; an attitude that Andi fought back against every time Miranda mentioned it in any form.

And then—

To have her base assumption about how everything in her life she was proud of was a misconception on her part had tipped her over some edge.

Meg happily led the way through the debris dropped by the scavengers. As Andi had said, it was a thin gleaning of the practical and the memento. And Meg—

Miranda stumbled to a halt and looked down at her dog.

Meg's sixth dog sense made her stop and look up at Miranda.

"How did you know?"

Meg wagged her tail in answer.

"How did she know what?" Lieutenant Noor stood close beside her. She shifted twenty more centimeters away.

"My dog is a highly trained autism therapy dog. She has a number of trained responses when I'm having...problems. But when I was so angry, she didn't respond at all, did she?"

"No, she sat as if watching a water polo match for the first time in her life. Bewildered but intrigued."

"I...wasn't having a meltdown?"

"No," Noor responded without hesitation. "It sounded more like a perfectly normal panic attack to me."

"Are you familiar with those?"

"I have seen them among some new recruits. Singaporean military training is not for those without strong intent."

"So, you're saying I had a perfectly normal emotional response to a provoking thought?"

"I would say yes."

Miranda looked down at Meg, who still watched her. "And you knew?"

Meg wagged her tail again.

"I don't know that I've ever had a confirmed purely emotional response before, at least not one of any magnitude."

"Something new every day, my commander always says. The path of success."

Miranda pulled out her personal notebook to write that down, but the thought was jarred aside by Holly stepping up to her.

"I was trying to avoid this, Miranda, but there's something I think you need to see. I know it's inside the plane and you aren't ready for that yet, but I think it's that important."

15

––––––––

Miranda mentally consulted her layered spheres, but their order had become all jumbled since realizing that the innermost one, people, might actually be the most essential. Did debris need to come before airframe? And did the order of outside to inside of airframe actually make a discernable difference to the ultimate findings of the investigation?

A deep breath, which she held as long as she could before letting it out slowly seemed to help. She imagined stepping through each sphere in turn until she reached... "Okay. Inside." Then blinked in surprise to see that she'd taken six physical steps forward as well.

The air felt thicker and thicker as they forged through the actual spheres themselves. She leaned into a palpable headwind pressing at the outer edge of the primary debris field —and almost fell on her face when there *was* no wind on the other side of that line.

Her thoughts had been so hectic she should backtrack all the way to the scavenger leavings, as she could barely recall them. Instead, she battered her way past the sphere of inspection of the aircraft's outside: final resting position, timing of multiple impacts as revealed by damage paths and estimated speed at first contact with the terrain, rock and foliage damage, and a hundred other external markers.

There would be no exterior view of the cockpit until cranes and welders arrived to cut away the collapsed television broadcast tower. Which also blocked the passenger doors.

However, the very rear of the fuselage was accessible because the tail had been torn off up at the peak. But it offered no entry. The direct impact of the falling steel radio mast had hammered into the Top Hat radar protruding above the fuselage and driven it down into the space below.

Peering into the wreckage, she spotted the contents of a battered toolbox scattered far and wide—though it looked as if the latches had been opened rather than ripped asunder. The heavy electronics cabinets were accordioned by the impact of the mast driving downward upon the radar's external element. Three of ten cabinet doors were open, each reflecting significant damage, but not sufficient to damage a *properly closed* toolbox.

However, the crew rest area was accessible through the missing door. In here, everything looked surprisingly normal other than the closest seat being missing. The metal should never have failed here, yet it had. Heavily distorted. Hadn't she seen a seat down on the road? Yes, she had, but she hadn't inspected it carefully beyond noting the distortion of its base— she had no measurements of support deflection angles and distances or damage indications at the actual attachment points or any of it.

Miranda *hated* doing this out of order...which was knowledge in itself. In the future, she'd keep her original sphere-model order.

To resist the urge to backtrack all the way to the seat, she considered the emergency exit itself. Had someone departed the plane after it crashed? Or, like the Asiana flight in South

Korea last year, had some passenger managed to open the door to jump out at the last moment before impact?

Looking down the hole that the seat had torn in the flooring, she could see that the whole area of framing had been crumpled. It was atypically damaged, perhaps due to a belly impact on the rocky peak. This was new. She wanted to inspect more carefully how the seat had broken free of the framing and knocked the panel, including the emergency over-wing door, loose—possibly without human intervention. Based on the damage she could see, a very large person must have been seated here as the seat itself would have insufficient mass to tear away in such a manner even with the damage from beneath.

But before she could take even one measurement, Holly was leading her forward once more. The others were trailing behind.

The Wedgetail's main cabin was surprisingly intact. Chairs lined up, most locked in the forward-facing position appropriate for crash preparedness. The emergency breathers weren't in their normal stowage positions and there was an open fire extinguisher clip on the side of a cabinet.

"The rope." She stopped and looked down at it.

"The rope," Holly agreed.

16

―――――――

IT STRETCHED FROM THE BASE OF THE FLIGHT COMMANDER'S
second-position seat to the cockpit door's handle.

The door was in the closed position, pinned closed by a section of the steel radio mast that had punched through the cabin roof. Miranda reached to work the handle, something felt wrong. The handle had been deformed. Bent—at an angle in keeping with a very high strain placed on it by the rope.

The bottom along the door jamb was bent outward into the cabin. She knelt down and extracted a flashlight from its assigned pocket in her vest as very little light filtered in through the various holes punched by the collapsed radio mast. Red paint along the crease and additional horizontal buckling to the door seal fifteen centimeters above the floor. As if something had been jammed in the door—something round by the nature of the bending.

"Lieutenant Noor," she called out. "There were two fire extinguishers in the collection of debris left by the scavengers. Could you please fetch the one that's lying east-west, perpendicular to the road, and bring it back?" It was chance that she remembered that. She was never, ever going to inspect a plane out of order again. Yet, now that she was this far in, she couldn't mentally fight her way back through the spheres and start over.

"Uh, yes, ma'am." She heard his feet trotting away.

She began calculating the pressure required to bend the door frame. With a caliper, she tested that the metal on a Wedgetail cockpit door was the same thickness as a standard 737. It was. A sprung pin punch proved that it was of the same grade of hardness.

We lost the pilots, had been the Wedgetail's final report. If the loss was due to an unpressurized cockpit and a fully pressurized cabin at forty-thousand feet... A rough calculation for the necessary pressure to bend the door in such a fashion offered an immense result.

"I'll have to write to the door's manufacturer."

"Why's that?" Barty asked.

"The stoutness of the door handle is quite impressive. It deformed but didn't fail despite a bending force of nine-point-five tons. No, wait, I failed to integrate for the angle of the door as it opened, so, an initial load of five tons, tapering rapidly to three. It was a good job that they doubled the rope—that's well past its single-strand breaking point."

Barty was staring at her in a way she didn't like, then he turned to Holly. "You weren't kidding."

Before Holly could answer what she hadn't been kidding about, Noor returned with the extinguisher—it had the paint scratches she'd recalled. She laid it on its side in the doorway but couldn't quite slip it in. Her attempts to open the door were resisted by the L-shaped piece of the radio mast that had pierced the cabin roof.

Holly wiggled it, then gave it a hard shove. Nothing.

She slid off her own pack and pulled out a tool about the size of a multi-D-cell flashlight. "Everyone look away." Then she pulled on welder's gloves and dark glasses.

Miranda scooted clear, covered Meg's eyes, then looked down at the carpeting and closed her own.

Even so, Miranda could see a brilliant arc of light shine for three seconds—a thermite cutting torch.

"That'll do," Holly grunted, then tossed a four-foot-long L-shaped section of steel into a corner with a loud clang.

Miranda opened her own eyes to make sure it was okay, then uncovered Meg's.

She opened the door enough to slide in the fire extinguisher. It fit the marks perfectly.

It was difficult to make notes in her notebook without the normal outer-sphere data on the first pages. Finally, she left room to add a table of contents to organize which sphere came in what order in her notes. She explained aloud as she recorded her findings.

"The cockpit was unpressurized and the cabin pressurized to normal at cruising altitudes. With the rope, they were able to open the door sufficiently to insert the fire extinguisher as a blocking object. Then, they must have reset the rope and opened it the rest of the way, or perhaps waited until the cabin pressure had equalized. That explains why all the masks are down."

Andi touched a finger to the door frame at Miranda's eye level as she knelt on the carpet. A patch of rusty brown.

"Dried blood," Andi whispered. "I'd know it anywhere."

"Yes, you would." They'd seen it on many crashes, but Andi had once had her entire cockpit sprayed with her copilot's blood when she'd still flown for the Army.

"Whoever inserted that fire extinguisher knelt exactly where you're kneeling, Miranda."

"The escaping cabin air would have driven her into the door frame." Miranda leaned forward and saw that the blood lined up with her forehead. "The person would have been my height and will have a pair of vertical wounds to their forehead."

Miranda swung the door fully open.

Andi stepped past her, then came rushing out. In seconds she was violently ill on one of the consoles.

"Why doesn't this look good?" Holly asked.

Nobody answered.

17

———————

Tuah bin Musa acknowledged the code from the Chief of Operations and hung up the radio's microphone. His thirty-meter service and pilot boat was already well out into the Strait of Malacca, two-thirds of the way to the ailing Arabian tanker.

"Finally!" It had been far too long. Not since the crippling of the USS *Theodore Roosevelt* in the South China Sea two years ago distracted everyone's attention had there been an opportunity like this one. Between a recently rebuilt but still annoyed American 9th Carrier Group, Singaporeans on the sea, and the Australians aloft, the Strait of Malacca was a hard place to make a serious profit from any less-than-legal operation.

He stared out at the scattered traffic, seeking a target. His was one of the smallest boats on the water. Three-million-barrel supertankers from the Persian Gulf, four-hundred-meter-long cargo ships carrying over ten-thousand forty-foot containers, and too many smaller vessels to count ranged across the waters within easy reach.

Though...he was already headed for a nice midsize tanker carrying a half million barrels of Persian crude.

"Get all the tankers moving," he told his first mate. The man was useless, but he was the son of the Queen's second cousin on his mother's side, so what was there to do? With the amount of money the Queen made flow in his direction, he was glad to bow and serve.

"All of them?" the man asked.

If he believed, Tuah would pray to Allah for a thunderbolt to strike his first mate down. For the heavens to open and Allah's great brown foot to come down and grind the man under his heel. But he didn't, so all he could hope for was that a stray bullet might one day solve the problem for him. Was that why the Queen had foisted the man upon him? Knowing his incompetence, did she hope Tuah would deal with the problem? Ah! Now it made sense, but he'd worry about that another time.

"Yes. Now! Every one that is empty. Time is already passing us by."

Tuah's small fleet of coastal tankers gathered refined fuel from big ports and distributed it to smaller ones, a marginally profitable operation. It was the big carriers who made all the money. Actually, not even the big carriers, but their multi-shelled corporate owners who were the lords of oil.

PETRONAS, Petroliam Nasional, had not built their Two-Penis Tower, as the Queen called it, to such great heights because they were barely scraping by. The Chinese National Petroleum Company lined the pockets of their power elite as surely as Shell and ExxonMobil owned America's politicians and BP owned the Commonwealth countries.

When the USS *Theodore Roosevelt* had been so damaged two years ago, all attention had focused on the South China Sea. Other aircraft carriers had rushed there, planes circled, and stupid people like China had probed for weaknesses in the American armor. Rumor said they'd lost several submarines for that miscalculation.

But with the world's attention on the South China Sea, no one had been watching the Strait of Malacca. He'd made a small fortune.

He didn't yet know what had happened. His useless spies, who wanted so much money, had offered him no more warning this time than two years ago. But fate, karma, or whatever it was had seen him perfectly ready—already underway in the strait with a full crew aboard.

"Did you tell the crew to change the sign?" His boat's real name on display across the stern was an invitation to a long jail sentence for all aboard.

His clueless first mate looked at him in surprise.

Not trusting himself to speak, Tuah tapped the compass heading he'd set on the GPS, pointed straight ahead, and stepped out of the wheelhouse. Hopefully the man was capable of letting the autopilot follow a straight course without wrecking them.

He let the fresh air and the scent of the sea clear his head. This. *This* is what mattered. A few gulls, too stupid to know that he was a pilot boat, not a fishing boat, circled and cried overhead. The breeze of motoring along at eighteen kilometers per hour washed away his anger. It reminded him of his days out on his father's fishing boat off the village of Bagan Lalang—before the Chinese built their resort there and pretended the locals didn't exist except when a new servant was needed.

He and his father would float for hours on the shore currents. Bapa would often joke about Tuah's name, "bin Musa. The son of Moses." The old man—somehow his father had always seemed old—would tap his own chest. Bapa was also named bin Musa for the centuries of fishermen who had come before him. "I parted the waters. Now you part the waters," and he would pat the gunwale of their small fishing boat.

Even when they caught barely enough fish to feed the family, the days were good under the hot sun. His father would make up great tales about any ship that Tuah pointed to. And even back then, there were always so many ships to choose from. Even now as he watched the traffic increase year-over-year, he didn't see the money flowing by. Rather, he saw a hundred stories, a thousand, ten thousand.

"Life is not so pretty, Bapa," he told the gulls.

He had set off to truly part the waters, sailing with the Merchant Marine. Off to see the wild ports, the dancing women, the dreams of an old fisherman who'd never traveled even the seventy kilometers to Malacca City. Tuah had learned that a cargo crane in Shanghai looked little different than an oil terminal off Amsterdam. That in most countries he wasn't even allowed off the boat because this customs man or that didn't trust him not to jump ship.

Instead, Tuah had sent all the money home to Bapa.

On his return, he'd initially been furious with the old man for spending it without asking first. But now he blessed his father.

Bapa had bought Tuah a berth as pilot on this very boat. It was slow and needed more work to maintain than a holy shrine, but it remained the flagship of his fleet that now ranged along three hundred kilometers of the strait.

Age and hard use had crippled Bapa's hands for fishing, but once ashore his father had pined for the sea. Tuah didn't begrudge a single *sen* coin to hire his sister's son, a strong but not ambitious youth, to fish with him each day in that same small boat Bapa's grandfather had built himself.

Tuah was about to signal the crew to change the name across the stern and the registry on either side of the bow. He'd bought a very illegal second AIS identification for his boat to match the *change.* He didn't dare approach the ship they'd been called out to service. His thrice-cursed first mate had drawn the attention of the Australian Wedgetail flying somewhere far above by not turning on the AIS at all after being trusted to start the engines. Tuah had placated them by pretending to be hung over.

But now he was on their radar, in their records. The worst situation.

He stared aloft, not that he expected to spot it. But having the Australian's all-seeing eye looking down at him didn't make sense with the signal he'd received. The chief's code had been very clear: *Safe to engage all shipping. All.* Why had he repeated the last? That could only mean that...there was no spy plane to watch him.

Had something happened to it?

If it was truly out of the sky...

Tuah looked ahead. The tanker he'd been racing out to service, the one moving slower than most because of a cranky Number Two engine, was expecting him. Would welcome him aboard without any questions, if he kept his service boat ID active. And even at this distance he could see that it was loaded to the waterline—no red bottom paint, only the black topsides showing along the water.

No one had ever successfully pirated an armed ship. That's why, when pirating, he posed as a pilot boat or an official safety inspector. But he'd already been invited aboard this one for the way this boat's crew made their living in normal times—as emergency mechanics.

He swung up his binoculars and inspected it again. It wasn't one of the great supertankers, but the Aframax-class ship would still carry a half million barrels of crude.

He ducked his head back into the wheelhouse.

"Turn off the AIS."

The Queen's second cousin's son did so without thinking to ask why.

Tuah didn't have him turn on the alternate AIS. He waited through one minute, then two. After five minutes with no response from the watchdog of the skies, he knew they were gone. "Turn it back on," because the tanker would expect to see it.

"Order up three boats to meet us." He listed the three closest. Then decided he should be even more specific. "Make sure that they're empty or order up the next closest." Tuah kept half an ear listening to make sure the dolt didn't mishandle even that simple task.

But mostly Tuah watched the big Aframax tanker. A half million barrels of crude. His three boats could handle a hundred and fifty thousand each. Even sold on the black market—PETRONAS's refineries paid half of the fair market value for *no-source* crude, pocketing the rest themselves—it would be ninety million ringgit for a day's work. And he knew that the Queen's power meant that was still double what PETRONAS paid other pirates.

He picked up the microphone for the legitimate trade channel, then double-checked that the idiot first mate hadn't mis-set the frequency before transmitting.

"Tanker *Ocean Queen*," he'd take the name as a good omen. "This is your service vessel ready to come alongside."

"Roger. Proceed to ladder on starboard side."

Boarding by ladder limited the ability of a team to storm the ship. But he had other ways to get men and arms aboard.

Every one of his mechanics had a minimum two years' military training, and their toolkits reflected that.

Except the Queen's second cousin's son, of course.

18

———

Miranda looked into the cockpit as Andi's retching continued to sound in the Wedgetail's main cabin.

Two people were in the pilots' seats, facing forward.

People.

She remained far from comfortable with the concept that the people were the most important aspect of a crash investigation. They were the least logical and predictable element of a highly precise machine. Yet here they were, at the very core of the plane. All the other bodies had been removed, except these two—hidden by the radio mast collapsed on top of them and the jammed cockpit door trapped by the same radio mast.

The pilot's body had been burned heavily enough to desiccate the skull. Blood had run down his shoulder and chest.

"That's unusual."

"What is?" Holly had moved up close behind her. "How the bloody hell did that happen?"

"Bloody is an accurate descriptor. I'm unsure of the Hell part of your assessment."

"I'm not." Holly sounded certain enough that Miranda wondered if, in order to understand the human factors more completely, she'd have to delve into metaphysical or religious studies. Neither had ever made sense to her. There appeared to be no practical basis for any of it, simply an unrooted *desire* for something to be true. And her efforts at self-exploration were generally focused on how to survive the world around her.

Something the pilot hadn't achieved.

"To bleed in this manner implies a severe hemorrhage within the head, releasing internal fluids at a high rate under pressure."

"So, what? His brain boiled over?"

Miranda considered. "That's an accurate statement. Is it also a metaphor in some way I don't understand?"

Holly shook her head, nodded, then swallowed hard before answering in a rough voice. "The metaphor is like a pot boiling over."

"Ah, thank you." Miranda nodded. "Making it a poor metaphor, because it more boiled out of his ears, eyes, nose—"

"No need to be quite so graphic, Miranda."

"Oh, okay."

"This really doesn't bother you?"

She looked again at the burnt corpse of the pilot. "I suppose it bothers me that someone took the life of a pilot. It does make me curious as to why. But knowing that I so rarely understand other's motivations, I've learned to make that less of an issue."

"The first four *W*s, is it?"

"Who, the pilot of an RAAF E-7A Wedgetail." Was *who* being first in the saying *who, what, when, where, why, and how* make the *whos* more important? And if so, was that something that the Grinch Who Stole Christmas understood, all of those whos in Whoville? "Wait!"

"What?"

"No, what's second."

Holly closed her eyes, "I've just entered a classic comedy routine."

"Who, what, when, where, why, and how. That's six *W*s, not five *W*s."

"Uh," Holly inspected the circuit breakers in the ceiling panel, though Miranda cataloged no unusual settings when she looked. "Can we table that for now as less relevant than, uh," she nodded toward but didn't quite look at the pilot.

"*Where* isn't usually considered one of the five *W*s," Mike said from the doorway.

"But that's—" Miranda stopped herself midsentence. "I suppose my noting that is illogical when *where* actually begins with a W but *how* doesn't." She took a series of three centering breaths and felt better for it. "I already did *who*. We'll know precisely *when* from the flight data recorder that Holly recovered. Wait, that's out of order. I'm getting all jumbled up. *What* comes next. It—"

"Holy Mother Mary! What happened to the pilot?" Mike focused down at him in profile from where he stood behind the copilot's seat.

"Exactly," Miranda nodded. "*What* is that the blood and brain matter poured out his skull's orifices. *When*— No, wait, I already did when. *Why*. Andi told me not to worry about *why*s because I'm so bad at them. And *how*. Probably by having his head superheated by a high-power infrared laser. Like..." she could feel there *was*—another *W*—a good metaphor somewhere nearby. "Like a..." she closed her eyes and— "Oh! Like a potato in a microwave if you forget to poke it." She doubled her fists together, then made a *ka-blooey* sound and tossed her hands open.

"Ka-blooey?" Mike asked.

"Not quite." She repeated the sound more carefully for him. "I had to blow up over twenty potatoes—twenty-seven to be exact, of varying sizes and varieties—before I could imitate the sonic profile sufficiently to demonstrate it to my mother. I never understood why she wasn't pleased. I thought it was a good first-order approximation of the average sonic discharge given the shortcoming of phonic reproduction of plosive sounds by human vocal chords and oral shapings."

"His head would have sounded like..." Mike didn't finish his sentence though Miranda made sure to leave him enough time to do so.

"I don't know. I never tried microwaving heads. Cleaning out all those potatoes was messy enough."

Holly leaned forward to look at the pilot more closely. "A high-power laser? Like that Chinese orbital laser that attacked the USS *Theodore Roosevelt?* What makes you say that?"

"I didn't say that."

"You said a high-powered laser."

"I did. But I didn't say anything about China, orbits, or similarities to the attack on the *Roosevelt.*"

"Okay, then what would you say?"

"A high-powered laser. That should be evident from the fact that I've already agreed that's what I said."

"Whose?"

"Is that another *W?* That would make seven. Well, six true ones and one false one. I have no idea."

"But it was definitely a laser?"

Miranda rolled her eyes. She felt them roll. Then she yelped loudly.

Andi pushed into the packed cockpit. "Are you okay, Miranda?"

"I did an eye roll, and it felt right. Was it right?"

Mike grinned down at her as Holly said, "Smack on, Little Sister." And held up a hand to high five.

Miranda high-fived all around.

"Yer a right strange crowd, sure enough." Barty had come around the outside of the plane and managed to slip through the wreckage to look through the missing window.

"Warned you," Mike told him. "Now, Miranda. What do we know about this laser?"

19

"GO AHEAD, MIRANDA." DRAKE ANSWERED THE SITUATION ROOM phone halfway through the first ring.

"Less non-topic-relevant than even your usual greeting. Most efficient," Miranda replied from half a world away. "Which was a non-topic-relevant statement from me. Sorry."

"It's okay. I'm here with Lizzy and Vice President Sarah Feldman." The three of them had been sitting around the table with far too little information, trying desperately to control the situation from half a world away.

The Aussies wanted revenge for their plane and their people.

Two experts from State had briefed them on the critical importance of the Strait of Malacca.

The Secretary of Defense was pushing to send a carrier group into either end, but with the latest hot spots of Yemen effectively closing the Suez, and China shoving hard against Taiwan, even the US's vaunted aircraft carrier capacity was getting stretched thin.

It was past midnight. Sarah had sent the President to bed an hour ago but neither she nor his wife had done him the same favor. Lizzy had been given her second general's star and now commanded the National Reconnaissance Office with a confidence that was hard to credit when he recalled the trepidation she'd shown when first taking over the NRO five years ago.

Hopefully Miranda would have something concrete. Maybe then he could get some sleep.

"Would it be a time wasting irrelevancy if I greeted them?"

"Not at all." He traded smiles across the table with the two women. Lizzy knew Miranda's peculiarities almost as well as he did. He and Miranda had first met about the same time he and Lizzy had—Miranda had stood as Lizzy's maid of honor. VP Sarah Feldman had caught on quickly as well.

"Hello." And that appeared to complete that item on whatever odd mental checklist Miranda used. "I was about to explain some things to the team and Holly suggested I call you and let you hear what few findings I have."

"We've been waiting on tenterhooks."

"I know the phrase, but what *is* a tenterhook?"

Drake opened his mouth, then closed it. "I have no idea."

"It's an old word for a hook used to attach a cloth to a drying frame," Sarah explained. At his look she answered, "Hey, Mister Chairman of the Joint Chiefs, you aren't the only one in this room who knows shit."

"Yes, ma'am. I'll remember that." He turned to the speaker phone. "Go ahead, Miranda. We'll take anything you've got." She turned on her phone's camera and some Marine monitoring the Sit Room communications routed it to the big screen mounted on the end wall.

A very black man stared so steadily at the camera that Drake wondered if he was one of the victims.

"You can see by the melting of the acrylic window laminate..." Miranda spoke up.

The black man looked down at the window edge by his

chin so abruptly that Lizzy and Sarah gasped in surprise. So, he hadn't been the only one fooled.

"...that a very high heat was induced in the material by a high-wattage laser. I'm unable to estimate the power yet as I don't yet know the attacker's distance."

"Could it have been orbital?" Drake shivered when he remembered how close they'd come to war over that one.

"No. The plane of attack, sorry, the *angle* of attack—to avoid homonym-based confusion—" She paused for the length of three heartbeats. "Sarah, when you're President, I hope that you will have more success at clarifying the English language than Roy did."

"I haven't been elected yet. And I doubt it. The language has been jumbling along for well over a millennium. I think it lies beyond my power to fix."

"Well, that's disappointing."

Drake had grown used to Miranda's ways. "You were saying about the angle of attack?" he prompted her back onto the key topic. He only hoped that whoever replaced him would think to do the same. President Roy Cole's second term would be ending soon, and Drake had long since arranged to retire the day *his* President left office.

"To have liquified the pilot's cerebral cortex, well back from the window, implies a low angle of attack—aircraft-to-aircraft rather than orbital-to-aircraft unless he was performing an atypically steep climb."

"To have done *what?*"

Miranda turned the camera from the black man still furrowing his brows at the melted acrylic to a horror directly out of a Hollywood slasher film. Lizzy gasped. Sarah gagged. Drake was glad of the time difference. Noon there, midnight here, so there was nothing in his stomach except a single cup of Navy-strong coffee that had barely been sustaining him.

"In addition to surficial charring, which you can see further evidence of behind him." Miranda shifted the camera to show the outline of the pilot's head on the seatback and then the shadow of the seatback on the scorched rear bulkhead of the cockpit.

It was a relief to no longer have the gory face upon the screen.

"He displays excessive flow of blood and...other liquified matter out of...multiple orifices. Based on the distension of his jaw, I would estimate that he was screaming when he died."

Drake wanted to close his eyes in case Miranda felt that another closeup was necessary to support her statement. Vice President Sarah Feldman had closed hers, but Lizzy stared fixedly at the screen. He'd known her for five years, been married to her for four, and General Elizabeth Gray continued to astound him. She'd been a US Air Force combat pilot flying F-16 Viper fighters. Who knew what she'd seen on the field of battle. It all should have been neat and clean in a jet, which always returned to base after a flight, but perhaps not.

Well, he'd been a 75th Ranger and would *not* be outdone by an air jockey, not even if she was his wife.

"The copilot," Miranda continued, "is quite a different matter."

She twisted around, panning across the other three members of her team squeezed into the cockpit and, in the cabin door, the face of a Chinese man in a military uniform that passed by too fast to identify.

He braced himself, but the copilot looked almost normal. His lower face was covered by an air mask and upper face appeared almost at rest except for the open and staring eye.

"His injuries did not come from the front, despite that window also being melted out."

The camera swung to again show the black man's face now peering sideways to inspect the other windshield.

"Instead," she panned to the burned-out side window, "he

was struck from the starboard side." She reached the phone around in front of the copilot's face.

He was revealed like some villain to have half a normal face and the other half distorted almost past recognition as human. Even the face mask was normal on one side and melted into his features on the other, adding to the alien demeanor.

"Like Two-Face," Sarah told him.

Drake didn't know the reference.

Sarah swallowed hard. "One of Batman's arch villains, brought to life. Come on, Drake, you must have read Batman as a kid." Her tone shifted to avoid the horror on the screen.

"Fantastic Four, Hulk, X-Men," he named off the ones he could think of, not that he'd ever read them.

Lizzy scoffed. She knew him too well.

Then they all looked back at the screen and the reality crashed down again.

But there was something else wrong. Something...

He scrabbled around until he found the RAAF crew manifest. "Something's wrong, Miranda. The listed copilot is a woman, a Mathilda Jackson."

Miranda's image swung down to focus on the copilot's unburned left breast. *Felton* was stitched above his pocket.

He found the name easily. "Squadron Leader Grant Felton. He was the systems officer."

"One of the women in the body bags." He didn't recognize the male voice with a strong Asian accent. "The Malaysian guard say her face so very badly burned. They find her in very rear seats of plane with great big man. So big his body take five men to carry."

"Thank you, Lieutenant Noor. Well done." Miranda addressed someone off screen. "You see, Drake. Everything is out of order. I need to go back to the beginning. None of the pieces fit."

"No, Miranda. Wait!"

There was a shuffling noise over the phone, then he was looking at Holly Harper's face.

"But—"

"She's gone, Drake, so deal with it. That's more info than I expected from the way we've been jumping her around. So, you've got a laser attack plane-to-plane at altitude."

"Two dead or critically wounded by the first laser attack," a thick Australian voice spoke up. "Changed out a pilot, who is struck by a second attack."

"Right. Good one, Barty."

A survivor? Would they have mentioned that? Drake glanced down the flight's manifest, but there was no Bart, Barty, or Bartholomew.

Some Marine monitoring the room proved how good he was as he flashed up the man's photo and profile on a side screen: Barty Kirwan, Chief Commissioner ATSB. A few moments later a bio scrolled up beside it. SASR (retired) like Holly, and as highly decorated. That was both interesting and impressive.

Holly continued, "There's something wonky about the cabin door, like—"

"They had to break into the cockpit," Andi spoke from off screen as well. "Rope and fire extinguisher. Jerry-rigged."

"Yes, that's it. They must have been on autopilot so the crew had time to break into the cabin. Systems Officer takes over and tries to bring them down safely. Until he's attacked again. Oh Christ!"

"What? Are you okay?"

"No," Holly paused long enough to leave Drake to wonder if they'd all been lased and he'd never hear from them again.

"Barty," Holly's voice was so low and dangerous that Drake could barely understand her. "We've got to see that Felton gets the biggest damn decoration ever."

"Why's that, mate?"

"It's why the crash is so clean. He completed the landing with half his face burned off."

When she abruptly hung up the phone, Drake couldn't feel offended. But he'd make damn sure that Grant Felton received highest honors if he had to fly down to Australia himself to do it. It was the least a fellow warrior could do.

20

———

Drake turned to the room but didn't know what to say.

"What's next?" Sarah was the first to recover. Good sign if she won the next election.

As Chairman of the Joint Chiefs of Staff, Drake was specifically nonpolitical. But he'd be voting for Sarah, no matter who they ran against her.

"Do we wake the President?"

Drake shook his head. "Not until we have something actionable, and concrete suggestions for him. There's no need, based on current information, for you to stay up. I can contact you if there are any new devel..."

He shut up when he saw her don't-be-stupid look. *What's next?* By the sound of it, Miranda would be offline for a while until she had a better grasp on what had happened. He'd have to trust her team. The Australian RAAF team was still nineteen hours out according to the latest estimates.

"The weapon," Lizzy said.

Drake wondered who was the CIA's top next-generation-weapons person. After all, if he was going to lose another night's sleep, it seemed only fair that she should too.

Lizzy dialed a number from memory and put it on speaker phone.

On the third ring, a male voice answered with a sloppy, "Uh-huh."

"Good morning, Jeremy. Sorry to wake you."

Of course. Miranda's right-hand man until he came to DC, Jeremy Trahn. The ultimate nerd-boy.

"Uh-huh." A wail started up in the background. "Uh-oh."

In the background, a female voice said, "I've got her," with an impressive lack of enthusiasm.

"Um..." Jeremy protested weakly, then seemed to recall he was holding a phone. "Uh, hello?"

"I'm sorry to wake everyone, Jeremy. This is Lizzy Gray."

"Uh-huh."

Drake recalled that Jeremy and Taz's baby had colic. Sure enough, the wail in the background sounded like someone was driving a knife into the kid. He remembered his second daughter's unsoothable agony, which had simply evaporated at thirteen weeks after putting them through three months of hell. Jeremy was probably running on a ten-minute sleep cycle, and they'd just woken the whole household.

Lizzy continued, "I'm in the Sit Room with Drake and VP Feldman."

"Uh-oh."

"Are you awake enough to answer a question? Then I'll let you try to get back to sleep."

"Uh-huh."

"Who can field a plane-to-plane laser powerful enough to melt the windscreens and, uh," Drake could see Lizzy swallow hard, "significantly burn the pilots?"

"What plane?"

"E-7A Wedgetail."

"Whoa!" Jeremy suddenly sounded very awake.

And his shout of surprise was loud enough to set off the

baby Taz had been soothing in the background. She'd been moving closer to the phone, probably to listen in, but now cursed emphatically and moved away again.

"At what range? What duration?"

"Unknown and unknown. Miranda's on site but was only able to give us preliminary information."

"Okay. Militarized Boeing 737…" he began mumbling material thickness and ballistic acrylic opacity factors, frequency spectrums and wattages, and all the other gibberish that was so frustrating to try to follow.

Drake had worked his way from a fresh-faced West Point grad to commanding the 75th Rangers before the Pentagon got him in their sights. As Chief of the Army and now the Chairman of the Joint Chiefs, it was his job to keep track of weapons developments and be able to offer advice to the President about them all.

Reminding himself that Miranda's people operated in a very narrow specialty didn't make him feel any better that he had to struggle to keep up. There was a reason they were his go-to people in these types of situations, but it didn't make his ego any happier each time he had to.

"How badly burned?" Jeremy emerged from his musings.

"*Raiders of the Lost Ark* melting heads," Sarah replied. She'd already learned Jeremy's language. "Plus charring."

Drake at least knew that reference. Only the reality had been so much worse.

"Uh-huh."

Drake was going to throttle the boy if he said that again. He returned to his musings for long enough that he, Lizzy, and Sarah had time to trade weak smiles.

"Okay! So," then Jeremy began speaking at high speed. "Base premise is strong infrared rather than visible spectrum. That simplifies it a lot. I'd have to run tests to be sure, but heating the acrylic enough to melt based on interstitial impurities and ninety-five-plus percent transmissivity, as well as cause catastrophic failure of the cranial containment—I've never studied that in detail—points to infrared frequencies without requiring enormous scales of power. US, China, and Israel definitely. Russia maybe, but I don't think at the necessary wattages outside the visual spectrum; I haven't heard of them having any success in those ranges prior to the Ukraine War and since then they've revealed quite how low-tech their thinking is—World War II artillery and tanks. And did you see the washing machine chips they used in the Kinzhal hypersonic missile's guidance system? We were so worried about that thing and half the time that they do reach the target they don't even detonate. Give me a break, that's beginner level. So, I'd say no to them. They can kill a satellite but not cause internal heating of the head as you described. India could build one but I haven't heard about it. And two, no, three, who have the knowledge, but no one talks about, are: Japan, South Korea, and Sweden."

"So, all the usual suspects," Drake considered. "Who are the unusual suspects?"

"That's a tough one, General Nason. Even a major ally like Australia or the UK would be hard pressed to achieve this without our knowledge. Someone could buy it, I suppose. Who do we sell heavy laser tech to?"

Drake glanced at Sarah. She'd been the National Security Advisor before replacing Vice President Clark Winston. She shook her head, and she would know.

"Not us," he told Jeremy.

"China isn't selling their tech to anyone, too afraid someone will use it against them."

"Which leaves Israel. With a possible but unlikely for India, South Korea, Japan, and Sweden."

"Best estimate, yes."

"Thanks. Sorry for waking the kid."

Another wail, this time close enough to the phone to pulse into the Situation Room and hurt his ears.

Then he heard Taz's voice, "And no, that doesn't make us even, General." But he heard her laugh before Jeremy hung up. Had becoming a mother softened Colonel Taz Cortez? Now *that* might be the strangest event of the whole evening.

"So," Drake asked, "who can we wake up in Israel?"

Sarah pulled up her contact list and keyed a number into the speakerphone on the table. "I'll let you do the talking, Drake. He and I didn't exactly see eye to eye when I was at USCENTCOM."

"Bad?"

"Good. Just a wide streak of self-righteous prick."

He was in a fine mood to deal with someone like that. Sarah made Drake almost sorry that he'd be retiring soon. Almost.

21

———————

Benny Muntz clocked the third kilometer on his treadmill and wished the Lord our God, Defender of the Universe, would smite this machine. What was the point of achieving the high rank of *aluf* in Israel's military if he had to do this? Did any of the US' two-star generals put themselves through such daily hell? He'd wager a thousand new shekel against it—at least not any of the sane ones, of which the Americans must have a few.

Benny hadn't intended to fall for a younger woman. He'd always confirmed himself as a bachelor, *I'm married to the military*—until Shira had breezed into his life.

Five K. Today he *would* hit five kilometers upon this accursed contraption. An *aluf* of the Israel Defense Forces would *not* be defeated by some machine. But if Moses had forced the Pharoah onto one of these, there'd have been no need for the ten plagues to free the Children of Israel from slavery. *Five K every day or break the bonds of slavery for the Children of Israel? Don't bother with parting the Red Sea, Moses. Take my ships. Keep them if you want. Here's some leavened bread to take with you.*

133

Shira, of course, had already leapt out of bed and run her five K in an easy loping stride that had been a wonder to watch as he slowly strove for full consciousness. She now did yoga while he suffered the distance. At least watching her gave him the goal to strive for. His bedroom had barely fit the treadmill, so she worked out on her mat in the only available space, directly before his eyes.

Behind her, the floor-to-ceiling windows revealed the early morning sun shining off the Mediterranean. He'd bought this place for the view, but watching Shira made it hard to remember quite which view.

And he wanted to keep up with her, far more than he'd expected to ever care about such things at his age.

Let's go dancing, Benny. The way she could move on the dance floor parted crowds faster than a Red Sea miracle. *Let's go swimming in Tenerife, Benny, when was the last time you took a vacation for yourself?* She swam like a mermaid along the white sand beaches of the Canary Islands. *Take me to bed, Benny.* Oh, yes.

At sixty, he'd settled comfortably into his body, still soldier fit—for an old soldier. At sixty-one he was ten kilos lighter with five to go and the fittest he'd been since the day he'd left his jet for a desk.

Four kilometers done. And Shira in those tight shorts and matching sports bra, done in the colors of the Israeli flag he served, did one of those backward bend arch things that he knew for a fact was physically impossible.

To hell with the machine.

He punched Stop, rode the slowing tread to the end, then stepped off.

Shaky legs, sweaty, stinking of his workout, he didn't care. In three strides he knelt between her feet. Too desperate to drag her onto the bed, he stripped off her shorts, collapsing that lovely arch. Her perfect ass dropped into his waiting palms. She giggled. The woman actually giggled as he fell on her and feasted upon her body like she was every part of a Passover Seder. He wished to consume her all at once.

She coaxed, teased, pleaded, and gave. Shira never stopped giving until they lay sprawled together on the yoga mat. Both naked except for those shorts snagged around her right root. The fresh sweat and their mutual gasps the only proof that they hadn't just died. That and the corner of the nightstand digging into his butt.

For now, he lay with his ear cushioned against one breast as he caressed the other and listened to her heart slow.

There'd never been a woman like Shira. A single year, one sixty-oneth of his life, yet it seemed she'd always been here. He'd cohabitated before, practically. But the women had always kept their own place for when the inevitable happened after a few months of fun. He'd certainly never lived with a woman before. Yet Shira had moved in within a week of the first time they slept together, three hours after first meeting at some party he no longer recalled. Well, the clingy dress, but what he remembered most about that was taking it off her.

In their year together, she'd never once mentioned wanting more. He listened to her heart's pace pick up as he slid his hand over her ribs and ripped stomach muscles. She slid her arms around his head and pulled him more tightly to her breast. As his hand slipped lower, her heart rate ticked up another notch.

He could never tire of exploring her body. It responded in ways his F-4 Phantom fighter jet's designers had only ever dreamt of.

She'd never asked for any promises, neither commitment nor a ring, but he could no longer remember what life was like without her.

He reached lower, caressing down one of her forever thighs to where her leg hooked over his. She never failed to welcome his touch. How fast *could* he make her heart race?

How would her heart sound if *he* was the one to suggest shifting from living together to a *life* together? His confirmed bachelorhood mien sloughed off so easily, like a tallit prayer shawl after leaving synagogue, that he barely noticed it falling away.

Her heart sounded so loudly in his ear that no other sound existed. Could exist.

Marriage? If that's what it took to keep her by his side, then...yes! It was no longer a question. He'd have to think about how to propose properly. Nothing conventional for Shira. But not when he lay here on the bedroom floor with his hand seeking the Holy Land either. Perhaps he could drive her so hard that she'd simply know? Create such an explosion in her body that she'd arch once more into that perfect, impossible—

Shira jolted.

And they cursed in unison at the blast from his phone—the harsh ring of an encrypted call. That elicited a half-laugh from her and a hatred for yet another aspect of modern technology from him. *Here, Pharoah, have a device intended to interrupt you repeatedly at the most inconvenient time imaginable.*

Shira didn't release the hold on his head against her breast, forcing him to remove his hand from the God-given gift of her body and reach behind him. His other hand was pinned to the floor beneath them, still cupping one cheek of that perfect ass. He found the corner of the nightstand, still digging into his butt, traced the edge up to the top, and managed to grab his phone as it blasted once more. He was a very heavy sleeper, especially if he and Shira had ravaged each other the night before, so he kept it loud.

"This had better be damned good," he answered, once he had the phone to his ear. Shira had shifted her embrace to let him hold the phone but didn't release him. He lay there with her breast pulsing against one ear and his phone against the other. She began to flex a single thigh muscle. The one pressed tight against his—

"Aluf Muntz?" a deep male voice asked. American by the accent.

"Yes."

"This is General Drake Nason."

Benjamin sat up abruptly. Or tried to. Shira's tight hold about his head threw him off balance. All he achieved was rising high enough to jam the sharp upper corner of the nightstand into his shoulder blade before he collapsed back onto Shira's breast.

He knew who Nason was, of course, though he'd never spoken to the man. It wasn't the most dignified position to be in for such a call, but he couldn't think of how to free himself. He'd have to practically castrate himself to get free of where he pressed against her thigh. But her leg, in turn was pinned by his.

Fine, he'd speak to the American Chairman of the Joint Chiefs while entangled in his lover's arms.

"What can I do for you, General?"

Shira stopped with the mind-numbing thigh flexion and began playing with his hair instead.

"I need to know if Israel has ever sold its Iron Beam laser technology to any third country."

"What? Why?"

"We're trying to trace an attack in the Strait of Malacca."

"Must have been one hell of an attack." That was an understatement, considering that Drake was the American's highest-ranked soldier.

"It was. And it was performed with a high-power airborne laser. That leaves very few of us as candidates. We need to know if it was one of yours and trace who might have used it." And the way he said it was accusatory rather than inquisitive.

Shira froze like she'd been cast in ice.

"I can, uh, look into that."

"General Muntz," the man's voice hardened further, "this is an urgent matter at the highest levels. You are listed as the commander in charge of Israel's advanced weaponry division. I need an answer now."

Focus, Benny. Focus. Lying tangled up in Shira didn't help but he managed.

"I would have to do a formal inventory to be certain. But there are no active missions, so they should all be hangared. We have two units out on evaluation."

"Who with?"

"Azerbaijan and…" he couldn't recall until Shira whispered with an impossibly small voice in his other ear, "Vietnam." "Vietnam," he echoed. Right, they'd chatted about that just a month or so ago.

Nason offered a thoughtful grunt.

"Oh, and your people, of course." It wasn't exactly a state secret who was evaluating it. Others had done so, but chosen not to buy in—yet.

"I need all the details as fast as you can. I need visual confirmation of every aircraft and every iteration of the weapon. Including all prototypes and next-gen devices."

"Don't be ridiculous, General Nason. That information constitutes highly classified Israeli state secrets."

There was a pause, long enough that he didn't like it much.

At least Shira had stopped teasing him so that he could think. Those cocky Americans were always so impressed with themselves and their power. For all he cared they could go and—

"General Muntz," Nason spoke up. "Would you rather Vice President Sarah Feldman called your Prime Minister in the next two minutes or the President himself? I should warn you that it's midnight here, and he's *never* in a good mood when woken within an hour of going to bed."

Sarah Feldman? He'd forgotten that she'd been made Vice President, was slated to landslide the upcoming election. A know-it-all pain in the ass—with an encyclopedic mind and guaranteed to recall how helpful Israel had or hadn't been once she was in office. "I'll see what I can do."

"I can be reached at this number in the Situation Room. If I don't hear from you inside thirty minutes, your Prime Minister will be calling you in thirty-one. Thank you, General." And, without an ounce of civility in his tone, the man was gone.

Benjamin stared at the dead phone. With the call ended, Shira renewed her teasing.

Fast? The man wanted fast? Well, if that was all he had time for, he'd show him fast.

With one supreme effort, using a strength and agility he'd partially recovered over these last months with her, he managed to disentangle himself from Shira and roll her over to kneeling on all fours on the yoga mat. Dog position down or something.

He reached around to cup her from the front as he drove in from behind. Fast and deep, he used all of his new conditioning to the utmost. He'd do the final kilometer of the workout into her body. She hung her head, disappearing beneath that soft wave of thick hair, and pushed back hard against each of his thrusts until her body shook with release and he emptied himself into her. Fast, but oh so good.

He let himself enjoy the intense heat of being inside her for a few more seconds before he forced himself to withdraw.

An Iron Beam laser aircraft gone rogue? That would be a disaster for which the US wouldn't merely berate Israel. They'd *punish* them.

22

———

Miranda couldn't stop backing up through the layers of spheres. Her movement lay outside her control, each one seeming to audibly snick shut behind her as she cleared it.

Away from the cockpit, out of the plane, away from the debris field, down the undulating rock path past even the false debris field created by the scavengers, until she and Meg stood once more in the midday heat, close by the Singaporean helicopter. Everywhere she looked was new—and wrong.

For the first time, there were a hundred holes offering views through every layer.

A battered fire extinguisher that should be out in the False Debris section now rested on the floor by the cockpit—worse, she'd put it there herself. Looking up at the fallen radio mast didn't hide the mental view of the dead pilots from her mind's eye.

Andi came trotting up to her, still far paler than usual. "Wow, did you book out of there in a hurry. I can't blame you, that was awful." She winced as if the words physically hurt her.

"Yes. The juxtaposition of incongruous information is very jarring. Is jarring an emotion? And what does that have to do

140

with jars? I jarred jam every summer on my island—" and her words stumbled to a halt. On her burned-over and lost island home. She could feel the wince on her own face. "Oh! I understand now. It isn't the words that hurt you, but the memories that they represent."

Andi narrowed her eyes in that way she had when reviewing one of their conversations. She finally offered an uncertain shrug. "I guess."

Those memories were now cluttering the present reality into a murky fog shimmering through the midday heat. But Miranda was sure she had the right of it.

The right of it.

That's what she needed.

"Okay," she pulled out the crash notebook, turned to the first page, and crossed out the *Report Table of Contents* heading. And then read the sparse notes there.

All the environmental factors had been properly noted before she'd been distracted. She looked at the sky, still a soft blue typical for high heat and humidity tropical climates. The temperature, she checked, had risen another three degrees. She noted that down—a fact corroborated by the sweat on her forehead.

Just to be certain, she let herself spend a few moments looking outside the debris perimeter. Liana vines dominated buttressed tree trunks, their stems in turn coated with mosses, lichens, and numerous other epiphytes. Flowers, especially in the pink and red spectrums, carpeted whole sections of the understory. Yes, the tropical rainforest had remained where it belonged.

Next, mapping the debris perimeter. That had already been done except for the wings. She took three deep breaths, which elicited a soft smile from Andi. Miranda had eventually matched that precise smile to *amused tolerance* (with Mike's help because it didn't appear on her emoji reference page). Did she need to spend the hour or more mapping the wings' debris fields over the steep and rough terrain when she already knew this had been the result of an aerial laser attack upon the pilots?

No. At least not yet. She noted that down.

On a last look at the environment, she noted that there was one element outside the debris perimeter: the ten body bags with their lone guard. Approach this geographically as they lay between the first two spheres: Environment and Debris Perimeter? Or logically, as they were people and would be part of the innermost Human Factors sphere?

"Andi, could you get someone else? I'm going to inspect the bodies next." They were often already removed by the time of her arrival on site, and she'd have to depend on photographs— if the rescue teams had thought to take any.

"You don't want me with you?"

"I saw and understood your reaction in the cockpit to all the dried blood. I didn't want to expose you to more of the same."

Andi hugged her for reasons Miranda didn't understand. "Good job thinking of another's feelings, Miranda."

Oh. That was still hard for her. But as Andi had just hugged her, she felt that was sufficient positive reinforcement that she didn't need to also pat herself on the back as Mike had taught her. Even if the hug had been a little damp and sweaty, it was Andi's and she could tolerate that.

"I'll start out with you, but I won't make any promises about staying." She looked around before calling out. "Lieutenant Noor, would you be willing to accompany Miranda and me on an inspection of the bodies?"

He too, Miranda noted, appeared far paler than he had before, paling further at Andi's question. Perhaps the light here was different than in Singapore. Inspecting her own forearms revealed no noteworthy alteration that she could detect, and she didn't carry a visible-light spectrometer to make quantitative tests. She'd researched them but had been unable to justify the space in her site-investigation kit.

"It's okay to say no," Andi told him.

"No. I wish to learn and be of helpfulness."

The three of them crossed to the line of ten body bags. Andi spoke to the lone guard through Noor. "There are two more bodies in the cockpit. You'll want to send in men with strong stomachs."

He nodded, gathered two empty bags, and went off.

"Why strong stomachs?" Miranda asked. "Neither of the men was particularly large and they'll also be lighter due to partial desiccation from—"

"Don't!" Andi held up a hand to stop her. "Please, Miranda. I know it doesn't bother you, but I find it very hard to look at or even think about them."

"But they're already dead. Do the dead dislike being looked at?" Miranda herself hated it when people stared at her. She could *feel* their eyes boring into her like ten thousand needles or a high-powered waterjet. But she couldn't imagine still feeling that way after she died.

"No. I... It's..." Andi looked at Noor, who shook his head. "It...uh, affects different people differently."

"You project *your* emotions onto *their* death experience. Whereas I don't. I'm only looking for the facts."

Andi nodded.

Miranda liked getting something right about emotions, even if she didn't share them the way neurotypical people did. "If you only focus on the facts revealed by their corpses, perhaps you could keep your emotions from becoming involved."

"Uh, I'll try. But most people—"

"Neurotypicals," Miranda sighed.

"—don't work that way."

Again, something she'd have to memorize but never really understand.

Miranda turned to the body bags. For the first time, she noted *how*—perhaps useful as a *W* word after all—they were laid out on the ground. The ten bags had been placed in the same pattern as the plane seats. She looked around, but there was no one from the Malay Air Force team close enough to thank.

Inside the first body bag lay a group captain; a First People's black woman with a bloody red bandage around her forehead. Yes, she would have been in the command seat, so her body bag had been placed one position closer to the cockpit than the others. And the bandage fit with—Miranda paused as she mentally stepped through three of her spheres—the group captain being the one to kneel in front of the cockpit door and place the fire extinguisher when it was partly opened.

She'd bled from the ears, but there were no wipe marks. Perhaps knocked unconscious because she hadn't braced herself before the escaping cabin pressure had dragged her forward into the door frame.

There was no instruction manual that Miranda had ever seen for how to break into a sealed cockpit when both pilots were disabled. Perhaps she should write one. If she did, she'd be sure to include a section on caution during cabin-depressurization-wind-tunnel effects in high-altitude / low-pressure environments. Yes, that would make a nice addendum to her final findings report.

The other body bags from the main cabin revealed no surprises. The first on what would have been the starboard side of the aircraft, the communications officer, had no blood or other obvious external damage. She alone of those in the cabin showed no bruising along the clavicle or waist where the five-point harness would have crossed. So, she was dead before the crash. She was also the only one without a broken neck caused by the force of the landing impact. Perhaps the abrupt change in cabin pressure had caused a catastrophic nitrogen bubble aerobullosis in her heart or brain, killing her instantly.

The final two bodies, from what would have been the crew rest area by their position, held far more information.

One was the missing female pilot. Burned as expected. An oxygen mask had stuck to her burned skin. She had a broken wrist. Miranda worked it a few times—Noor and Andi both caught their breath sharply. When she turned to look at them, they were both facing away. Miranda inspected the wrist more closely. The break was odd, not at the joint. Rather as if a great force had been applied directly over the inner-wrist pulse point. Slight bruises showed that a massive hand had clutched her wrist. But the bruise had barely colored, indicating she hadn't survived for long, if at all, after the break happened.

The final body, Wing Commander Nelson, had been a great bear of a man. His body showed no atypical damage; he still had a portable breather mask hanging about his neck. He had been mobile during the crisis, perhaps the one to transport the injured copilot to the rear of the plane. But why had he remained there?

"I need the QAR." She didn't have a black box reader with her, though she'd seen that Holly had recovered the cockpit voice data recorder and the flight recorder cores. But she could read the quick access recorder's data if it had survived. And with the remarkable smoothness of the crash, it should have.

Andi pulled out a radio. "Holly, can you get the QAR? We're over by the body bags."

"On it."

23

———

Tuah bin Musa topped the tanker's ladder and stepped onto the deck. Two men awaited him. One clearly the mechanic and the other a very junior officer. Good, no suspicion of what was about to happen to them.

"Tony Lamarr requesting permission to come aboard. This is my assistant." Ozell had come up the ladder close behind him.

They didn't even ask to check his ID, though he did have documents proving his name. Just as Ozell could prove his name was Omar when he had to. These guys were making it too easy; probably their first time being pirated. He'd enjoy giving them a new experience.

A quick scan of the deck revealed no surprises. Forward lay two hundred meters of pipe-covered deck. And aft rose the five stories of the tower block with the windowed bridge making the sixth. No one in sight except for his welcoming committee.

Tuah sent a brief prayer to Allah just in case he happened to be listening to a nonbeliever this afternoon: *Please let this continue so sweet.*

"If you can fix our engine, you are most very welcome." The

officer was Indian and spoke a lilting English. The way the mechanic followed the conversation by turning back and forth said that the Filipino didn't understand a word.

"Show us the way." Tuah checked his watch and then glanced about the strait. They were a hundred kilometers southeast of Kuala Lumpur and its heavy Marine patrols. The strait had narrowed to fifty kilometers wide, the first compression of traffic toward the southeastern pinch point. Still wide enough that the ships weren't convoyed into long lines, yet busy and crowded enough that his first two tankers coming up from astern weren't of any particular note.

He resisted looking aloft.

Time to hurry. He needed full control of the ship in the next fifteen minutes. He turned to Ozell but still didn't use his name. "You start on the engine. I want to chat with the captain." He turned for the bridge, leaving the junior officer no choice except to follow. Making a show of a bad hip he didn't have, Tuah was slow to ascend the six flights to the command level.

By the time he entered the bridge, he had details of the junior officer's family, what topics made the kid relax (he was a big Bollywood fan who laughed along when Tuah attempted some moves while resting *his hip* after the third flight), and as much as he could garner about his experience aboard ship. Asking about weapons training or security might arouse suspicions, but the lifestyle aboard sounded relaxed. Long voyages with nothing but the constant grind of standing watches and maintenance duties. Perfect.

With immaculate timing, he arrived on the bridge just as Ozell down in the engine room signaled to slow Engine One from cruise to headway keeping—the minimum speed to still maintain clear rudder control. Engine Two had already been stopped pending the arrival of their *service* team.

On cue five minutes later, Ozell called to the bridge. "I'm going to need the full team on this one, Boss. She's a mess."

Tuah barely had to glance at the Indonesian captain to get a nod of permission. "Roger that. I'll get you two more hands."

"Three would make this go faster."

Again, the captain's nod. *Yes, we're all such good friends here.*

"Okay, and as soon as I get our pilot up to the bridge, I'll come down and give you a hand."

"No need, boss. Rest that hip." That meant he already had control of the engine crew.

Tuah radioed his boat. Soon, four more crew were up the ladder and on deck. They disappeared out of sight as they entered the lower reaches of the ship's tower. One would head down to Ozell. The other three would work rapidly upward, deck by deck, securing any crew in the break areas or their rooms.

When all of them arrived on the bridge at once—masked and with their vicious-looking (the reason Tuah had chosen them) Ukrainian Malyuk bullpup rifles leading the way—the command crew surrendered instantly. Tuah had casually placed himself next to the radio to block any calls for help, but they were smart and didn't even try. It wasn't *their* load of crude after all.

"How many aboard, Captain?"

"Twenty-two."

Tuah glanced at one of his men, who nodded. The tally matched; no heroes hiding in the steel corridors of the ship.

"Okay, here's the deal, Captain. We idle along for a couple hours, transfer some crude, and you're on your way. If you promise to have no idea what we looked like or even what our boat name was, you and your people will be unharmed. We'll also have no interest in your personal valuables. However, any detailed reports about us *will* have future consequences if we see your ship transiting the strait ever again."

He didn't need to explain the other option with his armed

men circulating through the Bridge collecting cell phones into a bag.

"And there is the small matter of the ship's fund," Tuah tapped a foot against the safe.

The captain sighed but came forward to dial in the combination. All of these ships carried an emergency fund of cash in several denominations for bribes or paying for service—like the one he was supposed to be providing. It would make a nice bonus for his crew.

He glanced out the bridge windows in time to see that the rest of the crew had swarmed aboard and were catching the lines from his first coastal tanker to arrive alongside. The initial hundred and fifty thousand barrels of crude would soon be his.

It was an agonizingly long process to fill his three boats—a half million barrels of crude didn't flow down half-meter pipes in mere seconds. Glancing at the sky every thirty seconds as if he might spot the eye from above would give away his nerves. He kept resisting, but it was hard.

Halfway through the final boat, the tanker's ailing Number Two engine kicked to life. Ozell had always been a mechanic first and a fighter second.

"No charge," Tuah told the captain.

They shared a smile.

24

———

Now that Tuah had been dispatched to do what he did best, Rachel Yung sat in her office, facing out the window. But she had no interest in the bustling center of downtown Kuala Lumpur with its sharp high rises and vibrant low cityscape. Or any other terrestrial landform.

Instead, she did what so few others seemed capable of doing—she thought.

So many pieces in motion. An Australian Wedgetail down, and on Malaysian soil. She wished she'd sent a Special Branch squad to the site rather than an RMAF security team, but it was twenty-twenty hindsight and she never dwelt on what she couldn't change.

Someone had dispatched a high-priority investigation team on fantastically short notice. At such a high level, only her mole at the RMAF had known about it. No customs inspection, nothing. They must have been pre-staged at Changi Airport as if they knew it would happen.

A Singaporean Chinook helicopter and *persons unspecified* had crossed into Malaysian airspace—*No escort required.* Her contact at Changi Airport security had sent her a copy of an internal order to locate and transport a mixed American and Australian team. Two Australians, three Americans, and a Singaporean officer—all unnamed. Except for one Miranda Chase.

With few exceptions, Chase's public records were mundane. Though one in particular caught her attention. She'd flown out of Brunei into Kuala Lumpur five days after the partial destruction of the USS *Theodore Roosevelt* super carrier. Not noteworthy in itself. Except that she'd flown *into* Brunei within an hour of the same time as China's most VIP jet other than the President's own. It was an aircraft she tracked very carefully. Miranda's arrival in Brunei had coincided within minutes of the arrival of the Vice Chairman of the Chinese Central Military Commission.

So, they'd sent a *very* high-level investigation team. That meant an increased probability of discovering what had happened to bring the Wedgetail down. Once that was answered, events would happen very quickly. One didn't lose a three-trillion-ringgit airplane and a crew with several hundred man-years of combined training without forceful retribution.

Opportunity. She'd been thinking too small.

A quick ninety million ringgit for the three coastal tankers of stolen crude oil paid for her operations and more, but that was paycheck thinking. She must cast her nets farther and wider.

She didn't wish to rise higher. Political office was too exposed for someone who lived and operated in the shadows. And far too ephemeral. A single scandal or a bad vote, and such power could evaporate overnight.

Corporations were the true power—of the past. PETRONAS was perhaps the most powerful in all Malaysia, and her connections there ran deep as a drilled offshore well.

But the future and her specialty lay in security. Special

Branch had been founded as the premier counterterrorism unit.

She should—

Rachel tapped the phone and called in her assistant. Lee wasn't merely family, he was the sharpest mind in the extended Yung family save perhaps one as yet untested. He'd served her ever since she'd left the jungles of guerilla warfare for the office.

His eyebrows barely flickered as she hit the remote lock behind him.

"Who can we wholly trust across our departments?"

"The heads of Sea and Air Operations. Comms and Cyber." And he stopped.

They agreed on those. "But what about Tactical?"

Lee shrugged uncertainly.

Ham ka chan! She'd thought she had that department fully under her control. Curse their families to death—twice over!

Lee read her expression, something few could do, and explained. "He's good, but he came up through the force here in KL and has far too many connections to ignore."

Experience that made him incredibly useful in Tactical, but Lee was right—not solely her man. At times like this, she needed someone she could trust without question. Someone she could dump a cluster of problems on and who'd survive to walk out the far side unscathed.

Lee raised his hands and shook his head. "Don't look at me like that, Auntie." Aunt twice-removed in such a way that no one had ever tied them together. He'd long since made it clear that he wanted no part of leadership roles. A part of his brilliance came from standing outside and observing others' machinations.

She'd never been one to fidget, and she didn't now. Lee shared that skill and offered no unwelcome distraction while she considered.

"Okay, find out who sent the crash investigation team. Let's start with the Americans. I want to be able to call them in fifteen minutes and offer Special Branch's services."

"Suggestions?" Lee didn't write anything down, he never did.

"I don't know. Start at the top. Call the Director of the CIA. They're bound to be in on it."

Rachel was still thinking when her private phone vibrated. She tapped the remote lock on her office door and slid the phone out of her belt as it vibrated again.

It wasn't a text; it was a call.

25

IT WAS DONE. THE WEDGETAIL WAS DOWN.

Now all that remained was tying off any loose ends.

The Dassault Falcon would have to go, as would the crew that had flown it.

But how?

He studied the dark swirl of whisky that glittered in the sunlight coming through his office window. It was early, but he deserved a small celebration.

Scrolling through his phone's contact list, there was one other number that bothered him. All he had was a number and the initials RY. Before he'd learned more, his fool of a contact had crashed his helicopter into the ocean. He'd tried to trace the number without success; it was very well hidden.

This operation was done now and he wanted *all* the threads cut. Unless this RY could help him with the disposal of the Dassault and its crew. Perhaps it was finally time they spoke.

He hit Call and knocked back the rest of his whiskey while it rang. Being a professional, he didn't pour another.

26

RACHEL CONSIDERED THROUGH FIVE RINGS BEFORE ENGAGING HER voice-changer app and answering.

"I'm here." She could hear her own changed voice as she spoke and it gave her the chills. She had designed a setting that shifted her voice to a cross between James Earl Jones voicing Darth Vader and Jack Nicholson's Joker—deep, dangerous, and perhaps a little insane.

By the utter silence that lasted for several beats, she smiled. The man didn't know who she was. If he did, he'd have known she was a woman using a voice changer and remarked on it. Perhaps he was fishing for her identity with an actual call. It wouldn't work. Such poor fieldcraft shouldn't go unrewarded.

"Who are you planning to murder next?" her voice growled at him.

"I have a plane to dispose of." His recovery less steady than he probably hoped.

Rachel took her time considering.

He'd already killed off an E-7A Wedgetail. What plane would he want to kill off next? Actually, how did one bring down a Wedgetail from altitude at all?

Ah! From altitude? With another plane. A plane that would now hang about his neck like the Japanese prisoner-of-war chain her father had worn while interred at the infamous Changi camp.

This man possessed a weapon capable of downing a Wedgetail and now wanted to throw that away. Which meant the Wedgetail had been his sole target for this entire operation. A task not easily done. But that, in turn, explained this phone call. He was out of his depth—he'd failed to plan his endgame.

"You know," she needed to buy time to think, "they have a very high-level investigation team on site right now."

"An ATSB black fella they flew out." His scoff said how short-term his thinking truly was. If he knew about Miranda Chase and her team, he didn't understand them. Rachel was only starting to.

A light on her desk phone said that Lee had set up her next call.

"I will think on it and get back to you." And because the man was so much less than she'd imagined, she continued in her best Darth-Joker voice. "Take no action in the meantime."

Then she hung up, cleared her throat as if to shed the deep threatening tones of the voice changer, and picked up the already ringing line.

27

Clarissa blew her stroke when her cell phone blasted to life.

"Shit!" The handle of her rower machine slipped out of her grasp just as she kicked hard at the peak of her workout. The sliding seat shot to the end stop and hit it. Because she kept the toe straps loose to avoid adjusting them every time she got on or off the machine, her feet shot free and she tumbled off the back of the seat onto her carpet.

Her phone, set to blast over the TV feeds into her earbuds—she ran CNN, NBC, Fox, and Bloomberg in four quadrants of the screen, with the volume up on the first and last—rang again where it remained clipped to the rower's control panel.

Her legs were shaking with lactic acid as she'd powered out past eight thousand meters and into the sprint for ten. She checked the clock. One a.m. The world should stop long enough for an insomniac to have a decent workout, but she didn't even get that. She might not be sleeping much, except for exhausted collapses after workouts, but at least her body looked awesome.

Clark had been utterly wowed by her thirty-seven-year-old

body. Her conditioning now at forty-two would kill him, if the bastard wasn't already dead. A glance at the mirror as she lay gasping and flat on her back proved it. Six-pack abs for the first time in her life, the double sports bra and gym shorts didn't hide her figure or her killer legs. She'd let her white-blonde ponytail continue to grow to spite him for dying; he'd always been nuts for her hair. It now brushed her lower back—when she wasn't plastered on her tight ass on the carpet.

Looking hot, girl.

Not that it was doing her any good. A lonely CIA director didn't exactly hit the bars or a dating site for recreation.

Crawling on her hands and knees to the controls, not exactly dignified but better than standing up and having her shaking legs fold out from under her, she managed to silence the TV and answer the jangling phone. "What?"

"Good afternoon—"

"Morning!" she cut off the silky smooth voice on the other end of the phone. Then her brain caught up. The only place it was afternoon right now was the western Pacific Rim. A call to her private line at this hour meant something had happened.

"My apologies," the woman's voice remained unperturbed. "Good *morning.* I am sorry for the hour of the call but I am very concerned with the present security plans for the Strait of Malacca and wish to know how I might assist."

The strait? Why would anyone care about the strait enough to call the Director of the CIA in the middle of the night? "Who is this?"

"Police Chief—"

A cop was calling her? How the hell did she get this number?

"—Rachel Yung of the Royal Malaysian Police Special Branch."

Clarissa didn't know the name, but if she was who she said she was...

Managing to reach her feet, Clarissa staggered to her home office desk, dropping the phone hard on the surface, which would blast the woman at the other end. A quick search put a face to the name. Native Malay, fifties or early sixties, but with that whole ageless-Asian Michelle Yeoh thing going on.

"Would you mind giving me the year you graduated from the academy?"

There was a long pause. "I entered the jungle as a fighter at thirteen to fight the Malaysian Communist Party guerillas." That detail wasn't in the CIA's resume on the woman, but then neither was any academy listed.

"Okay, Rachel. Now what's this about the strait?"

Again, the long pause. "You don't know about the plane." It wasn't a question.

No, she didn't. And if she ever got her hands on the gonads of whoever hadn't told her, she'd crush them.

Plane.

Clarissa opened the reporting queue she'd had set up on Miranda Chase. Knowing her whereabouts had often proved informative. And… "Mount Ledang," she said to the woman. No idea yet why Miranda was there, but that was the latest GPS track on her phone.

"Yes," the woman sounded at least somewhat mollified. "The *loss* of the Royal Australian Air Force E-7A Wedgetail—"

Clarissa was glad she'd already set down the phone, or she'd have dropped it. Whoever had kept this from her wasn't going to have crushed gonads—she rip them off and make him eat them.

"—has significantly compromised the security coverage over the strait. Special Branch would like to offer its assistance."

"Have you spoken to anyone else about this yet?"

"You were my first call. I had your number. And as the D/CIA, I thought you would know who I should contact next."

Implying I don't have any other use than a contact list, you slick bitch.

"Hold one moment." She muted the call and speed dialed Drake. He picked up on the second ring; she didn't wait for a hello. "I've got the Royal Malaysian Special Branch Chief of Police on the line about a crashed Wedgetail. You've mobilized Miranda but couldn't be bothered to call me, you asshole?"

"We've known it was an attack for under thirty minutes, Clarissa. We've been busy."

"Well, I sure as fuck needed to know sooner, you asshole." She undid the mute on the first line. "Rachel Yung, we're now conferenced in with General Drake Nason, Chairman of the Joint Chiefs of Staff. Drake, Rachel is offering Special Branch's assistance on Strait of Malacca's security while Miranda continues her investigation of the Wedgetail incident." At least it *sounded* as if she knew what the hell was happening.

An E-7A Wedgetail gone down? Miranda had better prove that was an accident or there'd be major hell to pay.

"Hello, Ms. Yung," Drake did his fake gracious shit. "I'm also here with NRO Director General Elizabeth Gray and Vice President Sarah Feldman."

And Clarissa had just put on such a fine show of teamwork for the likely next President.

Fuck.

28

___

"I ALSO GRABBED THE MISSION RECORDER FROM THE commander's work station." Holly set down the end of the body bag she'd been helping to carry and held out the hard drive. "Hopefully it survived."

Miranda decided that any further information to be gathered from the corpses arranged in the TV tower's two parking spaces would best be performed by a medical examiner. The RMAF team's leader had been carrying the other end of the bag with Holly, though he looked ready to run away as soon as he set it down.

"You'll need to get refrigeration for these."

The officer looked around, blinked up at the sun, then nodded. "Right. I can do that." He pulled out his phone, glanced at Holly, and moved away quickly.

Holly's smile said she was very pleased by something. She always looked extra dangerous when she used that one. Miranda's tracking had proven that was an accurate assessment based on results.

Miranda took both the QAR and mission commander's hard drives, labeled and bagged them carefully in foil bags to protect them from erasure, then tucked them in the pocket of her pack that she reserved specifically for this type of incident-specific evidence. Once they were in their proper places, she could move to the next step. She withdrew the QAR, unbagged it, and plugged it into her tablet.

"Miranda, could we..." Andi started out but ended the unfinished sentence with a choking sound.

Mike, after a quick glance around—his skin was also very pale (again her own wasn't)—looked down at Meg. "Uh, don't you think your dog would be more comfortable if we moved to sit in the shade, farther from any smells coming out of the body bags?"

Miranda nodded and let Meg lead them over to the solid shadow created by the nose of the plane and the hinge point of the TV tower where it had bent to collapse along the top of the plane. Everyone followed Meg quickly as if in a rush to beat her there.

She sat beside Meg and began inspecting the QAR data. There were no voice channels, hopefully that would be captured by the cockpit voice recorder.

The altitude and control inputs, however, were highly illustrative. She narrated what she was seeing for the others.

"The flight profile is exactly as we worked out while inspecting the cockpit. Straight-and-level flight both before and after the attack. In fact, the lack of flight-level variance despite the perturbation of airflow caused by the loss of the windshields is a testament to the design of the autopilot; it compensated almost instantly."

She added in a view of aircraft systems and saw the double spike.

"The door-unlock codes were entered twice from the main cabin, two minutes apart. A hundred and eleven seconds after the second opening—presumably by use of the rope and fire extinguisher—a steady descent was begun to ten thousand feet.

After a brief seventeen seconds of level flight, a rapid descent ensued—one that included sporadic and often excessive control inputs."

"The burning of the second pilot," Lieutenant Noor spoke first.

"Technically the third pilot, but yes. He remained in some degree of control throughout the descent. That was exceptionally well done." She scrolled back to observe the original course data at the moment of the second attack. "On its original heading, it would either have been lost at sea or plunged into the city of Malacca."

"I have family there," Noor was the only one who'd remained standing, scanning as if on guard over their small group. "I am glad for what the pilot did."

There was far more data here, over two thousand aspects of the aircraft's performance and operations were tracked on the quick access recorder. But, as she now had the pertinent milestones of the incident itself, she would save that task for later.

Three deep breaths centered her enough to close and disconnect the QAR, rebag and store it, then extract the mission commander's drive. She'd never attempted to read one before, and after several minutes of trying, still hadn't made sense of it.

She knew that she was the best computer technician among her present team, but none of them were true experts. A quick tap connected her tablet to her satellite phone, and she hit the top number on her speed dial.

"Uh-huh?" A groggy voice mumbled out of the tablet's speakers.

"Jeremy?"

"Uh-huh."

"It's Miranda."

"Uh-huh." Then a high wail sounded in the background. "Uh-oh!"

"I'm going to fucking kill somebody with my bare hands!" Taz growled in the background, the last words fading as she hurried away from the phone.

Taz Cortez, Miranda knew, had proven her willingness to deliver on such threats. She held her breath, then realized she was being silly. Taz was presently fifteen thousand kilometers away in Washington, DC, and that was only by the most direct circumpolar route. Traveling via the most logical routes, Paris or Los Angeles, it would take most of a day's travel before she could kill Miranda with her bare hands, assuming she made good connections. So, the threat was not imminent. She set an alarm on her phone for twenty hours from now to remind herself she might be in danger soon.

"I have the mission commander's data drive from—"

"The E-7A Wedgetail," Jeremy's voice sounded clearly. "Drake and Lizzy already called us about that. He woke the baby a couple hours ago. That's why Taz is so upset. With her colic, we only got her to sleep...about twenty minutes ago."

"He called about the data drive?"

"No, about the crash and the laser. Was it really a laser? Do you know whose yet? My estimate was Israel, but that makes no sense in Malaysia."

"I can confirm it was a high-power laser. We do *not* know whose yet." And Miranda agreed that while Israel's Iron Dome weapon seemed the most likely candidate, it made the least sense. Of course, that was the aspect of investigation she never understood, the *why*. She had to close her eyes to remember— "I'm calling about the data drive. I don't know how to read it."

"Oh, hang on." There was a scrabbling noise in the background and the baby's wail increased, then decreased in volume. She could picture Jeremy moving past the baby's bedroom, proven by Taz's soothing string of curses, then down the stairs to his computer.

Moments later her tablet screen blinked up a message, and she tapped the Allow Connection button from Jeremy's system.

"I've never looked at one of these before." Her screen flickered from place to place too quickly for her to follow. "There is a serious amount of data here. The Air Force doesn't exactly post Wedgetail command console emulators on their website. Taz?" he shouted out. "I need your Pentagon access."

The baby's cry, though softer in pitch and intensity, became louder as Taz too came down the stairs.

Miranda considered the orientation of their home. Traveling due north along the circumpolar route, Taz had moved some nine meters closer to Mount Ledang, only six ten-millionths of a percent closer. She was still safe for now. If she continued to approach at that pace...but that was silly; Taz could always take a plane on her way to kill Miranda with her bare hands.

A minute later, her screen began to unscramble from data into organized information.

"Let's start with the intercom tracks." If people were actually at the core, perhaps they would tell her what they knew.

It took three more long minutes as Jeremy scrolled, zoomed, switched views, and tried different settings.

Then a voice sounded clearly from the speakers.

"I hate this place."

The dead were speaking to them.

29

———

DRAKE HAD NEVER BEEN A COMMO, BUT HE'D LEARNED TO respect what radio operators could do in the field. At the moment, he'd give good money to know how they did it.

He had Clarissa and Police Chief Rachel Yung of the Royal Malaysian Special Branch on one line.

Aluf Benjamin Muntz of the Israeli Defense Forces was on a second line.

Then a Marine overseeing the Situation Room announced that he had a call from Miranda on a third line.

"Fine. Gang them all together on the speaker phone."

VP Feldman raised an inquisitive eyebrow.

Perhaps *not* his best choice.

"This is General Drake Nason in the Situation Room. We are discussing the downing of the RAAF E-7A Wedgetail. Aluf Muntz of the IDF, you're up first. What's the status of your Iron Beam weapons?"

"I still don't understand why you think it was—"

"The weapon," Miranda spoke up, "was mounted on a Dassault Falcon 2000 business jet flying at forty-thousand feet over Indonesia to cross the Strait of Malacca. They were

166

breaking international flight regulations to do so, as Flight Level four-zero-zero should only have transitioning traffic." She sounded deeply and morally offended by the transgression.

"And breaking the small rule of attacking another aircraft," Drake couldn't resist.

"Actually, there is no specific agreement within the International Convention on Civil Aviation originally signed in Chicago in 1944 that prohibits an attack. And isn't the purpose of military flights *to* attack? No, Drake. No aviation laws were violated other than an inappropriate flight level forcing two aircraft into a dangerous proximity."

Lizzy was laughing at him, silently, but he knew his wife's face well enough to know that's what she was doing even if she was doing her best to hide it.

"And, Miranda, what countries mount their high-power-laser systems on the Falcon airframe?"

"To the best of my knowledge, only Israel."

"Thank you, Miranda." Drake shifted his mental attention from Malaysia to Israel. But before he could speak, Sarah leaned forward.

"VP Feldman here, Muntz. You know better than to keep fucking around with me. Account for that weapon." With that tone, he doubted even Lizzy would confront Sarah.

There was a groan. "I can't. Every one is visually accounted for except the one on loan to Vietnam for evaluation. That aircraft departed their facility for a test flight seven hours ago and did not return as scheduled. Vietnam is very reluctant to discuss the loss. I've managed to catch a rumor, but it's no more than that. Their scheduled test crew may have been found in a storage locker. Bound and gagged one would assume. This has not been confirmed."

"Tracking?" Lizzy asked.

"It's a military flight, tracking is turned off by default. We don't know where the plane is."

"Find it!" Sarah snapped out. "Find it fast!" And she tapped a button on the phone to hang up on him.

"Ms. Yung?" Lizzy spoke up.

"I'm still here."

"We'd appreciate any assistance you can offer in tracking that flight. Review radar logs, any anomalous sightings, and so on. I'm glad to call whoever you need to obtain the proper authorization."

Drake swore he could hear the smile in the woman's voice. "I am the Chief of Police for Special Branch. I require no authorization I don't already have." She gave him the shivers— she and Clarissa sounded like sharks of the same breed—and he already didn't trust one of them. Maybe potential damage could be mitigated by dividing their paths early on.

Lizzy was already on it. "Rachel, here's my direct number. You may call any time day or night. Do you need the assistance of our team on the ground?"

"Oh, no. They have given us all the information we need. We are aware of the sensitivity of the Wedgetail and are flying in a security team to lock down the aircraft until such time as the RAAF can place a force on the ground to guard it and recover any sensitive equipment."

Drake just bet she was, and planning a full inspection until the RAAF could put people in place. Thankfully, Lizzy had been a step ahead of them all on that one and mobilized a special team shortly after Miranda's first call.

"This is Vice President Feldman. We have a secondary team arriving in the next twenty minutes to protect the aircraft. We'll let you know if we have any other needs. Again, please call General Elizabeth Gray directly at the least news. She will know how to reach myself or the President as needed."

"I would be glad to do so. I will also coordinate with the Royal Malaysian Air Force to provide overwatch on the strait until such time as the RAAF, Singapore, or your own forces are available. Please keep me informed of all their actions so that we, uh, don't double up unnecessarily."

"We will do so," Lizzy assured her.

There was a click of disconnection.

That lone *uh* worried him. He could practically hear the gears of Rachel Yung's plans shifting on the fly. As long as they didn't involve the Wedgetail or shut down the shipping lanes, he couldn't worry about them at the moment.

"Clarissa, you still there?" Drake asked.

"Yes."

"Good, you know what to do. Find the bastards who burned that plane." He hung up that line before she could respond, which would be guaranteed to piss her off. Good!

Now they were down to just Miranda.

Before he started to ask her questions, he looked from Sarah to Lizzy, who were looking at each other.

He couldn't help sighing.

He'd thought to be done with the White House when President Roy Cole completed his second term. He would be retired, but Lizzy was nine years younger and not at the end of her career. And the synchronicity of the way she worked with Sarah...

Sarah Feldman had asked him for recommendations for her Chairman of the Joint Chiefs of Staff after Drake's retirement. He'd had several ideas, but he now knew the answer.

Come the election, Major General Elizabeth Gray was in for a hell of a promotion and his wife's new position was going to tie him to the White House for years to come.

30

———

It didn't take Rachel long to find out what had happened in Vietnam. With continuous relations reaching back to the fifteenth century, the bonds were close and the intelligence situation...fluid.

Since formal diplomatic relations had been established with the post-American War government, there had been a deepening regional cooperation. But that was not what had given Malaysia such access to information within Vietnam.

The Cambodian-Vietnamese War of the 1970s and '80s had driven a massive influx of boat people crossing the Gulf of Thailand to escape. That had created intelligence opportunities with both Viet-Malaysians who still had family in Vietnam and those who'd returned after the war, having lived for years in Malaysia.

Many had become agents of Special Branch's foreign network.

The Kép Air Base fifty kilometers north of Hanoi was a challenge. No co-located civilian airport, and so far north that it had limited options for placing multiple agents; but that didn't make her deaf there either. The answers were merely slow in coming, but they came.

The Viet equivalent of two American colonels and three staff sergeants had been found stripped of their gear—and their lives. Spilled paint in several colors suggested that the plane's ID had been altered quickly, though it was unclear to what. Those who had repainted the plane had probably departed in it. And, as the departure had been predawn, no one in the tower had a visual beyond the blinking navigation lights on the wingtips and tail as it was stolen.

A wholly predictable witch hunt had been unleashed as the Vietnam People's Air Force struggled to identify the perpetrators, the culpable, or just someone—anyone who wasn't them—to blame.

Rachel dispatched a message to her Chief of Operations to keep Tuah working. The Australians weren't going to plug this failure in air coverage quickly.

Which gave her an idea.

She contacted her second cousin in the RMAF, the one with the idiot son neither of them knew what to do with so they'd dumped him on Tuah. Within an hour, a Royal Malaysian Air Force plane was headed aloft to resume cover patrols. For a surprisingly small share of today's profits, he agreed to suppress all piracy in the strait—except Tuah bin Musa's. She doubled his requested share so that he could pass a percentage of that on to his brother-in-law in the naval patrols.

A quick note to her Chief of Operations told him to watch for bargains in shipping vessels over the coming months. The navy would be seizing ships for which they had no use. The state would sell them at auction. And she would arrange for Tuah to have exclusive first pick before any auction.

But for now, she wanted to bleed PETRONAS' back-channel black-market supply until she became their only source. Then they'd be forced to pay top dollar for the crude she stole before it reached their refineries. The executives depended on their share of the black market being sold forward at full price to line their own pockets with hefty bonuses. Until now, the split had been fifty-fifty even though she, well, Tuah, was the one taking most of the risk. Give her forty-eight hours and it would become seventy-five / twenty-five. A week? That could make a woman smile.

After all that was in motion, she once again turned back to her view of Kuala Lumpur.

Already, the tendrils of the CIA probed in her direction from Clarissa Reese, but that didn't concern her. Special Branch had years of experience sparring with clumsy Americans—they knew so little of patience. Dismissing them would be hasty and unwise, but neither did she feel more than a tantalizing frisson of anticipation crawling over her skin at dealing with them.

No, what was interesting was that, for the moment, she had the ear of the American heir-apparent to their presidency. And their Chairman of the Joint Chiefs.

How to use that?

She wished that she herself had traveled to the crash site. It would have sent alerts to the various powers vying to pull Malaysia into their personal grasp of how important this moment was. But she desperately needed information about what they had found to calculate her next move.

Something...something...

One of the last things General Drake Nason had said was that they had a team en route so there was no need for her to send a Special Branch team.

What the hell did that mean? The Australians had put on some serious hustle, but that site investigation team was still on the ground in Australia, at least a five-hour flight away.

The team she *had* sent to the site were too far down the

hierarchy to have any of her own people in it, making any direct contact untrustworthy.

Lee came into her office and handed her a quick note inked on a piece of rice paper. It was the way all ephemeral notes were moved around Special Branch—at least since she'd taken command. No electronic record. When done, drop the paper into a glass of water and it dissolved. Eating it was also an option. All department heads had a somewhat murky glass at their desk. She personally had a small, innocuous clay drinking vessel with a narrow neck and fluted lip that had been dated to the Malaccan Sultanate circa 1400 C.E. It reminded her that even the commonplace had value.

Then she read the list of six names on the note and couldn't help smiling.

31

———

"OH, THAT'S PRETTY."

At Lieutenant Noor's comment, Miranda looked aloft. "Are you commenting on the MV-22 Osprey or the parachutists?"

"Both, I think. The plane looks ungainly but dangerous, like a pterodactyl. And your parachute people must be very trained to fly with that neat precision."

"They're flying the PS-2 Multi-Mission System parachutes. That makes them Marine Corps." Holly shaded her eyes as she looked aloft.

As each exited the Osprey and opened their broad rectangular chutes, they dropped their packs on long tethers so that the pack's weight would hit the ground first, rather than applying strain on their body and knees. The sheer size of the packs declared they were coming to deal with any eventuality.

"Very well trained indeed to hold that spacing so neatly," Holly continued her assessment. "Twenty-seven, eight, nine. Thirty. That's...yep, thirty-two. Maximum load of the Osprey, but only if you floor-load them rather than giving them seats. They've been jammed against each other for hours with their butts on a hard deck to get here. Nothing worse than a grumpy Marine, is there, Andi?"

"Nothing," Andi agreed. "Except a grumpy Marine who thinks he's as good as a female soldier."

Miranda had no measure for that, but as Andi and Holly traded high-fives, she decided that they must be correct. Unsure how to record this particular piece of knowledge in her notebook—truisms, military relations, or some new, previously unimagined category—she reluctantly didn't try.

Besides, she was still connected to the Situation Room. "Drake, it looks as if your team has arrived."

"Excellent! They—"

The first Marine down landed less than ten meters away. As his parachute settled, it collapsed onto their heads.

Various calls of complaint from her team and a husky voice saying, "Sorry ma'am. Sorry sir."

From somewhere underneath, Meg added a great deal of barking to the confusion as the parachute was dragged clear.

When Miranda looked back at her hand, it was empty. She still had the tablet in her lap but the satellite phone was gone. Nor was it on the ground near her. Nor—she lifted Meg, who had grabbed a mouthful of the chute and was shaking it hard, making her very difficult to hold—was her phone under Meg.

Miranda spotted the golden oak leaf on the man's collar.

"Major. You have my phone in your parachute."

He grunted. "Well, that's a new one."

Other Marines were landing at various points spaced evenly around the perimeter of the plane. By the time they were all down, a complete strategic perimeter had been set up. The four-man RMAF team wisely didn't reach for their weapons, instead they stared at the overwhelming force that had just landed in their country.

They looked from Holly to the major and back several times. After a brief conference, they offered to help.

The RMAF team, Miranda's people, and the major in charge of the whole operation pawed through the three hundred and seventy square feet of ripstop nylon in search of her phone.

Two of them rang simultaneously.

One in Noor's pocket. The other still buried in the forty-two square yards of parachute.

"WHAT ELSE DO YOU KNOW, MIRANDA?" DRAKE ASKED ONCE she'd explained how a parachute had cut them off.

The protracted silence told Drake that he'd asked the wrong question. It was almost sunrise here in DC and he was way too old to pull all-night shit. He tried to rephrase the question, but it wasn't coming together in his head.

Miranda finally asked, "Do you mean relevant to your team's arrival, the laser attack, the crash, or some wider scope of information?"

It was the first time he'd heard Miranda anticipate the error in a wide-open question. He wanted to congratulate her but couldn't figure out how to do so without sounding condescending.

"The attack, please."

"As I mentioned before, the airplane approached at an illegal elevation. Oh wait," the phone shifted and clunked as if she was working its keypad. It rang once and Jeremy picked up.

"Are you okay, Miranda? What happened? I was getting worried."

"A parachute landed on me. Meg was very upset by that.

The Marine Corps major is most unhappy that she bit and tried to kill it. There's now a large hole in his parachute. I'm sorry, Drake. I'll pay to replace it."

"Don't worry about that, Miranda. Under the circumstances I think it was justified. Now," he blew out a breath, hoping that all the distractions were safely behind him, "about the attack."

"Oh, yes. That's why I remembered to call back Jeremy. Have you been able to back-trace the attacking airplane?"

"I'm working on that right now. Long before it was identified by the mission crew, while they were busy investigating a possible pirate vessel in the strait, the MESA radar picked up the Dassault Falcon's track. It was performing a back-and-forth patrol perpendicular to the strait, never passing over Malaysian territory. That means that it crossed the narrow dimension of the strait in eight minutes. Then it would turn, making a return passage for eight more minutes over the water, then ten more over the Indonesian island of Sumatra before turning and repeating the pattern."

"It was waiting for the Wedgetail." Drake felt sick to his stomach.

"It was waiting for the Wedgetail," Jeremy confirmed. "On spotting the Wedgetail, it made an early turn back from over Sumatra and intercepted the Wedgetail as it passed over Batu Pahat. That's when it attacked."

"And that's when we lost it." How was he supposed to search all of southwest Asia for a single twenty-meter long bizjet?

"Oh, not at all. Nothing wrong with the E-7A's tracking systems even if the crew were otherwise occupied after the attack. Moments before the attack, the senior surveillance officer switched the Top Hat MESA radar to threat-sector-analysis mode and focused it on the Dassault. We have high-resolution radar imaging and the complete track for as long as the Wedgetail remained aloft."

A Marine called from the Sit Room control desk. "Sir, incoming video addressed to you from Air Force Colonel Taz Cortez's account but it's signed Jeremy Trahn."

"Put it up." In seconds, it showed on the screen at the end of the room and began to play. It was a top-down view of the Malacca Strait on which two planes were highlighted and created thin white tracks behind them as they progressed.

A phrase appeared briefly over the image as if someone had scribbled it with a fat pen. *Please say Start.*

Miranda and then he said, "Start."

"Oh good, you're mostly in sync. Close enough." And Jeremy began narrating. "Here's the final crossing from southwest to northeast by the attacking Dassault Falcon 2000. This is the moment of firing the laser. You'll see no particular change in either aircraft, but that's when they lost the pilots and continued to fly on autopilot. After overflying the Wedgetail, the Falcon circles around to fly a course parallel to it and close alongside. Here they begin the descent, and here's the second round of firing."

The larger plane spasmed. It was the only word for it. It bucked hard, nosed down, rolled wing over wing, fought back to level flight, then plunged the other direction in a steep bank.

"Don't watch the Wedgetail. Watch the Falcon."

It was hard to do as the death spiral was so graphic on the screen.

At first, the Falcon followed the plane down, perhaps making sure it was going to die. Before it hit though, the Falcon turned and climbed back toward cruising altitude.

Then the simulation blinked out abruptly enough for all three of them in the Sit Room to gasp aloud.

"What lies in that direction?"

Miranda answered first. "Singapore and about eight hundred Indonesian islands, though very few with airports."

Drake glanced around the Sit Room and received somewhat dazed nods from Lizzy and VP Feldman.

"Jeremy, Miranda, and your whole team, thank you. With the Marines on the ground, the aircraft is secure. With your quick resolution as to the cause, I believe that your work is done. Jeremy, please make sure that this is received by the appropriate authorities in the RAAF."

"Do it as soon as we're done here. Taz," there was a distant wail of a small child as if from the next room, "and Amy will pass our findings on to the investigation team, which is now in the air."

A thick Australian voice sounded over Miranda's phone. "Oi. I'll be hanging here waiting for them. We'll complete the investigation and secure the aircraft as needed."

Drake recalled the image of the Australian Transportation Safety Board Chief Commissioner standing outside the airplane's cockpit looking in.

"Excellent..."

Barty, Lizzy mouthed to him.

"...Barty. We really appreciate that. Miranda, I believe that means you can return to your original vacation plans. We'll try not to call you with too many questions."

"How many is too many?"

Drake laughed. "I don't know, Miranda. I don't know."

33

"Nenek?" Noor had answered his phone carefully once he was clear of the collapsed parachute. Other than his birthday or family gatherings, he never had direct contact with Grandmother. Her life kept her firmly in Kuala Lumpur and his in Singapore since his family had moved there shortly before his birth. They were rarely both in Malacca at the same time.

"Hello, Apu." Only Nenek and Ibu, Grandmother and Mother, used that nickname for Adiputera. For all others inside the family he was mostly Adi, first-born. Outside the family, Noor was more acceptable to the many races of Singapore.

"Are you well, Nenek?"

"I am. But it is you I wish to speak about." Nenek was rarely subtle, though when she was, no one ever managed to second-guess what she was up to. "You are traveling to interesting places with interesting people."

"I am?" He was, but how did she... Oh, the plane. It wasn't his grandmother calling, it was the Chief of Malaysia's Special Branch. Calling about Miranda Chase and her team. "I am."

"Talk to me."

It was unlikely her to ask such an open question. He hadn't

yet had time to organize his thoughts around all the day's new experiences.

So, first he described the arrival of the US Marine Corps security team on Malaysian soil.

Then, glancing down to where Miranda sat cross-legged in the shade of the fuselage with the tablet in her lap, he began to narrate in a low voice what Jeremy was saying. Meg had decided to rest her front paws on Miranda's thigh to watch the tablet as well. No one pushed the dog aside. Instead, there was a shuffling as everyone else shifted their position to gain an unobstructed view.

Nenek made no interruptions to his narrative. As he spoke, he thought about Mike's initial question on the helicopter ride about his clearance level. But there didn't appear to be any secret information here, simply facts about the attack and flight.

After Drake had signed off and released them, he stepped away so that he could speak more comfortably. The big Marine watched him carefully, so Noor kept his rifle slung over his shoulder and his other hand nowhere near his sidearm. He approached and silently showed his ID to the man, who read it twice and then nodded with a mere scowl instead of the deep frown with which he'd been watching Noor.

Clear of the security perimeter, he found a patch of unoccupied shade not far from the body bags.

"I definitely need more training in security clearances."

"Yes, I would highly recommend that."

"Sorry, Nenek, I was merely thinking aloud."

"A habit to be cautious of if you are going to begin traveling in such circles." *Such circles*, like those Nenek Rachel Yung traveled in.

That gave Noor pause. He knew little of what she did. Ibu certainly never spoke of her own mother's past or doings beyond the limited scope of her interactions with the family.

Balance.

Noor received very positive reviews from his superiors on his balancing of priorities versus niceties. His initial meeting with Miranda Chase in Changi Airport was perhaps the worst transgression of his career.

But Rachel Yung was using plain speech in a way he couldn't recall her doing before.

No. She was talking about choices.

If he stepped aside from *such circles* as she referred to, his career would progress as any other bright young officer in the Singapore Armed Forces. But if he stepped into those circles? He would be leaping into the unknown with both feet.

He could feel her waiting. Not the austere matriarch of the Yung family—for though his bapa was a Noor, his ibu led the family and Nenek above her. He reminded himself that the woman awaiting his response wasn't his grandmother but instead the Chief of the Malaysian Special Branch.

And she wouldn't wait for long.

"My life and my career are in Singapore," he vacillated between saying Chief Yung and... "Nenek."

"Of course they are," she sounded as amiable as she ever did. "The question is what kind of future do you want *there*?"

Her slight emphasis on the final word confirmed that she accepted his choice to remain in Singapore. But what else did she want from him?

Balance or the knife edge? This wasn't only a test of his preferences but also of his decisiveness.

Did he want more than the average career? And did he have the wit and determination to grab it?

He thought of his commander at the airport. Stubborn, hide-bound, entrenched in managing airport security. An important role and one he did well if gruffly, but already Noor could see the man's shortcomings. And they weren't only *his* shortcomings, but of the role itself.

He looked around. Miranda's team were done with their call and were preparing to depart. The Marines stood as a dedicated guard force, facing outward from the aircraft with one hand on their rifles aimed at the ground as they kept watch.

The leader of the small RMAF security team was very obsequiously conferring with the Marine Corps major. The MV-22 Osprey, perhaps having departed to refuel after its hurried journey here, returned. With no space big enough to land, it lowered a basket, and the body bags of the Wedgetail's flight crew began heading aloft.

Life could be so short.

Finally he looked to the peak of Mount Ledang, where the tail section of the Wedgetail still perched with its own contingent of Marine Corps guards. A place of legends and dreams. A place of exotic adventures—and women.

He was modern enough that Miranda Chase and Andi Wu being a couple did not bother him, though he'd caught many disapproving looks from the RMAF security team once they noticed. Holly Harper was the most amazing woman he'd ever met. Not for him, she was far too old, but she gave him definite ideas about his own future.

One last look, but no celestial princess appeared from the depths of the thick rainforest. And that was the final piece. As a Singaporean soldier he could only expect so much. But if he himself could somehow become more...

He moved away from the noisy lift operation toward the parked Chinook helicopter that had brought them here. He spoke as soon as he felt there was some chance of being heard over the roar of the Osprey hovering high above.

He hesitated one last time. Was he putting family ahead of duty? No. Nor did he think that Rachel Yung had either. She'd been a fierce warrior in the defense of Malaysia for over fifty years. And she had accepted his choice of Singapore as the place he would defend. But how much more could he achieve with Nenek's guidance and connections?

"Grandmother," he shifted to English for its more formal sound. "I very much look forward to discussing the possibilities with you further."

"I look forward to that as well, Adiputera." *First prince.* The first time she'd acknowledged his full name that he could recall.

Quite what path he'd set his feet upon was unclear. But it wouldn't be dull. Maybe there *would* be a celestial princess in his future. This trip to Mount Ledang looked to be very fruitful. He offered a bow of thanks to the trees, just in case the spirit was watching.

"For now," Grandmother informed him, "find out as much as possible about the NTSB investigation team."

That he could do. Outside of his grandmother, they were perhaps the most interesting people he'd ever met.

Then she began giving him instructions.

34

Miranda stared down at her dinner. It had been a very confusing day. They had overnighted in Hawaii the previous day to break up the flight, but not left the airport hotel.

Mike and Holly had each given different explanations of why it wasn't worth scheduling in the extra days for going to the beaches (Miranda had always preferred forests herself). The openness of beaches left her exposed, and the dense crowds of people could induce agoraphobia in even a neurotypical introvert, never mind an autistic one. For her, such experiences bordered on the much more specific enochlophobia—being enclosed by crowds.

But she'd become so confused by Mike and Holly's overlapping yet incongruous explanations that she'd had to ask Andi to explain after they'd curled up together in bed that night.

Apparently Mike and Holly had enjoyed a *very* good vacation in Hawaii, becoming closer as a couple. Andi said that they found this so upsetting that they didn't want to revisit the location in case it somehow drew them even closer.

"Why is that a bad thing?"

"It's..." But Andi had been unable to explain it to Miranda's satisfaction. She liked that she and Andi were closer than ever. Having put the choices of the past behind them—which had led to Miranda being kidnapped by Russia—Miranda felt safe around Andi.

In the hours since leaving Hawaii, they'd arrived in Changi Airport, been dragged out to a crash investigation, dealt with a wide variety of ground personnel, including thieves and the Situation Room, before being whisked back to Singapore.

With the last flight for Darwin, Australia, or any decent connection already departed, Noor had arranged hotel rooms for them. Then he'd made reservations for them at Violet Oon's Kitchen inside the Jewel building of the airport. The massive glass enclosure boasted a five-level mezzanine packed with entertainment and dining, all gathered around a courtyard that had been built around a tropical forest and a rain vortex. The last feature was enormous and filled the center like a whooshing tornado of water lit in ever-changing colors. Now that it was evening, the shifts from brilliant blue to red to green and so on were quite disconcerting. She was far more used to the ocean, where water stayed ocean-colored from dark gray to turquoise-blue based on its turbulence, aeration, and localized chemistry.

The restaurant disconcertingly mimicked the rain vortex. The floor was fine tiles, the walls and ceiling elaborate dark wood paneling, and in the center, a towering welcome station and bar in jade green. When they'd been escorted away from that space and into an equally lavish but far quieter private dining room, it was a huge relief.

She could feel herself slowly expanding outward. She'd always liked airplanes, and that was how she tolerated airports —by using them as her primary focus to shut out other noise. Here in Changi's Jewel, no planes were visible. Instead there were shops, crowds, the rain vortex, more crowds, and, high above them all, bridges and game parks and probably even arcades. She couldn't tolerate arcades, even with noise-canceling headphones.

Here, the dining-room staff was polite, quiet, and they'd given Meg a bed, water bowl, and a plate of cooked chicken. Except when the staff door opened to the pantry that must connect to a subterranean kitchen, all she could hear was the voices of her four companions.

"I think they pay you too well," Holly waved a chicken satay stick to indicate the table and the room.

"No," Noor smiled, "they don't. Grandmother thought you would appreciate it. It is her way of saying thank you for your quick work resolving the crash today."

"Nice grandmother," Mike sipped his wine.

"She...can be."

"Well, thank her. This is a fine end to the day. What's her name?"

"Rachel Yung."

Holly spit a mouthful of satay onto the table, causing Miranda to become even more skeptical about her dish of food than she had been—Holly was not one given to spitting out food of any type.

What *was* Nasi Goreng Bakso, anyway? Noor had described it as twice-fried rice with spicy meatballs. But she could see the rice was thick with little bits of shallot, red pepper, and scrambled egg. Tucked in around the edge of the bowl were sliced cucumbers, tomatoes, and lime wedges. Smells of garlic, chili paste, and several things she couldn't identify filled the air. Everything was touching each other. She didn't like her food doing that; it was confusing. Who knew, there could even be mushrooms lurking in there just waiting to make her teeth feel all funny.

"Rachel Yung?" Holly gasped out. "*The* Rachel Yung?"

Miranda looked at her. "There must be more than one

Rachel Yung. Neither the given nor the surname are particularly rare. A singular *the* Rachel Yung seems statistically unlikely."

Holly ignored her and faced Noor, waiting for an answer.

Noor answered slowly. "She's a chief in the Royal Malaysian Police."

"Chief of Special Branch," Holly stated flatly. "That's some grandmother you have there, Lieutenant Noor."

Mike asked for details while Andi whispered with an attendant topping up water glasses. Then Andi leaned close. "She says there are no mushrooms in it, Miranda."

"That's good. But I will continue to approach this meal with a great deal of caution."

Andi glanced at her own roasted black pepper tiger prawns on pasta topped with arugula and didn't offer to switch. They looked scary and Andi would know that. Instead, she took a clean fork and test-tasted the rice and a small meatball. "It is good, Miranda."

She considered giving a meatball to Meg for testing, but she'd finished her meal and fallen asleep in her dog bed. Taking a deep breath, she took a small forkful, then closed her eyes so that she didn't have to watch all her food touching each other. A careful bite revealed the complete lack of mushrooms. Also, no cherry tomatoes that popped so unpredictably in her mouth. Other than the look of it and that it was happening all at once in her mouth, it was actually quite good.

Holly still wasn't eating.

"What?" Noor asked.

"I'm debating about whether to warn you about her, Rachel, or to ask what she's like."

"What do you mean?"

"I mentioned before that I was Australian Spec Ops. Regionally, we keep our ear to the ground. She was in the field before my time, but her reputation was…" Holly shuddered, "…terrifying. I'm not sure I'd ever want to meet her."

"Well, she thinks this team is most interesting."

"Which is the reason she's having you host this dinner," Mike nodded. "No complaints from me."

Miranda braved another bite, with closed eyes, during the ensuing silence. When she opened them while she chewed, trying to taste only one bit at a time, she looked across the table.

Holly's skin might have turned even paler than it had been in the Wedgetail's cockpit when they first found the pilots.

35

Noor rose an hour earlier than anyone else to personally escort the four members of Miranda's team through airport security and onto their flight.

"Are you really going to do survival training in the Outback?" He tried not to sound overeager, but would another opportunity like this one ever come his way?

"You make it sound so hard," Holly laughed at him.

After he'd reported to Grandmother last night, she'd suggested he try to accompany them. His protests about his commander not liking him missing another shift at the airport were brushed aside. She would take care of it.

"I've only ever trained here in Singapore. Oh, and I have hiked Mount Ledang many times."

"Still after your celestial princess?"

"A boy can have hopes."

Holly glanced sideways at Mike, who shrugged in answer.

Noor could read neither the answer nor the question.

"Fine by us," Andi answered from close behind them.

Holly stopped him at the edge of the gate waiting area. "Okay, mate. You want it that bad, we're game. If you can get yourself on the plane, you're welcome to come play. We'll probably be out a week at most. Beyond that, I haven't planned, but it won't be *desert training.*" She surrounded the words with air quotes. "We're talking about the deep Bush."

He pulled out his phone, unlocked it, and turned it to face Holly.

It was a paid ticket, in economy but still a valid ticket.

She punched his shoulder hard enough to knock him into Andi, who shoved him back the other direction like she wasn't twenty-five centimeters shorter than he was, more like she was made of steel.

Mike steadied him, then tapped his own arm. "I feel your pain, buddy. I feel your pain."

36

Darwin International Airport was so much smaller than Changi that it was hard to believe they were both called airports. Darwin had one small terminal with five small jetways, of which three were presently empty. Changi had twenty-eight jetways servicing four terminals that were never vacant for more than a few minutes.

After they retrieved their luggage—he'd grabbed a field kit last night—Noor asked where they were going. Holly merely smiled as Andi led them out of the terminal into the blazing sun. It was different here. No pale blue sky dulled by the thick tropical moisture. Here it was a dry crystalline blue.

"I've never been to Australia before." Grandmother had arranged for a visa from the Australian embassy for him yesterday.

"Lived here too long. Far too long." Even though her tone was morose, Holly looked as if she belonged here. She stood taller, as if posing for a statue without being aware of it. As if her feet belonged on this soil.

Noor looked down. On this *pavement*.

"Rule Number One," Holly slapped a water bottle into his

hand, "Drink up. Rule Number Two, this water is cold. Don't drink it too fast or you'll be whining about stomach cramps."

"Stay hydrated, no whining. Got it."

It earned him another punch on the arm. More painful than the first, as she had the annoying habit of hitting exactly the same spot. He decided it was her version of a friendly gesture.

"So, are we going to walk straight into the Outback from here?"

"Patience, Padawan."

"I'm not some naive and inexperienced *Star Wars* character! I'm a lieutenant of the Republic of Singapore Air Force." Noor took a deep breath when he realized he'd been raising his voice. "Why did you bring me along? I had bet Grandmother that you wouldn't, and now I owe her a thoughtful gift."

She stopped and turned to him as the others continued ahead. A long assessing gaze.

"I wasn't sure at first. Partly so that I could keep tabs on Rachel Yung was my first thought."

"Is my grandmother so fearsome?"

"If you want to survive this bloody game, never ever doubt that for a single second."

This time Noor waited her out while he reconsidered quite what he'd stepped into.

Holly turned away to scan the horizon as if she was simply making sure everything was where it should be. "No real bush around here. If you're going to go deep, you don't do it in the Top End of the Northern Territory. Bush here's no worse than a stroll down a country lane. We're headed south past the Kakadu and into the Barkly. That's a bit of the true bush that Miranda insists she wants to see. Gotta be a right smart cobber to walk out there."

Still he waited.

After a deep sigh, she faced him once more. "The other

reason? Because you remind me of me, you little shit!" She snapped it out, then closed and rubbed her eyes as if in pain. "Or maybe what I might have been. You have hope and belief that people can be good. I'm only learning that bit of magic this late in life, from these people. If I can give you some survival tools so that you can hang onto that, I'll consider it a job well done."

"You've taken me on a personal survival course to help me be not like you?"

"I guess. It sounds about right. If you want the deep thinker, talk to Mike, not me."

It made him wonder if he could step back out of the path Grandmother envisioned? No, that decision point lay firmly behind him and he wouldn't second guess it. But neither would he blindly step forward again.

They started walking to catch up with the others. He figured that topic was closed—at least for now.

"So, how are we getting to the real Outback?" He attempted to strike her casual tone but knew he missed it badly. Both the Noors and the Yungs tended to the serious side. Past girlfriends had asked if he ever laughed. He was sure he did, he simply couldn't recall when.

Holly waved a hand as if in answer. The others had led them past the corner of a small hangar west of the main terminal. Parked out on the tarmac sat a helicopter. Mike and Miranda waited nearby. The helicopter had three blades, which was quite distinctive, but he couldn't place it.

"What's that?"

"Uh-oh," Holly shifted away.

"It's a Eurocopter AS350 Squirrel," Miranda answered, "the B2 variant. You can tell by the addition of the aerodynamic strake added to the tailboom to break up a turbulent wrap-around airflow. It also has a different angle on the engine exhaust that improved handling. That places it after the

Eurocopter AStar designation but before it was rebranded as the Airbus AS350 Écureuil. The B3 variant, which came next, added higher performance attributes that allowed it to be the first helicopter to truly land on the top of Mount Everest. In 2005, a French pilot, Didier Delsalle, needed to rest on the peak for two full minutes to set the record; he landed twice, for four minutes each. The Squirrel has a range of seven hundred kilometers up to fifteen thousand feet. It's driven by—"

"That's probably enough detail for now," Mike said softly and Noor almost jumped aside when Miranda slapped a hand over her mouth.

"I'm pulling a Jeremy." When Noor squinted at her, she continued mumbling through her hand. "A former teammate, the one we called in DC about the mission commander's flight tracking. He enjoys explaining things."

"At length," Holly agreed.

"Who's going to fly that?" But his question was answered as Andi Wu began inspecting the helicopter in a highly practiced manner. Noor worked at an airport and recognized a preflight check when he saw one.

"Remember when we first met you?" Mike asked.

Noor cast his thoughts back to the confrontation by the Changi Airport koi pond. "Uh, Holly said that Andi was the dangerous one. Special Operations but she didn't say what kind."

Mike simply pointed at the helicopter.

Noor had assumed the look on the little Chinese woman had been all bluster. Apparently not. Again Nenek's words about the circles he was now walking among came to mind. Yes, he could already see so much more than he had even a day ago.

Once ready, they took off to the south. The land looked stark and empty at first. There were occasional low trees, and patches of scrub as far as he could see to either side of the arrow-straight two-lane highway they followed. Soon even the underlying scrub grass gave way to increasing stretches of red soil. Out here the world had rusted and only the occasional plant rose more than a few meters above it.

"Why is it only green along the road?"

"Dew condenses on the pavement at night and dribbles off the edges. You need big bull bars on your vehicle to drive the Outback at night. All sorts of critters, especially hundred-kilo 'roos, come to eat those plants on the verge. Cave in your front end but good if you smack one."

Holly continued pointing out features that told a deeper story. A water tank twenty meters across and five high built fifty kilometers from the prior water source. "It was a real lifeline to the old drovers who'd driven mule and even camel trains over this landscape. Folks passing down the Alice still use them." That's what she called this stretch of road that traveled the eighteen hundred kilometers from Darwin to Alice Springs with only two real towns between.

Next up was a roadhouse, which was little more than that; one or two families running a small general store with a gas pump out front. "At a hundred kilometers apart, they often have a small cafe and a big freezer chock full of ice cream bars."

On the narrow two-lane highway twisting below, the occasional road train raced along. A tractor-trailer truck with three, four, even five trailers in tow. "How do they stop and turn?"

"Carefully, Padawan."

Apparently he was stuck with that for now.

"*Very* carefully. My dad was a truckie his whole life. Died hauling a load. Probably well-oiled when it happened." Noor assumed that last was some form of obscure trucker slang. The biggest trucks in Singapore were the fuel trucks at the airport.

Holly also had them fly low over a river pointing out logs that burst to life under the beating sound of their helo.

"Those are *crocodiles?*" They were huge.

"Eat you as soon as look at you. The salties are the nasty ones. You have a few up your way, down here we have a couple hundred thousand. And the biggest ones?" She pointed emphatically downward as if marking the continent, not just this muddy bit of river. "But they're rare past fifty kilometers from the coast. For that we have freshies. Fresh water crocs are about half the length of a saltie, but you can find them hundreds of kilometers inland. No dogs in our public parks." Holly turned to address the dog, "Sorry, Meg," then whispered barely louder than the engine and the pounding of the rotors. "Dogs are too stupid to run and crocs know this. So a barking dog sounds just like a dinner bell to these boys."

They overflew a wild water buffalo herd that merely watched them go by, and spooked a couple packs of kangaroos who bounded away with surprising speed. By the time they landed in Katherine, an hour to the south to top up their fuel tanks, he wondered that anyone thought of the Outback as barren desert.

On landing beside the small airport terminal, a Hawkei armored truck gathered up Miranda, Mike, and Holly and whisked them away before Noor knew what was happening. That left him and Andi to watch as a fuel truck headed their way.

"Why didn't you go with them?"

"They're debriefing about a fixed-wing crash. Doing it in person since we're passing through." She tapped a knuckle against the side of the helicopter. "This is me. One of these go down and Holly can go shit with the bears in the woods for all I care."

Despite her sunglasses, a lifetime in Singapore where three-quarters of the population were of Chinese descent made reading her expression beyond the words easy. "You *really* do not like her."

Andi glanced up at him, sighed, and told the fuelie as he arrived, "Full up. Thanks." before leading Noor aside.

Katherine Airport was a single long runway. At one end, a half dozen buildings and hangars were grouped near a small terminal building. More than enough to handle the six flights a week that stopped here.

The interesting part lay across the runway. That was RAAF Base Tindal. There was no vast parking area for planes. Instead, it was a warren of narrow taxiways leading to thirty or so hangars able to hold one or two planes each. Most of the hangars were open to both sides because here the danger was the sun, not the weather. A plane could roll in under its own power, and roll out the same way. In one of the bigger hangars, he could spot another E-7A Wedgetail. Most of the others had pairs and trios of fighter jets.

But even more interesting was the little hundred-and-sixty-centimeter woman walking beside him, Andi Wu. Grandmother had uncovered very little information about her, about any of them. It was intriguing that Grandmother was as interested in these people as he was. He doubted it was mere curiosity on either of their parts but he'd wager their reasons differed. For him, they were a shining example of teamwork at levels he'd never given thought to before. For her? That was a question he'd ask the next time they spoke.

Unlike Holly always gazing off into the distance when thinking—or Miranda *never* looking at people—Andi turned to look him square in the eye.

"It's not that easy. I don't hate her. Holly and I have...had our differences." From a Chinese Singaporean that implied a battle to near-death. But did that translate to one born and raised in America? "Sometimes that slips out. Just ignore it."

And by the set of her jaw, that's all she was going to say on that. As he had a thousand other questions anyway, he moved on. "Mike said that you were Special Operations."

"When did he say that?"

"At the airport, when you were preparing to beat me into the concrete slab of the concourse with your bare hands."

That earned him a half smile. "Oh that. I was perhaps a little too distracted to be listening to Mike." He noted that she didn't apologize or even look chagrined. That's when he connected a few pieces. "Special Operations. You're a specialist in helicopters. Isn't there a helicopter team in the US military just for that?"

Andi nodded. "The 160th Special Operations Aviation Regiment. You might know us as SOAR or the Night Stalkers."

Not *it* but *us*. Even though she was no longer in the service, just as she'd said about the AS350 helicopter parked behind them, *This is me.*

That meant... "Does Miranda really need a former SASR operative and an elite Night Stalkers pilot to do her job? And what is Mike?"

"Yes, in ways you can't imagine. And no one knows, Mike least of all."

The fuelie called out and Andi turned back to pay the man.

That left Noor to stand in the bright sun—though without Singapore's oppressive humidity, it barely touched him. And nothing to do but peer through the heat shimmer rising off the runway at what else he could see in the distant plane hangars.

37

THERE SIMPLY WEREN'T ENOUGH AIRPORTS IN THE NORTHERN Territory. Other than abandoned WWII strips still scraped into the dirt alongside the Stuart, there were only four: Darwin, Katherine, Tennant Creek, and Alice Springs. They stretched out in a thirteen-hundred-kilometer-long line with nothing in between except a few cattle stations and even fewer roadhouses. Their little helo could reach from one airport to the next, but it couldn't skip any along the way.

That landed them in Tennant Creek in the afternoon, with no one willing to continue on until the next day after a such a long morning of travel.

Holly didn't even know where to begin. There were so many places here she didn't want to revisit, so many people she'd never expected to see again. How to avoid them all? Pulling her Matildas soccer team ball cap low wasn't going to help. Shaving her head and putting on a dress for only about the third time in her life would do it. But since neither of those seemed likely, she'd go with putting her head down like a water buffalo and plowing straight ahead—with force.

They made it out of the airport clean. The kid working the

fuel truck had probably been in diapers when she'd skipped town. She'd skipped the car rental issue by letting Mike go in and rent it.

"It was the best they had." He handed her the keys to a Mazda CX-30 compact SUV. She tossed the keys back, forced Noor up front with Mike, and squeezed into the middle position in the rear seat. Normally she fought for the front because she had the longest legs on the team. But the less she saw of Tennant Creek and the less TC saw of her, the happier they'd both be.

Mike saw her choice and nodded. The others looked at her strangely. Holly rarely piloted aircraft, but when they were in a car together, no one else got the wheel.

Seated in the back between Miranda and Andi, it was a tight fit even though they were both small women. Andi gave her a nasty look.

"Eat shit, bitch. I'm hiding, okay?"

Andi glanced up, around the windows, then nodded. "Oh, okay. I thought you were trying to get between..." she nodded toward Miranda who was busy talking to Meg—one of her standard self-reassurance practices.

"You think I'm *that* stupid?"

Andi shrugged a maybe yes / maybe no.

"You and me, we're gonna have a serious yabber."

Andi cricked her neck like it hurt at the thought.

"Yeah, mine too. But we've got to, for..." She knew her mistake the moment she tipped her head to the side. Miranda was autistic, not deaf or stupid.

"Me," Miranda sighed heavily but continued speaking to Meg. "They're going to talk about me when I'm not there. I don't think that's a very good idea, do you?"

Meg appeared to think about it before putting out her tongue to pant a little in the over-warm car (idiots had parked it in the sun and the AC hadn't caught up yet) and appeared to smile.

"You think it's better if I'm not there? I'm not sure, but... okay." Meg curled up in her lap.

Holly figured Andi had to have the patience of Job to be in love with this woman. "Later," she mouthed to Andi, who nodded.

"Whoa! What just happened?"

Holly hadn't been paying attention, but a glance out the window told her. "I warned you. Take a right."

The biggest town for five hundred kilometers in any direction, Tennant Creek stretched a grand four blocks long. A third of the one-story buildings still had the same tenants, the same faded sign, and probably the same dust in the window. A third had new ownership since she'd left, though she wouldn't place bets on which might last. And, as usual, a third had For Sale or For Lease signs in vacant windows. About half of those had steel fences around the perimeters of grass-cracked parking lots—a sure sign of the long abandoned. Few buildings dared risk the rarefied air of a second story.

"I said it wasn't much."

Then she realized what she'd done. The last right turn at the end of town was Standley Street. No question, the gods hated her.

She opened her mouth to protest, but Mike was watching her in the rearview mirror. Even with only his eyes visible, she could read the sympathy there.

"Like ripping a bandage off the wound?" she asked.

He nodded.

Three deep breaths like Miranda used didn't help. Neither did the fourth.

Meg stood up and walked from Miranda's lap and into hers.

"I'm not having an episode, you crazy little beast." But it did feel nice to dig a hand into Meg's thick fur. "Okay, the last road before the water-and-power works. It's called Marla Marla but there were never any signs. Yeah, left here," she closed her eyes. "Go to the end and stop. If that shithole is still standing, you'll be there. If it isn't, I just might believe that there's some god or other watching over me."

The car stopped. "Is this the place?"

She opened one eye. It was.

She opened the other. And it wasn't.

It had a coat of paint. The piles of Dad's trucker shit—worn tires, blown electrical and hydraulic harnesses from tractor to trailer, and worse—were gone from the front yard. A front garden had been coaxed to grow in the sandy red soil. Not much to brag on, but there were vegetables and a few flowers.

"What the hell?" She plopped Meg back in Miranda's lap, then reached past Andi to open the door and shoved her out. Andi barely managed to avoid sprawling onto the ground.

Holly stood where she'd been ten thousand times, at the head of the dust driveway. But she couldn't move any closer. The biggest change, other than looking in better condition than any moment in the sixteen years she'd lived here, was the heavy board fence around the property. There was even a gate. Though it stood open at the moment, there was a steel guide track across the dirt threshold that showed active use.

"Oi! Who the hell are you?" A native woman stepped into view with a handgun on her hip. "No strangers allowed."

Holly studied her face. If the woman had been a girl... "Jedda?" She'd been some years behind Holly.

The woman blinked twice, then barked out a laugh. "We all thought Quint was lying when he said you weren't dead." Jedda spoke fine English, but if you did that in Tennant Creek, it would sound like you were trying to be better than everyone else.

"Not last I checked."

"Then whose lazy ass is lying under that gravestone?" She nodded to the south.

Holly shrugged. Her parents had declared her dead after she'd run away from home at sixteen—and buried her. Something she'd learned after flying in to see their final resting places and dealing with what little business remained. She waved a hand at her old home. "What the hell?"

"Couple years back, Quint say you give it to Julalikari Council. Even forged signature."

Three years back, she'd spent a single night and morning in town after surviving a plane crash. The copilot of the sabotaged airliner had been Quint Dermott, just twelve when she'd left town at sixteen. By the time of the crash, he'd grown up—a lot. She was careful not to look toward Mike for what he might see on her face. They'd already been sleeping together by that time, yet she and Quint...

"No, that was me that signed it."

"Don't that beat all. Well, the council say what da hell and turn it into women's shelter—that your doin' or Quint?"

Holly shook her head. It had been all Quint. Hard not to like him for it.

Jedda offered a slight smile and a thoughtful hum that any woman would recognize. Then she glanced back at the house and the smile went away. "It's for them as got to get 'way from where they livin'."

"You?"

"Me? Naw. I working woman. No one as messes with me." She patted the gun on her hip. "Though never had to do more than pop some cobber inta foot to make him rethink goin' to *fetch his woman*. Might've even enjoyed it." Her smile was infectious.

"You with Quint?"

Again Jedda laughed. "You thinking of that time you caught us."

"Might be." She'd spotted a young Quint and a just developing Jedda doing *show me yours* out on the edge of town —this edge of town. Remembered doing that herself some years before in exactly the same spot behind the plumbing supply center with Jedda's cousin Yarran, so she'd just nodded and walked on by. It had also been the start of her friendship with a younger Quint just a few months before she'd bolted out of town. One that had ultimately led to her scragging him a quick one last time she was in town.

Jedda read the look easy enough. "Don't think Quint's the settling type yet. But been awhile since I looked in on him." Again that thoughtful smile.

Holly spotted several faces now peeping out from the shadows beyond the open windows. A battered women's shelter. Her parents had been cot cases who were never sober by choice—at their best when laid out and snoring off another bout. But they'd never come to blows but the once—Mum had punched her in the nose hard enough that she'd likely bled a pint and Holly had replied with a kick between the legs that had left Mum on the floor long enough for Holly to bolt for good.

Mike came up beside her.

"*You* can come in, I s'pose. But no men allowed." Jedda patted her sidearm again to make her point, offering Mike and Noor a glare.

"No, thanks. This is closer than I ever wanted to come."

Jedda nodded like that made some kind of sense.

All Holly knew was that her skin itched like it had been overtaken by a swarm of goblin spiders just from being in the same territory. "Say hey to Quint for me."

Jedda raised her eyebrows.

"Or not."

They shared a half laugh. If Jedda was going after Quint,

she wouldn't be mentioning Holly any time soon. Holly turned back for the car. No one gave her any strange looks this time when she returned to hide in the rear seat center position.

38

———

HOLLY HADN'T BEEN LAUGHING ONCE THEY WERE ALONE.

It took no imagination to see what her home had been like. Simply looking at the run-down dwellings to either side of the women's shelter had answered that. The struggling town; one in which they'd parked their car inside a steel-gated lot and been told not to walk off the main street after dark. And that town of three thousand people looked lush compared with her old home dominated by the low throb of the big diesel generators next door that supplied Tennant Creek's electricity.

The long stretch of unbroken red soil past the last house must have looked very attractive to the kid trapped there.

After they'd dropped off the others, she'd bought some flowers at the only grocery store in town. He'd refused to leave her side, so she'd let him drive her to a graveyard south of town where she laid them on the strangest graves he'd ever seen.

She hadn't so much as spared a glance for her parents' graves, but the one with Holly's name and her brother's had cut her to her knees. She brushed all the dust off his side and laid her flowers by his name.

While he'd watched over her, the sun had set. Once down,

there was no way to tell direction as the horizon turned pink all the way around. In minutes it traveled through orange and red to shades of blue and finally black. The first stars showed in the unblemished arc of sky before Holly struggled to her feet. When he stepped up to help, she'd shaken her head. Not said a word since.

Mike had wanted to question her once they'd curled up in the hotel room together. But she'd just laid her face against his shoulder. She hadn't sobbed or shaken. But he'd felt the slow trickle of hot tears land on his skin for a long time before she fell asleep. Even that was extreme for her, so he simply held her and let her be.

It had left him wide awake to connect the confusing images on his own.

He considered his youth in the orphanage and, for perhaps the first time in his life, wondered if he hadn't had the easier life. He'd had his parents until they died in a car crash when he was nine, watching them bleed out from where he'd been trapped in the back seat. The orphanage had been run by Sister Mary Pat, a long-time friend of his parents, so he'd had it easy. As easy as it ever was in a Catholic orphanage.

Both he and Holly had hit the streets at sixteen, except his had led into the comparatively rich urban wasteland of San Bernardino, California.

Hers had been covered in red sand in every direction.

39

He looked at the reports he'd managed to get copies of. Far too much detailed information after a half day's investigation. One of those threads could lead to places he didn't want it to go.

Whoever RY was—with that creepy-as-shit voice—he'd been right. Hang onto the Dassault Falcon with the Iron Beam laser and its crew until all of this was settled.

There was still cleanup to be done.

40

———————

"LET'S TAKE A TOUR OF THE AREA FIRST," HOLLY ANNOUNCED over breakfast the next morning.

The cafe was a brand-new place that served good coffee and a seriously tasty fry-up. Except for the vegemite. Holly had tried to hook him on it, but it still tasted like something he'd only scrape off his boot with a long stick...while wearing latex gloves.

"Some remote places that are worth seeing since we have the helo. Places we won't walk to any time soon." Holly sounded a little too cheerful for Mike's comfort about doing a helicopter ride today.

He'd wager that once aloft, she'd lead them on a tour that ended nowhere near Tennant Creek. Out here that meant either going back the way they'd come from Katherine to the north, or heading south to Alice Springs. He figured he'd won his bet when Holly sat in the front of the helo with Andi and guided her over Tennant Creek to the south—she didn't look down as they passed over the cemetery.

Mike sat in back with Noor and Miranda. Meg had a seat all to herself by the window but she kept strolling back and forth across all of their laps to look out one window and then across again to peer out the other.

"I figured we'd start with a short walk around the Amelia Creek crater. Give everyone a feel for what's out here."

"Crater like bomb or..." Mike couldn't imagine a war happening here.

"Or," Holly answered as she pointed Andi east away from the thin ribbon of the Stuart Highway, the only sign of civilization he could spot. "The impact was big but not an extinction-level event. The asteroid that whacked-in a half billion or so years ago was probably only a kilometer across. The crater is twenty kilometers wide and probably killed everything within a couple hundred kilometers. But I wanted you to see the contrast with the lush landscape around Tennant Creek."

Mike coughed out a laugh. "Lush?"

"Just you wait, mate. After that, we'll head north to the Barkly Tablelands. It's not this barren, much easier to find water and a bit of bush tucker for grub. I figured to save us a half day's hike to really get into it by flying there."

"Wait, we didn't stock up. What about water and food?" Noor exclaimed.

"You wanted to do a bit of a survival course. That's about getting dumped somewhere with whatever you're carrying and your wits. And we've got it easy," she thumped the helo on the dash. "We can leave any time. In a more extreme case, if we crashed, then we'd be talking about what we could salvage from the wreckage. But let's not go there. After the crater, we'll fly up into the Tablelands. We'll walk a big circle there, never more than a day from the helo if we decide as a group to bail out."

Mike's earlier assessment of Holly's intentions of getting them away from Tennant Creek had been wrong. By turning aside into the Outback, the helo had insufficient range to reach any other town without first returning to Tennant Creek for refueling. Knowing what yesterday had put her through, it was incredible that she was delivering on her promise to the group. Beyond mere tenacity, her resilience was astonishing. If anyone knew what that took to do, it was him, and he loved that about her.

Thinking the *L* word, one they'd never used with each other, should have been at least as uncomfortable as Holly's return to Tennant Creek. Instead, Mike found it comforting, which was unnerving in itself but no less true. He'd wager that saying it to her out loud anytime soon would not be a good idea.

And with each passing moment of watching the arid landscape sweeping by below them, this trip didn't look like such a great idea either.

41

THE AS350 B3 SQUIRREL HELICOPTER CRUISED AT TWO HUNDRED and forty-five kilometers per hour. Using that, her watch, and the angle of the sun, Miranda attempted to follow Holly's navigation without peeking between the pilots' seats to read the instruments. Her research had told her that accurate navigation was an essential survival skill.

Four-point-oh-eight kilometers per minute. She checked the hour and the shadow angle on the scrub below and decided they were flying on a course of three-four-zero, north-northwest.

But that made no sense. She knew they'd flown southeast over Tennant Creek because the town lay south of the airport.

Then the world seemed to twist under their rotor blades, leaving her a little nauseous. They were *south* of the equator, so the sun lay to the *north*. Which meant their shadow-indicated track lay at approximately one-six-zero, south-southeast. That made far more sense, and her stomach settled quickly after the abrupt reorientation.

She tried to start a page in her notebook, but Meg kept pacing back and forth over their laps, never spending more than nineteen seconds at either window with an average of eleven seconds and a first standard deviation of…

Meg barked out the window. Miranda noted the direction of Meg's attention. An aircraft was approaching them rapidly—a white sparkle in the distance. Within seconds it resolved into a small jet. It was unusual for a jet to be this low, as Holly was guiding them close enough to the landscape to see the details. They were below five hundred feet extrapolating from the angle of the sun at 9:37 a.m. and the apparent length of the shadows stretching from the scrubby trees below.

The jet flew at the same level. This far from any town, it should be at twenty-thousand feet or above.

"You can't really see it very easily," Holly was pointing, "it's been eroding for an eon or three, but that's the crater rim there." They were approximately a hundred and fifty kilometers from Tennant Creek.

Miranda was about to point out that there had only ever been four eons in Earth's history and the globe had probably been largely molten for the first one, so the likelihood of it actually being three eons old didn't make sense.

But then she saw the jet's type, a Dassault Falcon 2000. Except the shape wasn't right. It had an additional form attached on the belly.

"I think that's the plane that downed the E-7A Wedgetail."

"Okay," Mike said. "Hold it. Repeat that."

He knew she hated repeating things, so she pointed instead.

Mike peered out the window. "Medium bizjet? Holly! At our flight level! Nine o'clock!"

Miranda wasn't sure why he shouted so loudly; they were all wearing intercom headsets. Well, everyone except Meg.

Holly glanced to her left and leaned forward to look across Andi in the pilot's seat, but Andi must have slammed over the controls. They turned abruptly to the south. Seconds later a section of her side window melted away as did—Miranda snatched Meg into her arms—the side window that had been facing the jet moments before.

Andi had spun the helicopter so that the rear and body of the helo were exposed to the infrared laser rather than the people in the cabin.

After three long seconds, and the air in the cabin heating abruptly to sauna levels despite the gaping holes in the side windows, the engine sputtered. Several red lights appeared across the console, including a raucous Master Alarm.

"Get us down," Holly called out. "Act like we're crashing or they'll fire at us again."

"News for you, Harper," Andi's voice was the dead calm that pilots left on every cockpit voice recording during a dire emergency. "We already *are* crashing. Everyone brace."

Miranda knew the chances of keeping both arms wrapped around a thirty-pound dog if they impacted with any significant g-force was slim. So, she placed Meg in the empty seat beside her, ran the lap belt through Meg's therapy dog vest, and snugged it down. Meg grabbed it in her teeth and wrestled with it until Miranda told her, "Leave it."

Andi had instinctively attached not just the lap belt but the two over-the-shoulder straps. Holly now struggled to do the same against the thrashing flight of the wounded helo. The back seats had lap-and-shoulder belts like a car for her, Mike, and Noor. Meg was too short for the shoulder belt to be of any use.

The two men started to lean forward to brace against the back of Andi and Holly's seats, as you would in a plane crash with only a lap belt.

"No," she tugged on Mike's shoulder. "Lean back, let the belt take the impact. Centered across your chest. Nothing underneath it like a zipper or button."

Mike in turn pulled Noor upright, though the man had

braced so hard forward that Mike had to shake him quite severely before he'd move.

Miranda pictured the jet's flight path. "Andi, keep rotating to the west and then the north as we descend. The Falcon was moving at full cruise. The laser housing and load will significantly increase its turning radius, so it will be coming around to our south."

"I'll see what I can do about that."

The engine had begun clattering horribly when the fire alarm blared. Holly pulled the Engine Fire T-handle to cut the fuel and release the extinguisher. Miranda could feel by the slewing sensation in her stomach that the rudder controls of the rear rotor were badly compromised.

Straight ahead, the rocky ground below filled the windscreen. They were steeply nose down.

"Down!" Holly commanded.

"Going that way," Andi actually sounded like she was growling the way Meg would.

"No, down into the deepest ravine you can find."

"Without killing us?" The helo swirled right, then left, then right again.

"Right. Without killing us." Holly's voice shifted. "Everyone, the second we're down, get out and away from the helo. You have to hide fast."

With the engine finally stopped, the silence was almost... Miranda had to think about what emotion this might be...eerie? Now didn't seem like the moment to ask if she'd gotten that right. Only the thud of the windmilling rotors and the roar of the wind through the missing windows. It was nice that the wind cooled down the cockpit air after the laser attack had heated it so abruptly.

"You want to be well clear of the helo—" Holly shouted as the intercom failed.

"If we survive," Andi injected with a shout.

Everyone pulled off the now dead headsets.

"—but more importantly invisible from above. Don't look for the jet. Our friends will be looking for you. If you can see them, they can see you."

Friends didn't sound like an appropriate descriptive to Miranda. Their actions against the E-7A Wedgetail and—as she had little doubt it was the same plane—against them were distinctly *un*friendly.

"There, that way." Holly pointed out the windscreen, her finger moving in the opposite direction of the helicopter's spin. "There's a cave in the rock. Get us close to that, Andi."

"Can't." It was a bitten-off sound.

"Then close to the cliff wall."

"Can." And with a final counter-twist and a hard flare, the nose rose abruptly. Two hundred meters directly ahead, Miranda spotted the darkness of an overhung rock. Cave was a distinct exaggeration for the deep depression in the rock face. Close by her melted-out window, a steep cliff rose twenty or thirty meters.

And then they hit.

42

HOLLY CONCENTRATED ON STAYING LOOSE. MANY INJURIES IN A crash happened from over tensing, the body fighting the fall. When parachuting, especially if in a heavy landing, the trick was to relax and roll, letting the collapsing knee-thigh-hip-shoulder landing dissipate the impact energy.

Also, concentrating on her body's position kept her from grabbing the controls and stomping on the rudder pedals. She was little more than an amateur helo pilot and Captain Andi Wu was one of the best in the US military before the PTSD had sidelined her. That didn't stop Holly's instincts from trying to do anything to save them.

Andi had imparted enough last-second lift that the helo actually bounced after the first hit. Not high. This wasn't a Black Hawk with big wheels and massive shock absorbers, but the skids were rigid enough that she bounced. She slammed down the collective as they hit again.

The skid on Holly's side crumpled. She could feel the helo tip toward the sideways roll-and-thrash that was sure to cause damage and injuries.

But Andi did some form of magic with the collective, cyclic, and damaged rudders. They balanced on the tipping point for at least three heartbeats—that resounded like a multiple strike of two hundred and fifty-kilo bombs—before settling on one skid and its belly.

"Go! Go! Go!" Holly shouted the moment she knew she was alive.

The five of them streamed out, Meg at Miranda's heels. The starboard side was crumpled into the dirt and those doors wouldn't open, so Holly was the last out of the helo after scrambling over Andi's seat.

"To that overhang!" Holly ignored her own instruction and moved aft to throw open the luggage compartment. This side had sustained very little damage.

She shoved bags to the sides.

Miranda reached in to pull out her field pack.

"Bloody hell! I told you to run." Holly didn't have time to argue. She flicked open her Glauca Bɪ knife, the French counterterrorism guys had taste in choosing that, and rammed it five times through the cloth at the back of the cargo compartment, giving each strike a hard twist before withdrawing the blade. The holes she punched in the crash-resistant fuel tank mounted behind the cloth began dumping fuel.

She moved back, staying one step ahead of the leading edge of the spill.

Five precious seconds she waited before pulling out her keys. Then she swung the two-inch-long flint rod free and struck it with the edge of her blade. The third spark jumped to the edge of streaming fuel.

Holly grabbed Miranda's arm and dragged her into a full sprint. It was only then that she became aware of Andi hovering close to Miranda's other side and Mike close to hers.

"You're all idiots!" And she loved them for it.

The fuel had dumped onto the sun-scorched rock and started evaporating fast. In seconds it would—

Whump!

Even being braced for it, she was knocked to her knees by the air blast as all of the vapors lit off at once. She didn't need to look back to know that a column of fire bloomed twenty or more meters above them.

As fast as she could, she dragged everyone to their feet and raced again for the overhang as small shrapnel, and some not so small, rained down around them.

A glance behind showed the utter destruction she'd wrought.

From obvious to oblivion. Barty would approve, if she lived to tell him about it.

They reached the cave, which turned out to be little more than a well-shadowed ledge, and dove in. With Noor's help— the only one to follow her orders—they were packed tightly into the shadows. They'd crashed on and run across a wind-cleared slab of rust-red rock, so there was no trail leading to their hideout. At least none that wouldn't take an experienced tracker on the ground to follow. From the air they were invisible.

Moments later the jet roared by low overhead. It cut a wide circle. Once. Twice. Then, apparently satisfied, it arrowed north.

"I'll know you the next time I see you, you bloody bastard."

"Tindal Air Base."

It took Holly a moment to recognize Noor's voice, her ears were still ringing after her proximity to the explosion. "Say that again."

"I saw that plane in a hangar at Tindal Air Base while I was waiting for your debriefing. With the RAAF markings on it."

She grabbed his shirt in a fist and yanked him close. "And you didn't say anything?"

"I only ever saw the plane that attacked the Wedgetail as a little radar image on Ms. Chase's tablet. I'm not trained to interpret that. I only am knowing— I, only, know, that I thought the aircraft at Tindal had a shape I hadn't seen at Changi Airport before. Was it the same one?"

Holly let him go, barely resisting the urge to slam him against the cave's back wall as she did so. That had been close. Far too close.

She turned to stare out at the helicopter. Her attack on the fuel tank must have mostly drained it before she sparked the fire. With the initial fuel-air explosion over—which had shattered the Squirrel into a kajillion bits and bobs mostly smaller than her hand—there was little left of the fire. Out here, the nearest soul might well be forty or more kilometers away. Had the fire and smoke even reached past a hundred meters to be visible along the horizon at such a distance?

No. They were on their own.

Miranda reached into the pack she'd risked her life to rescue and pulled out her satellite phone. At least they wouldn't have to trek out through—

"No! Don't!" She grabbed the phone and turned it off.

"But..." Miranda rubbed her hand where Holly had wrenched the phone from her grasp.

"Tracking. If these blokes up to Tindal think we were enough of a threat to come and kill us, they'd certainly be watching for any signals. In fact, everyone turn off your phones and give them to me. Does anyone have some aluminum foil?"

"But a single call to Drake and..."

"And guess who he's going to call—Tindal Air Force Base. And if we tell him not to? Then he's calling someone too far away to help us before Tindal could land a major *oh-so-sorry-about-your-team* mishap on our heads. It's a no-go, Miranda. We're on our own now."

"I still don't understand." Miranda dug into a pocket of her pack and pulled out a couple of foil-lined pouches like the ones she'd used to protect the QAR and Mission Commander's drives before turning them over to the RAAF team earlier.

It was Noor who decided to explain. "Ms. Chase, the only people likely to know where to find you would be the people you spoke with at Tindal Air Base while they were debriefing you about the Wedgetail. Did you give them your plans?"

"Shit! Shit! Shit! Shit!" Holly pounded her fists against her thighs.

"Who?" Mike asked.

"There was a chap who seemed genuinely interested in our plans. He told me to be sure not to miss Amelia Creek crater, one of the fifty biggest craters on the planet. Never saw it before myself, so it caught my interest."

"And," Andi finished, "no one would be better equipped to watch for any signs of our survival than an officer of the Royal Australian Air Force."

"Oh," Miranda coaxed Meg into her lap. The dog settled in for a nap. "So what's next?"

"What's next? That's all you have to say?" All Holly was aware of was a need to throttle someone. It itched against the inside of her palms.

"Our helicopter is broken." That earned Miranda enough barks of laughter for Meg to pop her head up. There wasn't a piece left that couldn't pass easily through the hole in a truck tire. "We can't call for help. So, what's next?"

Holly looked out at the baking red rock stretching away from their cramped bit of shade. They were in a broad ravine perhaps three hundred meters across. And she could already see the heat rising off the rock blurring the far wall.

"We sort through our gear and then lie down to conserve energy until two hours before sunset."

43

"That's why I stayed at the helicopter, to gather my pack," Miranda explained before Holly could yell at her for not running like she was told. "In his book *Outback Survival,* Bob Cooper made it very clear the importance of husbanding all your resources."

They were all huddled close together in the narrow shade of the cave. Holly and Miranda were the only ones who had grabbed their packs.

"You read Bob's book?" Holly twisted to face Miranda. "No better reference out there. Bugger's a civvy but he ran my SASR survival course. Four weeks of bloody brutal, even to someone with all my skills. He gave me top score of my gang of twenty-three—that ticked off a couple of the boyos something fierce—but still I thought he'd kill us all more than a time or two."

"I thought everyone would have read it." The others shook their heads. "We were coming to the Outback. I thought that researching how to survive here might be a good idea."

"Well done, you. So what treats did you bring, Miranda?"

She spread out her pack's contents. The way she did so made it clear that it was the exact pattern she'd used to organize it all for packing. Holly wanted to kiss her on top of the head for being so damn cute. And as she kept laying out more and more of her kit, she wanted to kiss Miranda's feet in thanks.

She herself had grown soft and stupid. Her civilian instincts had her grabbing her travel bag, not the small survival kit she'd assembled. What she could now offer to the group held little more than a couple changes of clothes and toiletries. Well, other than the several weapons now hanging about her body.

When Miranda set out the rolled-up burlap bag next to the post snake-bite compression bandages, Holly snatched it up, leaving a blank space in Miranda's layout—which froze her in place. "What the hell, Miranda?"

"I'm sorry. I couldn't find jute bags in Seattle, so I bought burlap. I hope that's okay."

"But...why?"

"In chapter two of his book, Mr. Cooper relates his experiences in the SASR survival course. He said they were each given a jute bag and fifteen minutes with a thread and needle," she held up a sewing kit, then set it back in precisely the same place, "to alter the bag into a garment. Then they were stripped naked and had nothing else to wear for the next week. Are you going to make us do that? It is very itchy material."

Holly handed it back, shuddering at the memory. "No, Miranda. That is not only itchy, but painfully abrasive in some very uncomfortable places. After a week you'd almost be happier going naked if not for the sunburn and the cold desert nights. We won't be doing that."

"Oh good." She went to set it aside.

Holly stopped her. "Never throw anything out when you're in a situation like this." She looked over the other equipment Miranda had assembled. "You didn't bring a compass or any food."

"That would have defeated any lessons in solar and celestial navigation and bush tucker. I looked for a good book on that but there were so many, and they didn't agree."

"Next time, feel free to pack a little food. And a compass." Holly was going to miss both, but especially the compass.

"Okay." She pulled out a notebook from the pack's side pocket and added the note, then tucked it away. After they finished going through everything, Miranda reloaded her pack.

Then she closed her eyes and took several deep breaths.

When Noor started to ask a question, Holly raised a hand to stop him. The rest of them knew this was a sign of Miranda gathering herself back from the edge of panic. She was the most prepared of all of them, so why was she panicking?

That's when Holly realized that Miranda had been carefully keeping her back to the opening. Here, in their shadowed notch in the cliff, she must feel safer not facing the unknown.

Halfway through, Andi took Miranda's hand and synced their breathing. However annoyed Holly still became at the memory of Andi's betrayal, she couldn't deny how good the two women were together. Which only made her feel like more of a shit for driving them apart. And—

She caught Mike looking from them to her with a strange expression on his face. As if having slept together for so long, he abruptly saw her in a new light. One with a question in it that she wanted to avoid at all costs.

"So, uh, *Noor*. You had a question."

"Yes. What's next?"

Holly sighed. "That's a tough one. We're a hundred and fifty klicks from Tennant Creek. I could walk that, but I don't think we all could. I'm torn between the Stuart Highway, seventy kilometers to the west or the nearest water, which lies thirty kilometers almost directly away from civilization to the east. Water is the key. Weeks without food, you can struggle through. Three days without water and we're dead."

"Seventy kilometers. We can walk that in two days. Can't we find water on the way?"

"Over this terrain, it's probably closer to four or five days. And to the west, we might find enough water to sustain one or two—not five. And if that cobber up at Tindal is smart, he'll have patrols along that stretch of the Stuart watching for us stepping out of the bush just in case we survived the crash."

Noor looked disappointed. Miranda had opened her eyes and was at least listening.

"To the east-northeast, and only thirty kilometers away, there's a kilometer-long stretch of the Frew River called the Old Police Station Waterhole that holds water even during the Dry. That's the season we're in now. Only have two in most of Australia, the Dry and the Wet."

"It gets wet here?" Noor leaned out to look up and down the ravine.

"Not often, mate. When it does, it'll try to kill you."

And Holly wished she could cut out her tongue. That's how she'd killed her older brother, driving into a flow that had risen from nowhere to overtop the Stuart during the Wet. It had dragged him to his death and left her alone with her horror show of a family.

She hurried on to try to shut her mind against that gaping wound. "But add another ten degrees or so during the Wet, that's Centigrade, and you'll likely collapse from heat stroke before your corpse desiccates."

"Oh."

"One or two of us could strike out fast and alone. But if we don't find help soon, anyone we left behind would die of thirst. There won't be any water here for at least six months. No decisions until two hours before sunset." Between the five of them, they'd ended up with four one-liter bottles of water— two were Miranda's per Bob Cooper's book, the others were Noor's and the one she'd jammed into her own luggage.

"Everyone drink one cup of water and lie down in the shade to conserve energy. We don't have enough water to move during the heat of the day."

As they lay down on the cool shadowed floor, Holly felt a far colder chill. Five people, five and a dog. How the hell was she supposed to get them out of Amelia Creek crater alive? And even if she did, would the RAAF be hunting them?

Her last thought before she let herself fall into a doze was about Lieutenant Adiputera Noor. His grandmother, *The* Rachel Yung, had positioned herself to know everything about the Wedgetail E-7A crash. Even having her grandson push himself into joining them.

Yet she couldn't make it fit that she would have any part in an attack on her grandson. If Noor knew more, she was too exhausted to pin him to a wall and find out what.

Last night, after she'd managed to convince Mike she was asleep and he'd finally slept for real, she'd moved to the chair beside the bed and watched him by the bathroom's nightlight leaking into the room. The man had become the anchor in her life, even more than Miranda.

Miranda had created a team, a place for Holly to exist and help.

Mike had created a place she wanted to *be*. She'd never have made it through the day without him—might have died draped over her and her brother's gravestone without him.

She'd resisted as long as she could, but shortly before dawn, she'd slid back into bed beside him and simply held on. And despite her sending him to safety, Mike had waited beside her at the helicopter. Their fates tied together in that moment more surely than the way he'd held her while the tears forced their way past her defenses.

Despite the heat penetrating their shelter, he rolled close enough to lay an arm on her chest—his hand resting over her heart.

Damn the man.

44

____

Noor wished he could kick himself. He'd followed Sergeant Harper's orders and run when he was told to. He'd been the only one to do so. But even if she was enlisted (released) and he was a serving lieutenant, her orders had the authority of command. His instincts hadn't hesitated.

Only as they were sorting through their gear later did he realize that his field kit had been blown up along with the helicopter. Until that moment he hadn't considered its potential usefulness in this dire situation. He'd clutched a water bottle as he'd ridden in the helo because Holly had told him to remain hydrated. After two cups of tea and a large orange juice with breakfast, he was so _hydrated_ that he'd nearly burst a bladder before slipping out of their hidey hole to take a leak. All else was gone. Including the sidearm he'd signed out. Now he'd have to complete all the paperwork involved in its loss. Which, he supposed, wasn't all that important in the scheme of things.

When the area of the destroyed helicopter had shifted into deep afternoon shadow, Miranda had slipped out to inspect the site. Holly went with her and Noor followed close behind.

"See, Miranda, sometimes it *is* useful to know how to destroy an aircraft."

"I still don't like it. It was a perfectly nice helicopter."

"Until it was fried by a military-grade laser. I simply leveraged the opportunity to keep us alive."

"I still don't like it." Without another word, Miranda turned to study the wreckage. She even took photographs and made notes in one of her little books.

Holly stared at Miranda's back before twisting away to stare out at the terrain.

Noor moved up beside her. "Is that how she says thank you for saving her life? How angry is she?"

Holly scowled at him. "She's not! She's—" Then she looked over her shoulder at Miranda's back before turning once more to face the distance rocks still shimmering in the afternoon's heat.

"Who knows? Not even her. Her autism makes it hard for her to know her own emotions, never mind anyone else's. But her certainty has a didactic quality that can..." Holly glanced at him as if realizing who she was talking to for the first time "...be uncomfortable."

"She should meet Grandmother."

"Not a chance in Hell, Noor. Don't even think it!"

Her vehemence rocked him back on his heels. Perhaps it was a taste of what she felt from Miranda. "I was only referring to Grandmother's didactic self-assuredness of always speaking absolute truth."

"Rachel Yung's reputation for that reaches far and wide. And she has *nothing* in common with Miranda."

Then she ended the conversation by stalking over to Miranda. Rather than continuing the...argument, to all external appearances they were simply investigating yet another aircraft incident together. He fell in close enough behind them to overhear their conversation but far enough to not be part of it.

Yet all they discussed was evidence of the crash and the results of Holly's triggered explosion. They methodically circled the rather large debris perimeter, though Holly wouldn't let Miranda leave the deep shade to enter the area that was still sunlit.

She also wouldn't let them walk anywhere that had scorch or char on the rocks. "No footprints."

As he circled, he tried to understand Holly's vehement reaction to Grandmother Yung. She was certainly a tough lady. But Noor had been raised to excel and he understood that instinct that drove him ahead. That drove him to simply say yes and walk into, uh, *through* the door when Nenek had opened it.

He learned no more from overhearing their analysis walking about the wreckage, but he did find his sidearm. It had been blown aside, unblemished, though no other sign remained of his pack. He slipped it into his back waistband under his shirt. Thank God he wouldn't have to fill in all that paperwork.

<h1 style="text-align:center">45</h1>

———

HOLLY KICKED DIRT OVER THE TINY FIRE SHE'D STARTED WITH HER flint. It was so much more space efficient and practical than the bow-drill fire starter kit Miranda had purchased, that she tried to toss it away. "No, keep it in case we get separated," Holly had insisted. "And leave no evidence behind that we were here."

As the fire died, they drank their second cup of water of the day warmed and flavored with the tea bags Miranda had packed.

"I hope the flavor is okay. I didn't know whether we would want caffeine or not to enhance our chances of survival. But it does taste good. I always liked blueberry tea." And she did. It was a happy tea that made her feel better.

While she was packing away the cups, Holly had asked for Miranda's burlap bag. She'd split the side seam and cut it into five roughly equal pieces.

"Thankfully, you all have caps. Need to get Noor one from the Matildas."

"Matildas?"

"You can't think that your Singapore Army ball cap could be even a tenth as good as one for the Aussie women's national soccer team, mate. Get a grip." And she moved on before Noor could respond. "Cover your hats and leave it wide on your shoulders and down your back. A burlap square isn't *all* that different in color from the soil and rock. I don't want us showing up on satellite more than we have to. But I also want to cover as much ground as possible before dark. We don't want a line of bobbing headlamps anywhere close to where they think we died just in case they're still watching."

They had two headlamps: Miranda's and the one Holly had found among the wreckage as well as a couple of batteries that tested okay once the carbon was rubbed off against a rock.

"Travel in single file whenever possible. When we're on sand or dirt, I'll go last to cover our tracks. Most importantly, believe it or not, talk to each other. This is going to be a long and hard slog. If we're crazy lucky, we could be there by morning. If not, we'll have to hole up for another day. Even with water, we don't have enough containers for us to travel in the heat. After water, the next biggest survival factor is keeping your head in the game. Tom Hanks and Wilson the soccer ball in that movie *Castaway* is totally real. That's how he survived, not ingenuity and a coconut cookbook."

"I don't know what to talk about."

"It doesn't matter, Miranda. Just whatever comes to mind."

"What about Meg? That comes to mind. Should I talk about that?"

Holly looked down at the terrier aghast. She'd forgotten about the dog. The small terrier would end up bloody-pawed if she walked the whole way. But far worse, she'd leave unwanted tracks off to either side as she investigated smells, perhaps getting bitten by an annoyed snake, and a myriad of other unpredictable events.

She took her pack and quickly sorted through the contents. Some went into her pockets, some tossed aside, and most of the clothes were pushed to the bottom. She scooped up Meg and dropped her in the pack so that her head poked out.

Andi gathered the discards. "I'll carry these until we can bury them somewhere well away from the site."

Before she could shoulder Meg and the pack, Mike stepped forward and gently took the straps from her.

"No, Mike. I can do this." Her voice sounded oddly strained, even to her own ears. How must it sound to the others?

"I know that. You can do anything, Hol. But we need you mobile. I've got her." After he shouldered the pack, Mike turned his back to Miranda so that Meg was facing her.

"Miranda, you follow behind me and keep an eye on Meg. Talk to her so that she knows everything's okay."

"You're coddling me." Then she closed her eyes for a moment as if thinking hard. "Right now, I think I should say thank you." Then she looked at their small hideaway one last time before turning to face Meg.

"I liked it here, Meg. Safe on three sides at least." Then she turned, took three deep breaths, and stepped away.

"Head for that cleft, there," Holly pointed. "I'll catch up." Then she began removing any sign of their presence.

46

———

"Okay, Noor. Where's our starting point?"

He looked out at the sun kissing the horizon. He didn't see anything familiar, though he'd been watching behind them as often as he remembered. At a loss, he made his best estimate and sliced a hand to the sun's left. Despite this being only a five-minute break after two hours' walking, Holly was spending it hunkered down with him.

By her smile he knew he had it wrong. "What did you forget?"

He looked down at his own shadow striking east. The sun was west. Holly had said their desired track was twenty degrees north of east and he was pointing twenty degrees south of the sun.

"Think about—"

"No, don't!" He cut her off. He could do this. Again he checked his shadow, now so ridiculously long that it could cross mountains. After a two-hour hike up and down the walls of successive ravines that crossed their desired path, he wished he could stride as easily as his shadow over this arid terrain. It would cross the coast at—

He twisted back to look at the sun. "It's midwinter. And we're below the equator. The sun sets farther north in the winter."

"How much?" Holly prompted him with a smile.

"No idea."

"We're close to the Tropic of Capricorn. On June 21st, midwinter solstice, it sets twenty-five degrees to the north of west."

He shifted his hand from twenty degrees south of the sunset to forty-five degrees. "Whoa!" As if by magic, all of those tiny features he'd tried to memorize but knew he'd failed at, were there in a line. "We're dead on track."

"Pretty close." Holly set a stick on the ground, pointing along the track, then a rock at either end. "This is the most dangerous time to navigate. You think you can walk through civil twilight, but features that your eyes recognize will become hard, then impossible to see. We need to wait for a few planets and stars to show up before it will be safe to move on. Go tell the others they actually have at least twenty minutes, but they are *not* to take off their boots."

"Right." Once boots were removed after a long hike, feet swelled far too much to fit back in. The only cures were time or soaking your feet in cool water. They had neither, but the others might need reminding. Well, not Andi as she was a Special Operations officer. And probably not Miranda because she knew everything as far as he could tell. It felt weird telling just Mike. He was Holly's boyfriend. Someone sleeping with Holly made him think uncomfortable thoughts.

You're a Singaporean military officer, Noor. Get your peacocks to walk in a line.

So he told Mike, making it loud enough for the others to hear in case they needed a reminder.

"Got it. Thanks."

He was halfway back to Holly's lookout when he remembered they'd have a longer break than expected.

Thankfully twilight had progressed enough that they couldn't see his blush for forgetting Holly's initial message.

"Careful, *Padawan*," Mike teased him. "Getting taken under Holly's wing isn't as safe as it sounds."

"Nor is my grandmother's." Then he smiled in the dark. "Or I'd be kicked back and eating a slice of pizza with my squad right about now."

They both laughed at that. Holly had found a few vaguely turnip-like tubers for them to crunch on. *No time for hunting or much foraging. Middle of the Dry is the wrong season for berries or fruit.* It made him thankful for the food, but a pizza sounded spectacular at the moment.

His empty stomach growled loudly enough to earn him another laugh.

47

———————

Holly wished she dared turn on a phone. She'd like one reliable fix. Next time she'd study the damn map before going into the bush. One quick glance to find Amelia Creek crater and give Andi the coordinates. A second look had told her that the terrain was far too rough for an inexperienced mob like this one, and they'd be better off testing themselves against the Barkly to the North.

Then she'd folded the map and stuffed it into her pack; her blown-up pack would have made this a far more comfortable experience if she'd grabbed it instead of her clothes. She'd stocked extra water bottles, electrolytes, energy bars, and a whole kit of other gear she'd really appreciate at the moment—like a pro-grade compass.

Instead, she was swinging their lives from the tiny needlepoint of skills she hadn't used in most of fifteen years. A SASR operator kept up on their survival skills more as a game than a need. Sure, if you missed an extraction, you might have to lie low somewhere hard for a day or a week until the next possible pickup. She'd solved that the way any SASR operator did, by never missing an extraction.

This was the age of GPS locators and electronic maps. But she'd been out of SASR for—bloody dingo farts—six years? That meant that she and Mike had lapsed into five years together, which was beyond insane.

But it also meant her last celestial nav course had been…

It gave her the shudders.

She'd *pretty close* to lied to Noor while she prayed he was right. One glance at a paper map and no compass wasn't much to go on. Oh, they were holding the course she'd set, despite the brutal hill-and-ravine territory they were scrambling over. That in itself constituted a minor miracle.

But where were they headed? If she was off by more than a degree and a half, they could cross a dry riverbed during the night and never know they'd missed the only water hole she knew about.

Past that? The next stop would be Mount Isa city, five hundred kilometers on. A mining town so rough it made Tennant Creek look friendly. Those two years slaving away as a waitress there after running away from TC had taught her the hard way how to defend herself. But it had also taught her to keep everyone at a distance.

After leaving Yarran behind in TC, no one ever got close to her—she'd made sure of that.

Until Mike.

He now sat with the others twenty paces away, having put his life in her hands. She could save Miranda's dog. That much she could do. But Mike had taken Meg onto his own back and now she had to keep the four humans alive in order to save the dog.

As usual, all thoughts of Mike tied her in knots.

Keep control of the now.

Right. Bob Cooper must have said that a thousand times. If she died here, she couldn't solve the next problem. So, she'd work on the now.

Except she'd *been* working the now.

Holly had hustled ahead at the bottom of every ravine so that she could scrabble holes in the dry soil without anyone seeing that there was no hint of moisture below the surface this time of year. She'd ranged back and forth across the south side of every hill, seeking *gnammas,* rock pools that might hold water from a recent rainfall. The ones to the north would, of course, be dried out by the hot sun. But, damn it, those to the south were dried out as well. It probably hadn't rained out here in months. Not even any pigface or other succulent plant whose leaves could be chewed for a few precious drops of bitter moisture.

No animal tracks bigger than a thorny devil lizard and a couple of elapids. While the latter were okay in desperation, she wasn't in the mood to chase after a snake with deadly neurotoxins on its breath.

She looked up at the stars. The brighter beacons now shone forth. She remembered their names at least: Fomalhaut, Achernar, Sirius mapping the zenith from west to east across the winter sky. To the north, planets marked the ecliptic, a notably unreliable measure unless a person stayed abreast of the planetary motions—which she hadn't!

For now, the hunter was rising in the east, lying upon his back this far south of the equator. No, here in Australia, Orion's belt was three fishermen in a canoe that stretched from Rigel to Betelgeuse. They'd been banished to the sky for illegally catching a great king-fish marked by the arc of Orion's bow.

She rested her hand on the stick she'd anchored in the dirt to point where they needed to go.

Yes. To start, she'd follow the lost fishermen and hope that they led her to water.

And when they'd risen too high in the night sky to be a reliable guide?

By then Hydra would be cresting the horizon. She could

only hope that the monster of the sea didn't consume them all for daring to cross the desert.

48

———

Twelve hours.

The helo had been down for twelve hours.

No cry for help.

No phone calls.

No trace of their numbers when he'd scanned for them.

The Dassault Falcon had brought back images of the massive fireball from the crash. The satellite image had shown the utter devastation of the aftermath—the AS350 Squirrel helo shattered past recognition. So remote, no one had come looking for the cause of the fire. Except possibly crazy geologists a decade in the future visiting Amelia Creek crater for who knew what reason, no one would find it tucked so deep in that narrow ravine.

He allowed himself a cautious breath.

No. Impatience had almost tripped him up before.

He couldn't keep monitoring the crash site and their phones for long without arousing suspicion. Perhaps for one more day.

But the patrol roving along the Stuart Highway? Them he'd keep looking for three days. Maybe four.

49

———————

"Straight to voicemail." As Drake Nason hung up the line, Clarissa didn't dare so much as breathe.

"Miranda's allowed a vacation. Who else could answer the question?" President Roy Cole sat behind the Roosevelt desk in the Oval Office.

Roy had asked Clarissa to stay behind after the last meeting. She'd been ready for the hammer to land on her head for how she'd yelled at Drake, with Feldman and Lizzy Gray in the room. The three of them had been asked to stay as well.

Bracing herself for the blow hadn't been as easy as it used to. When married to Clark after she'd made him Vice President, she'd become untouchable. A quality she hadn't understood until some bastard had offed the poor sod. Since his death, she'd done everything she could to make herself and, specifically through her, the CIA indispensable.

And *still* Drake shut her out at every turn.

Except the hammer hadn't fallen.

Instead, the question on the table had come from the RAAF. They wanted a formal safety assessment before lofting a replacement E-7A Wedgetail over the Strait of Malacca. Drake had tried calling Miranda to weigh in as well.

Clarissa pulled out her own phone, tapped a few queries—then flinched. *Shit!* She used to be better at subterfuge. Her skills were getting soft. Maybe no one had noticed that—

"What?" Drake asked.

"I... Nothing." She glanced at her phone again, then tucked it away when she caught herself.

"Clarissa."

She put on her best D/CIA not-saying-a-word face, which only lasted as long as it took her to see that she had everyone's attention. "Okay. Fine. I keep a tracer on Miranda's phone. It tells me things like where the Wedgetail went down in Malaysia when you're being too goddamn righteous to tell me things I need to know."

"It was a developing situation, Clarissa, and at midnight local time you didn't need to know."

"Until the Chief of the Royal Malaysian Special Branch called me personally at one a.m."

"Until then," Drake concurred with that annoying complacency he wielded like a familiar sidearm.

"Well, right now her trace shows squat. No signal from her phone, her satellite phone, or Holly Harper's."

Sarah Feldman spoke up. "Are you monitoring those with or without their permission?"

"Seriously? We're the CIA. I'm not tapping their calls. I'm merely tracking their locations. Get real, Madame Vice President." She needed to sit the woman down, before she won the election, and have a long talk about just what the CIA could do for her once she was in office.

Drake looked annoyed. But General Elizabeth Gray, as Director of the NRO, appeared to understand. She'd bring her husband around if anyone could.

Drake picked up the phone beside the couch again, dialed, then put it on speaker.

"Again?" Taz snarled when she picked up.

On cue, mere seconds later, a baby began wailing in the background.

"Jeremy," she called out, "feel free to kill Drake for me while you're at it." Then her voice faded away.

Clarissa could definitely get behind that program.

"What do you need, General?" Of course, Jeremy Trahn, perhaps the NTSB's top crash investigator after Miranda, would probably never harm a fly. A pity.

"We're trying to reach Miranda but she's not answering. Have you heard from her? If not, can you trace her phones?"

There was a pounding on a keyboard. Within seconds, it sounded as if there were a thousand ring-tone buzzes emanating from the phone. One after another, they picked up:

"This is Mike. Please leave a message…"

"Andi here, but not here. Say something."

"You have reached the voicemail of Miranda and Meg Chase. We're…"

Meg? Clarissa mouthed to Lizzy.

"Her dog."

And finally, in Holly's voice, "So say something already."

Jeremy cut them all off and again the roar of the keyboard overly close to the phone's pickup on his end.

"No current signals. The last trace was thirteen hours ago at 20.848 degrees south, 134.924 east. That's the location of… Amelia Creek crater deep in the Australian Outback. It's one of the fifty largest impact craters that have been found on the Earth so far. Twenty kilometers across? Wow! That means that the asteroid was probably a kilometer wide when it impacted. They've only been able to date it to one-point-one billion years ago, plus or minus a half-billion. That would have set off a—" He stopped himself. "Sorry, too much information."

Lizzy Gray had keyed the coordinates into her tablet. Then she gasped in shock. Manipulated the screen a few times, before looking up at Drake in horror. Roy hurried out from behind his desk. Clarissa was the last to gather around her and look down at the screen lying across her lap.

It gave her the least advantageous view, upside down, but it didn't matter much.

As the Director of the National Reconnaissance Office, Gray had gone straight to calling up the latest satellite view of the area. Spread across the entire image were a thousand pieces of debris. A lone chunk of rotor blade said that it had once been a helicopter. The immediate area, and when Gray zoomed back, the entire cliff face, were scorched black by what must have been a horrific explosion.

Jeremy's wail of despair—filling the otherwise silent Oval Office as he must have found the same image—echoed the baby's in the background.

50

"No, General Nason, I hadn't heard about any accident in that area." Without conscious thought, Group Captain Julian Osborn had risen to stand at attention. He was the equivalent of a colonel and General Nason wore four stars, the equivalent of four stripes above the bar in the RAAF. One was for merit. Two meant someone excelled in the political game, few of those reached three except by competence. But four? He knew what that meant on a man's epaulet.

"You're our nearest asset. Are you able to send a team out to search for survivors?"

"It would be my pleasure. Amelia Creek crater lies in quite the remote area, I must say. And it's after dark here in Australia. I can dispatch a team to arrive at sunrise, that would be in eleven hours."

"Sooner is better." Julian knew a command tone when he heard one.

He considered for a moment. A recommendation from America's top soldier might be just what he needed to relaunch his career on an upward trajectory. More than one way to skin a dingo. He'd like to trade in his senior-officer four thin stripes and get him the heavy bar of air commodore on his own uniform.

Julian checked the roster. They did have a Spec Ops team that might appreciate the training opportunity.

"I can have a jump team there in ninety minutes," he should have thought of that sooner. "Then I'll send in a helicopter team behind them to arrive at dawn. Would that be satisfactory, General?" He considered adding false assurances that he was sure the general's people were all right. But they were both career military men and knew better.

"Wonderful. Thank you so much, Osborn. I look forward to hearing from you in under two hours." And he was gone.

The familiarity was a bit presumptuous, but he was American. Julian would take it as a good sign. Perhaps a *very* good sign.

51

"There was one other member in their party," Lizzy told him by the time he got off the phone with Australia.

"Who?" Drake asked. He didn't recall any new NTSB investigator being added to Miranda's team.

"Jeremy found a fifth phone number co-located with the others at the time of the accident. He's tracing it now."

Jeremy sounded over the Oval Office speaker phone. "A Lieutenant Adiputera Noor of the Singaporean Army. His phone track follows Miranda's back through Tennant Creek last night, Singapore the night before, the Wedgetail crash site, and all the way back to Changi Airport before they diverge significantly."

"How did he tie up with them? Can we get his profile on the screen?" Clarissa called out to the room. She might be a pain in his ass, but it was a good question.

And there it was. His grandmother.

Clarissa dialed the number from memory. So much for keeping the two of them apart. At Drake's sharp nod, she rolled her eyes but switched it to speaker.

"Hello, Rachel. Director of the Central Intelligence Agency

Clarissa Reese here. I'm sorry to call you this late in your evening, but have you heard from your grandson Adiputera today?"

"Good evening, Director. Not a problem. No. We haven't spoken since last night. Should I be worried?"

"Rachel? Drake Nason here. I'm sorry to inform you that we have some cause to believe that he was involved in a mishap deep in the Australian Outback along with one of our teams. We're mobilizing forces to investigate even as we speak."

There was a long silence before she managed in a tight voice, "There's no mistake?"

"His phone was co-located with others. The nearest team is two hours out. Can you tell us why he might have traveled to Australia with our people?"

She cleared her throat carefully, but still sounded shaken when she spoke. "He was befriended by a Holly Harper at the Wedgetail incident site. He received permission from his commander to travel with her for an impromptu Outback survival course. He's a very eager and skilled young officer."

"We'll keep you informed as soon as we have any news."

"I would appreciate that." Her voice had taken on a different tone before she hung up—like Holly Harper when she was preparing to rain Hell down upon some poor unsuspecting soul's head.

At first he thought he was imagining it, until he saw Clarissa's wince of caution. From Holly Harper, Clarissa of all people would know that tone well. He wondered who had just landed on Rachel Yung's shit list.

52

———

Rachel set the phone down very carefully, struggling to not smash it through the floral marquetry of her seventeenth century desk from the Dutch colonial occupation.

What in all creation could she do from here? Kuala Lumpur lay five thousand kilometers from the Outback.

If those clumsy Americans had gotten Adiputera killed…

And then she had a horrid thought.

Adi nearly worshipped the people who investigated the Wedgetail crash. And he was an exceptionally bright boy. The events of the last few days had motivated her to approach him sooner than she'd planned, but she'd been watching him for some years—the best of his generation in the family.

What if the Americans had *not* been the problem? Their general had said that his team was also caught up in the incident, whatever that had been. What did the team have in common with Adi? They'd all been at the crash-site investigating the E-7A Wedgetail. A plane's demise that she'd been forewarned of by her contact.

She'd been entering her apartment atop the PETRONAS

tower as the phone had begun ringing. She'd navigated through the apartment to her office by the lights of Kuala Lumpur shining in the wide windows. Now she turned on her a small Tiffany lamp. Crossing the vast oriental rug to her safe, she keyed in the code, then thumb-printed in the secondary lock. She extracted the file she'd built on her contact, relocked the safe, and took it back to her desk, spreading it open on the ornate surface.

She studied the pictures of him that she'd acquired. You could tell much from a man's face, but one had to take care to not see what one wanted to. She'd seen him first as an unknown and then as a crafty ally.

But if he was an enemy?

That too was visible in his features.

Then she began sorting through the other information she'd gathered. A wife, divorced. No sign of a mistress. Impotent? Or perhaps other-driven enough to not care about sex? Only a fool didn't care about sex. Since her husband's death, Rachel chose her lovers carefully, but enjoyed them immensely. Her present one managed the Prime Minister's schedule—young but exceptionally imaginative...and virile. And useful.

Her contact, perhaps thinking himself still safely anonymous, had two children. Son and daughter. The son off on some backpacker tour of Europe. But the daughter...

Something didn't quite line up.

Rachel returned to that page to read her background more carefully. Top of her class at Monash University in Melbourne —a top-fifty university worldwide. No record of her for two years afterward, until a placement at the Australian embassy in Singapore so generic that it might mean anything. Two years without a trace could simply be a gap in her investigations. Or, had the girl been a student in the Australian Secret Intelligence Service's graduate program? Not so different from Special

Branch, they recruited heavily from the best in Australia's universities.

Digging deeper, she was estranged from her powerful father, so of little use to Rachel as leverage. But...

Rachel flipped back to her picture. The girl was quite pretty in an overly healthy Australian manner.

And—Rachel turned to the next page—unattached.

She allowed herself a bit of hope. One that counted on Adi's survival, but hope nonetheless. Though, of course, he was too modern to ever accept any matchmaking from his grandmother. She'd have to find a way around that.

Then she set aside the daughter's file for later consideration and returned her attention to the father.

53

———

"Down! Down! Down!" Holly shouted. "On the east side rocks or under anything you can find."

It might be too late to hide, but maybe not. The sound had teased her, at the very edge of hearing, until it had pounded into her conscious thoughts with all the power of a kangaroo kick.

"Hercules C-130J," Miranda whispered from close beside her. "With the six-blade Dowty propellers by the sound. Couldn't we signal them for help?"

"Do you see anything? Peek to the side, not over the top." Holly had made sure she'd pulled Miranda out of sight.

Miranda did. "No, I don't see anything."

"Exactly. No running lights. In this sky, the blinking red of the port wing-tip light should be glaring at us. They're running due south, probably coming out of Tindal Air Base. If you watch closely, you should be able to see the red interior light when they lower the tailgate for the jumpers."

"Jumpers?" After a long hesitation, Miranda said she didn't see anything.

"Look lower than you'd expect."

"Yes, I can see the red light."

"Combat insertion? That's a Spec Ops trick. I don't know why they waited until after dark. But if they'd come in daylight, I'll bet it wouldn't have been good for us."

Miranda was quiet but Holly could hear the unspoken question that Miranda was struggling with. Questions about human motivation snarled her up worst of all.

"If Noor and I are right, one of the people who interviewed us at Tindal Air Base not only downed the Wedgetail but also our helicopter. Yes, this could be a rescue team, using it as an excuse for a combat-style exercise. But I'm not willing to bet out lives on it."

"But...why?"

"That, Miranda, we won't know until we get out of this— alive. Let's go. Time is shorter than I thought."

After it dropped the team, the Hercules turned north, switched on its lights, and headed back to base.

"Okay everyone. Drink a cuppa and we're on the move double time. We have to get where we're going by dawn."

Or else they really would need a rescue team and Holly didn't like the odds of that.

<h1 style="text-align:center">54</h1>

<hr>

"No sir. No sign of any bodies." Jannali had hated the Outback as a kid, even more as a recruit, and ten times that during SASR training. And now? Doing a night jump into the arid wasteland to track down some lost idiots who'd wandered too deep into the Great Australian Fuck All.

"Nothing?" Bloody officer sitting so cozy back at base.

"Not so far, sir. We've scouted the immediate area, but can't see any tracks out of the area either. Could be another helo came for them."

"Expand your search. We need to be sure."

"Yes sir." Jannali clipped his radio back onto his harness and turned to his men. "Okay, boys. Pattern search. Shifting outward in five-meter stages centered on the crash. Seeking any signs of survivors or departure direction." All the wishing in the world wasn't going to turn four grunts into twenty. Or fifty. Jannali had walked enough of the Outback to know even that wouldn't be enough, especially if someone didn't *want* to be found.

Now why might *that* be? The question was above his pay grade, but he was a Spec Ops Flight Sergeant, as high as a noncommissioned grunt could go. They were already talking advanced training and making him a warrant officer, so maybe he *was* paid to think now.

He still couldn't imagine who in their right mind would try to walk out of here.

After twenty minutes, Harris called him over. He wasn't a great tracker, but he pointed at a wall of rock.

"You?" Jannali asked.

"I was about to, Sarg. But spotted this."

Jannali whistled and the other two trotted over.

The four of them stood in line staring at the wall through their night-vision goggles.

"Any of you?"

No one answered.

"Okay. New center. Five-meter grid search from this point."

Fifty meters north of the wreck, someone had peed against the rocks. A man, standing. He'd been careful though, none of it had flowed to outline his boots or feet. No sign of a track to or from on the hard rock.

Jannali looked north, then double-checked the map on his phone. Tennant Creek lay a hundred and fifty kilometers off in that direction. A hell of a walk. He only hoped he didn't have to do it himself.

Three hours later, they'd found nothing except for a possible displaced soil slip another four hundred meters north. A 'roo or a survivor?

He called it in.

The terse instruction had been, "Start walking. Helos arriving at dawn."

55

HOLLY FELL TO HER KNEES AS IF SOMEONE HAD CUT THEM OUT from under her.

Mike almost fell over her when she did. He stopped, remembered, and braced just in time as Miranda ran face first into Meg. They were all moving pretty much head down at this point. Thirty pounds of dog on his back during a fast march across impossible terrain was...

And then he saw it.

They'd each had their final cup of water at three a.m.

The predawn light had turned the whole sky pink. And from the rise, he was looking down upon a shining crescent of pink. Sky reflected off water—*beautiful* water. He'd never seen such a lovely sight.

"You did it, Hol!" He managed to croak out as he collapsed beside her. "You goddamn miracle worker."

Her tears were glistening tracks down her cheeks through the red dust that covered all of them.

He gave her a small shake, but she might have been dead for all the attention she paid him. Her gaze remained fixed and unblinking, staring out at the water.

Mike imagined himself in the James Stewart role for the last scene of *The Flight of the Phoenix*. After weeks of rebuilding a crashed airplane in the deep Sahara and rescuing themselves, desperate and long since out of water, they'd flown to a distant oasis. Together the men had plunged down the hill to dive into the water. He staggered to his feet and headed down the slope toward the water. He wished he could run, but his feet were too sore, his throat too parched.

Stagger? He'd take it.

Holly had led them to water and he couldn't wait to plunge his entire body into it.

He'd made it halfway when Holly tugged on his arm.

"Don't." Her voice was even croakier than his.

Mike shook her off and managed a fast shuffle.

This time she took him out at the knees, splaying him onto the powder dry soil. The pack with Meg slid up his back, piling her onto the back of his head and driving his face into the dirt.

"What the hell?" At least that's what he tried to say. Instead, he made puffs in the dust like, "Wad duh hul?" Then he began coughing and choking on the soil he inhaled.

"Freshies!" Holly shouted in his ear loud enough to hurt.

"Right. Water. Fresh." He managed with only four choking coughs.

"Fresh. Eee. Croc. O. Diles." Her voice was in no better shape than his.

Blinking hard, he managed to clear one eye. He'd gotten so close. No more than fifty meters to water. And now he could see them lined up like logs along the shore.

They weren't as big as the saltie cousins in the north, but he didn't want to meet one in a dark pool either.

Holly dragged him back to his feet. "Not. Eat humans. Much. Dogs? Yum!"

The load that had burdened him so during the everlasting

night was now the comforting weight of Meg still in the knapsack.

The others came up to them.

"We can't drink for another half hour. Miranda, we'll need your purification tablets." Holly began collecting their precious water flasks. "I'll refill. Noor, you can come with me. If the freshies get fresh, shoot off that popgun hidden in your waistband. First round in the air. Second, about ten down the row. The others will attack the wounded croc."

Instead of digging for pills, Miranda simply pointed.

Mike managed to follow the direction she indicated.

There, a few hundred meters down the far shore, a caravan was parked behind a pickup. And people were standing in front of it staring at them.

"Or we could go talk to them?" Mike managed.

Holly just nodded and set off.

They fell into the same line they'd been in all night. Holly in the lead, Mike with Meg close behind, Miranda following Meg and Andi keeping an eye on Miranda, with Noor keeping up the rear.

That trudge, so close yet so far, seemed to be the hardest stretch of the night.

Right until someone put an ice cold juice box in his hand and said, "Drink that slow, mate. Real slow."

56

———————

"Outback Telegraph," Holly told Carlisle. An odd name for a Black, but he seemed to like it. "At least four steps."

"Someone be huntin' you?"

Holly nodded.

"You de good 'un or de bad 'un?"

She rolled her eyes at him and he laughed.

They were speaking in a mashup of Warumungu and broad Strine that no one except a local would follow. It didn't matter that they didn't know each other, they shared the tribal language unique to the region.

"Who and what message?" Carlisle kept it light, which considering the shape the five of them would be in without him, was a gift.

"You know a lady by the name of Jedda?"

He slapped his hip where Jedda had worn her sidearm.

"That one. If Quint is in town, tell him to come here with his plane, but to leave town to the west first."

Carlisle pulled out his emergency radio and called a brother who ran the Ti-Tree Roadhouse three hundred kilometers south of Tennant Creek. He'd call some cousin, who'd call...

She had no idea. But that's how the Outback Telegraph worked. The messages traveled. Sometimes directly, sometimes not. Until she'd traced this back to its origin, she'd appreciate the less-than-direct connection back to her.

When Carlisle had finished his call and they'd sat in silence for a bit, he asked, "Why not message to the man hissself?"

Holly smiled. "I've got my reasons."

57

Holly woke when she heard the plane.

"Beech Bonanza with the Hartzell three-bladed propeller," Miranda announced with her infallible ear before it came into sight. It landed on the dirt track that led up to the waterhole after wandering far and wide over the Davenport Range.

Her feet hurt too much to do more than sit up as he taxied to a stop and shut down the engine. Quint clambered out and strolled over like he was king of the walk.

"You've got a goddamned crease in your trousers."

"Doin' better than you, Hol." He grinned down at her and she couldn't help grinning back. They'd each taken a sponge bath from a bucket of water, but this wasn't any kind of swimming hole.

"You're lookin' good, Quint." And he did.

"Haven't we already played out this scene before?" He turned to look at the others. "Miranda. Andi. Hey, Mike." They traded cautious manly nods. "Who's the kid?"

"I am Lieutenant Adiputera Noor of the Singapore Armed Forces at your service. I am not a kid."

"Christ, Harper. You trapping baby minnows now. Don't you

know there are rules about when to toss them back in?" He winked at her.

Noor, apparently at a loss, kept his mouth shut.

"Need a lift, Quint."

He nodded. "So Jedda said. Haven't seen that girl in a bit. She's looking very fine."

Holly glanced up at the sun. "That what took you so long a-comin'?"

Quint's grin said it just might be. "You're just lucky I wasn't out on a flight."

"You still on the LA to Sydney route?"

"Hoping a pretty lady might be stepping on my plane sometime soon."

The main reason she'd chosen to come in through Changi and Darwin rather than Sydney. An entire flight with Quint on the hustle might make Mike's brain explode. Though the one morning of sizzle she'd had with Quint didn't fire her up any more. He was still too handsome for his own good, but—

She glanced over her shoulder.

—Quint wasn't Mike Munroe. She offered Mike a smile, which he was a little slow to return.

Quint must have picked up on it. "So, where's this aerial bus ride going?"

"Tindal Air Base."

He squinted at her. He would know that it shared the field with Katherine's civilian airport, but she hadn't said Katherine.

"And there's a couple Aussie squads on the ground somewhere, maybe with air support, that we want to avoid." She waved a hand vaguely to the west.

That brought back Quint's smile. "Full on military search-and-rescue according to the telegraph. They're halfway to Tennant Creek—the hard way." He tramped a couple times in the dirt.

Good. That made for fewer people to pay attention to a small Beech Bonanza flying in from the depths of the Outback.

58

Drake groped for the ringing phone and found it on the nightstand after the third try.

Holly Harper flashed on the display.

"Holly, where are you?"

Lizzy tackled him. Normally being tackled by his wife in her light summer nightgown was just the kind of invitation he hoped for. Tonight, she dragged the phone far enough from his ear that she could listen as well. The fact that she had to wrap herself around him to do so was a pure bonus he'd collect on later.

Except no one answered.

Instead, there was a crinkling like aluminum foil and then footsteps.

Lizzy raised herself enough to twist the phone a bit more and read the display. "Hey, video."

He pulled it from his ear, saw she was right, and punched for video. "Holly? Are you—"

"Oi! You can't come in here. It's—" A man's voice was suddenly choked off. All Drake saw was someone in a Royal Australian Air Force uniform dropping to the floor.

"Don't kill him, Andi." Holly called out.

"No promises."

They were clearly meant to be silent observers.

There were only jittery glimpses. Hallway. A very closeup view of Holly's denim-clad leg, then a view behind. Andi tying up the guard. Then the phone swung forward again. Pant leg, hallway, and finally a door sign as she tucked the phone into a breast pocket with the camera facing out.

Group Captain Julian Osborn.

That was the man who they'd talked to about the loss of the E-7A Wedgetail and who'd dispatched the search-and-rescue team to go find Miranda and her people.

"Why's Holly showing us this?"

Lizzy just shook her head. At least he wasn't the only one in the dark. Literally. He turned on the bedside lamp without looking away from the phone.

Holly didn't knock.

She didn't bother with the door handle.

A boot came on-screen just long enough to kick the door inward, splintering the door jamb.

"Who the hell are—" Then the voice choked off.

"This is where you say how glad you are to see us safe, mate," Holly spoke calmly. "Oh, did you think we carked it in Amelia Creek crater when your laser plane shot us down?"

The man merely gaped. He started into denial.

"Wait a minute." Drake felt suddenly sick. "Him? The RAAF group captain? But I trusted him."

"Me too." Lizzy didn't sound any happier.

That's when Andi slid into the frame from the side and held her knife blade an inch away from Osborn's nose. "Can I carve it off? Please? His nose to spite his face."

The phone's view shifted as Holly sat down in front of the desk. Then her boots filled the lower part of the image as her heels landed on his desk. The view shifted up to his face again as she tipped back her chair.

"I think you only made one real mistake, Julian, my old mate. You're the one who told me about the crater. Then your men didn't manage to kill us there. Oh, don't worry, they aren't coming to save you. The RACMPs were only too glad to cart them off for questioning. By the way, there's a reason those idiots weren't accepted in SASR; my regiment has much higher standards than you do. Like those poor sods who picked up my false trail toward Tennant Creek—I'm proud of those boys, I was being subtle. I needed them to stay in tracking mode, moving much slower than hot on a trail."

Holly then held up a fist in clear view of the phone for Osborn to see.

"Cover your ears, Miranda."

"She's alive!" he and Lizzy whispered to each other. Pure relief flowed through him. Drake couldn't imagine how he'd live with himself if he'd sent her to her death with this investigation.

She must be standing out of view of the camera.

Holly showed what lay in her hand, a demolitions trigger.

She pressed it.

A massive thump shook the room. A window shattered loudly but no one turned to look at it. Through it Drake could hear fire sirens begin to howl in the background—disconcertingly like Jeremy's kid.

"...I can't imagine that plane will be bothering anyone much now. Nice trick hiding it in plain view. Aussie markings, and you'd be the chap to authorize the paperwork to park it here."

Lizzy buried her face against his shoulder to muffle a laugh.

Drake felt it was a little drastic, but it was hard to argue. The general in him disapproved of the wasteful destruction—the Israelis would be pissed as hell. But the former 75th Army

Ranger in him gave her a full-on *Hooah* that set Lizzy laughing again.

Holly tossed the control to Osborn, who caught it instinctively. Now it would be his fingerprints on the trigger. Andi reached into Osborn's jacket pocket, extracting his phone. She held it up to his face before tossing it to Holly.

Unlocked, Holly began scrolling through the menus. The first thing Drake noticed was that she turned off the Phone Lock. Holly paused at some screen that wasn't at the right angle for Drake to read, a phone number. He could tell by the wobbling of the image that she was keying something into her own phone. More scrolling, then a second phone number received the same treatment before she tucked Osborn's into her pocket.

"The only thing I couldn't figure out was why you took out the E-7A Wedgetail. Then I had a pal do some digging. Group Captain Julian Osborn, former commander of the E-7A Wedgetail, facing involuntary retirement. Ignobly forced out with no honor guard, no rank bump, nothing but a handshake. Two years shy of full pension, too. Now *that* had to hurt."

"Shit," Lizzy's curse was soft but emphatic. "We missed all that. We trusted the bastard."

Osborn's face had traveled through a number of emotions, but that last was one too far and tipped him into blind fury, probably Holly's intent all along.

"It was that Abo!" He looked ready to blow a blood vessel.

"Group Captain Rowena McCain?" Holly asked in the most innocent of voices. "Oh dear. And I was so sure that *Abo* had gone the way of wop, kike, and nigger in America. I must be wrong."

Osborn visibly tried to reel himself in, not realizing it was far too late. "She set out to undermine me. Took my seat! They were already talking about giving her the promotion that was rightfully mine! To some black bitch who never should have left the kitchen."

"Top of her class. Sterling record. Unlike yours, rife with complaints and mediocrity. Yes, that must have been so vexing." Then Holly turned the phone on herself. "Heard enough, mate?"

Drake tried to reply, but he was still on mute.

Instead, the easily recognizable voice of the Australian Governor-General sounded on the call. "Quite. Consider past travesties forgiven, Ms. Harper."

"Thank you, sir. I was...just a little annoyed when I tried to choke you with my bare hands prior to my departure from the service."

"I may have noticed. Should you ever wish to return to—"

"I'd rather cross the whole of the GAFA on hands and knees. But I do apologize."

"Gaffa?" Lizzy whispered to him.

"The Great Australian Fuck All. The Outback."

Lizzy's laugh joined his.

Holly turned enough to show three MPs and a senior officer crowding into the room. As the MPs reached for him, Osborn threw himself over the desk at Holly. She kicked away, doing a backward roll to land on her feet as the chair slammed onto the floor.

He screamed as Andi's knife laid a long slice from his nose, gouging deep across his cheek and ear.

"Good!" Lizzy whispered. "Misogynist bastard."

That was his fighting lady. He held her a little tighter, appreciating the strength of her slender form as Holly's phone steadied on a new image.

"Damn it!" Andi held up her blade. "Idiot lunged too suddenly. Now it's all icky." She began wiping the blade clean of blood on the ass of Osborn's pants while the MPs pinned the raging man to his own desk.

59

———

"SEE YOU LATER, SWEETHEART." SHIRA PULLED HIM CLOSE AS SHE did every morning after checking that his uniform was up to her standards for an aluf of the Israeli Defense Forces.

Benjamin appreciated every square centimeter of contact.

After her workout and shower, she'd tugged on one of his t-shirts that swirled tantalizingly at the very top of those lovely thighs. His hands roamed over his favorite curves, her cheek down to her breast and the other down her gloriously toned ass.

"I can't be late today," which was their signal that he couldn't afford to undress and then dress again—this time. The office had mostly adapted to his somewhat erratic daily starting time, but he had an early meeting today at Israeli Defense Headquarters in the center of Tel Aviv. Traffic was hell at this hour.

For her on-line work from home, Shira was on no particular schedule. He envied that. More than a little, but he wasn't going to be quitting Special Weapons research anytime soon to join her.

He bent down to nuzzle her neck before leaving.

She gasped, then froze as rigid as a statue.

"Haven't even kissed you yet."

She didn't respond to the joke. Instead she stared wide-eyed over his shoulder. Frozen like the time his F-4's engines had choked deep over Lebanese territory. His body had gone rigid in terror, knowing what happened to Israeli pilots ejecting over Lebanon during the five long years of the Second Intifada. He'd managed to restart one engine and make it home safely, but he'd never forgotten the feeling.

Still holding her close, this time with his arm wrapped protectively about her shoulders, he turned to see that her attention was focused on the sliding glass balcony door. No, on the two men in full gear who had just rappelled onto his balcony.

As they crashed through the glass, the front door to his apartment blew open. Literally blew open—Benjamin recognized a breaching charge even though basic training lay four decades in his past. The shock wave sent both him and Shira staggering into the living room.

These weren't Air Force security people, they were Mossad. Two over the balcony, two through the front door.

He hadn't done a thing—had he?

Before he could act, they knocked him aside. Face into a wall. One man pinned him there.

Two others threw Shira to the carpet, ignoring his t-shirt riding up to her waist as they zip-tied her hands, stuffed a gag in her mouth, and bagged her head. The last stood in the far corner of the room with his weapon raised and ready for any surprises.

"What the—"

He stopped when an agent swung his Uzi to center on Benny's face.

The moment he stood there with his mouth agape was one too long. He was cuffed and gagged as well.

"Strip the place," the leader called out. "Phones, computers, files. You know the drill." And the team began to destroy his apartment.

"General. You've been harboring a foreign agent responsible for providing key information, provided by you against the state secrets laws, facilitating the theft of a Dassault Falcon 2000 and a highly classified Iron Beam laser weapon. The agent is also implicated in the destruction of an E-7A Wedgetail, the death of its crew, and an attack on a helicopter carrying a US military team. The US's NSA was able to provide us with a tape of the phone call in which she provided this information. It has been voice-matched."

An agent walked in from the bedroom with Shira's phone, unbagged her only long enough to unlock it, but not long enough for them to look at each other.

"Number and call time match," he announced seconds later.

As they bagged his head, they didn't bother reading Benny his rights. This was Mossad—one of the most effective clandestine agencies in the world. They didn't waste time with someone's rights once they'd found the guilty.

Judge, jury, and executioner.

60

———

Rachel had worked different scenarios until she was cross-eyed.

Julian Osborn had cut himself off from the society of his family. He had no friends she could trace. Her reach into an Australian Air Base deep in the Northern Territory was limited mostly to satellite images like any normal person. She didn't have a single agent on the ground there because, until this moment, she'd never needed one. Australia was so upstanding and forthright that not only did it limit her tools to leverage subversion, but she hadn't needed one before now either.

Besides, both her and Special Branch's resources were limited and were far better placed in a hundred other locales both domestic and foreign. No one on the Lao People's Revolutionary Party could sneeze without her knowing if it was allergies or a life-threatening disease that could destroy the balance of power. China might think they were inscrutable, but she had people embedded all the way to Beijing.

Nothing in an Outback military base.

Having missed the prior night's sleep, she'd finally

collapsed into bed at ten, having heard nothing from anyone about the fate of her grandson.

Four hours sleep was all she ever required, yet she could barely drag herself from bed after sleeping for seven. Halfway to the shower, she hesitated.

Something...

She took a silk robe from the hook and wrapped it around her as she stepped into her dark living room. Nothing but the sweeping view of Kuala Lumpur in the five a.m. darkness. She could entertain five or a hundred and five in this room with equal ease.

Her office door was ajar.

She stepped through into the darkness. There was...

Rachel dove to the rug. A hand slap to her belt, but she wasn't wearing it. And it no longer contained a stiletto even if she did. It would have a miniature cell phone in need of a charging.

At her desk, only three meters away, she'd hidden—

A soft click and the room's indirect lighting rose to a gentle glow.

There, at the center of the room, an empty chair where none should be that had triggered her subconscious into defensive action. And in the corner, facing her, with her back to neither door nor window, sat a woman with long gold-blonde hair.

It wasn't Clarissa Reese, the director of the CIA. Rachel had studied what images she could find. That woman was very full-figured over a trim waist, and her hair was lightest blonde.

This woman she'd never seen before, yet she felt as if she knew her. It would take someone with exceptional skills to arrive undetected past her guards and alarms—her inaccessibility perhaps the one aspect she most appreciated about living at the top of PETRONAS Tower Two.

"Holly Harper?" It would fit, though Rachel had found no

images of her. She'd found the other members of the team, but never the former SASR agent. To all appearances...unarmed, though Rachel doubted that.

"Rachel Yung," the woman replied with only the slightest trace of an Australian accent. In a way, she looked like nothing special. Tall, pretty, a yellow baseball cap, a black t-shirt, jeans, and Army boots. "You still have some moves, *Datin,*" she paid high respect in jungle Malay.

Rachel stood slowly, careful not to reveal how much that dive to the carpet had hurt her hip—the one that a communist bastard had shot as she'd gutted him with a knife forty years before.

Holly waved her to a seat.

It was a good choice. Six meters from where Holly sat, it would be nearly impossible to charge her faster than she could draw a weapon. The chair in the center of the room was away from the desk and any other furniture. Not that it mattered. She could see that Holly had stripped the room by the pile of weapons laid out neatly across the red leather of the Chesterfield sofa. A quick inventory revealed that she had investigated more than Rachel's office.

She moved carefully toward the chair but, like her, Holly was a professional observer.

"It sucks, doesn't it?" She switched to English, leaving Rachel to wonder at just what had been her past actions in Malaysia. "I recently had occasion to go on a stroll across the Outback. We were lucky, it took barely sixteen hours, yet I can still feel it in my muscles and my reaction time."

Rachel sat and neatly arranged her floor-length green silk robe over her legs before looking at Holly and asking the most important question. "Noor?"

Holly merely shrugged. His fate or even the news of it would wait until something else was answered. "On the floor beside you."

Rachel looked over the far side of the chair. There lay the small phone normally kept in her belt—her belt that even now lay in the dressing room close by her bed. And yet she hadn't been awakened.

She declined to pick up the phone. "We could have used your skills in the jungle against the communists."

Again the shrug, though it did not look comfortable. "Tell me about the man on the other end of that line."

Rachel felt both heat and hope. Heat of fury that the man had shot down the helicopter carrying her grandson and the hope that because Holly Harper sat here, perhaps Noor survived as well.

Holly Harper sat *here*. That meant she'd caught the man, accessed his phone, and impossibly traced the texts to the one lying beside her chair. Her computer people must be even better than Rachel's own, and she'd paid for the best.

"Please tell me the bastard is dead."

"He'll never see the light of day again. Is that good enough?"

Rachel nodded. "I'd rather have gutted him myself, but it is acceptable."

"What was your part of the deal?"

"Scheduling information only." And here she must tread carefully. She explained the process—how he'd told her when there was no aerial coverage above the strait, and her providing him with information of when Australia was the *only* air coverage. Rachel didn't mention how she'd taken advantage of the opportunities Julian Osborn had created. Nor did Holly ask. That was irrelevant to this conversation; her instincts told her that Holly could no more be bought than she herself could. Offering her a profit share would be an egregious insult, perhaps a deadly one.

"The E-7A?"

"The first I knew of it was the text you've already read on that phone, despite its security." She nodded to where it lay.

"You knew what you were dealing with." Holly picked up a file from the small side table. *The* file. Every detail she'd been able to gather on Julian Osborn's life. A glance at her safe showed that it, too, stood ajar. Again, the how was irrelevant but it was beyond even her own skills; she'd made sure of that when she'd had it installed.

"Yes. But I did not know how extreme he could be. Prior information from him was related to gaps in air coverage above the Strait of Malacca due to unanticipated delays of the Australian security flights or an aborted patrol. Gaps of mere hours that harmed no one." Except for the owners of the ships Tuah bin Musa had pirated for her.

Holly flipped through the file quickly, proving she'd already read through it and was merely hunting for a particular page. When she reached it, she studied it at length.

The silence—Rachel knew the power of that particular tool —but this time it worked against her. When she could stand it no longer, she gave voice to her initial question. "Noor?"

Holly studied her, then looked back down at the file. After a long moment, she tore out the page and tossed the rest of the folder aside. With Julian Osborn down, she was right. It *was* no more than paper for the burn bag.

Holly Harper pushed out of the chair, walking as if her feet were still sore. She halted a mere step to the side of Rachel's chair. When there was no killing blow—and Rachel had little doubt she could deliver one—she looked up at Holly's face.

They watched each other for a long moment. Holly gave no sign of her thoughts as she assessed Rachel's future.

Rachel didn't brace herself; what would be the point? Holly Harper was thirty years younger, thirty years fresher, and her fieldcraft skills, unlike her own, had remained current.

No sign of a decision showed on her face as Holly set the single saved page in Rachel's silk-covered lap. "Tell him: Holly said *Celestial Princess.*"

He lived.

Her eyes blurred as she looked down. She could barely make out the features of the lovely girl who had nothing to do with her father but would be so perfect for Noor's future.

Not a single alarm triggered as Holly Harper slipped away.

61

"I think that vacations are...problematic." Miranda stated as she stroked Meg's ears where the dog lay in her lap.

"I couldn't agree more." Except Andi was looking at Holly instead of Miranda.

Too exhausted to squirm, Holly merely flapped a hand at Andi as if to say, *Yeah, yeah. You and I still need to talk.* While the others had slept off their ordeal in the comfortable beds of Changi's airport hotel, Holly had spent the night paying her visit to Rachel Yung in Kuala Lumpur.

Besides, Miranda was right. Their first team vacation had turned into averting a new World War by staging a one-woman invasion of Russia—and kicking Andi off the team and out of Miranda's life for eight months. This time had been close—too close. Ironically, if anyone other than Andi had been at the controls of the Squirrel helicopter when they were lased, none of them would be sitting here in the Changi airport's *forest* awaiting their flight home.

She looked up at the trees but seemed to see her Special Air Service Regiment team's last mission among ones not so different. The drug runners who had tripped over their ambush meant for another criminal of far more importance. The gun battle. The explosions that Holly had triggered in revenge that had finished the clash and ended her career in the Australian Special Air Service Regiment.

What if she could now leave that in the past? But if she did, what lay ahead of her?

When she looked down, Mike was watching her; their chairs so close that the arms were touching.

"You should have seen her face, Mike," she whispered just for him.

"Whose, Miranda's? I just saw it."

"No, Rachel Yung's. When it came down to it, when I really backed her into a corner, she only cared about one thing."

"Her life?"

"Her grandson's. With her life on the line—and trust me, it was a close thing and she knew it—she cared most of all about Noor. Family. Might have even surprised herself with that."

Mike offered one of his teasing grins she knew so well. "Does that mean you want to have babies with me, Harper?"

The angle was wrong to slam a fist into his gut. Besides, she was too tired. Instead she took his hand and watched with only minor surprise as their fingers interlaced.

"No, you idiot. But, Mike..." Holly took a deep breath and did her best to leave all her past behind her as she let it out. "It *does* mean that you have nothing to worry about. As long as you'll have me, I'll be there."

He raised their joined hands and kissed the back of hers. He knew better than to mess it up with words that she could latch onto and worry to death. Mike was always so good with people, including her, because that's what he did better than anyone she knew. Maybe she'd let him keep doing that— without *too* many complaints.

When she noticed the deep silence in their small circle, she turned to look at Andi and Miranda. They too were holding hands.

Andi wiped at her eyes. "God! That was so sweet, Harper."

"I'm not sweet!"

"That," Miranda stated, "is true."

They all stared at her in surprise. Then they burst into laughter together, even Meg added a bark. Because, as usual, Miranda was absolutely right.

For perhaps the first time since she'd run from Tennant Creek after her brother's death, Holly knew she'd found a place she belonged.

She looked around at her friends.

Not too shabby, Harper.

AFTERWORD

If you enjoyed Wedgetail
please consider leaving a review.
They really help.

More Miranda coming soon.
In the meantime,
keep reading for an exciting excerpt from:
Night Stalkers Reload #1, Guard the East Flank

Be sure to visit:
https://mlbuchman.com/fan-club-freebies

- *Bonus Scene/Story*
- *Recipe from the book*
- *Character list, place maps, plane pictures, and more*

NIGHT STALKERSRELOAD #1 (EXCERPT)

IF YOU ENJOYED THAT, YOU'LL LOVE…

GUARD THE EAST FLANK (EXCERPT)

"When was the last time you flew?"

"Yesterday. Or was it Tuesday, Emma?" Mark glanced her way, but didn't give her time to respond. "Yep, thinkin' it was Tuesday." He pointed westward at the abrupt upward break of the Montana Front Range. Their twenty-thousand-acre ranch ended there and the million-acre Selway-Bitterroot Wilderness began.

She, Mark, and Colonel Cassius McDermott had stopped their horses in the shade of a white birch copse atop a crest of the rolling landscape. It was one of Emily's favorite views. They were on a lazy afternoon ride a couple hours from the ranch, and this would be their turnback point.

The sun glinted off the sharp peaks of the Lewis Range, emphasizing the alternating light and dark strata that slashed through the mountains like the insides of mile-tall layer cakes. Being born and raised in DC, even six years living here hadn't decreased Emily's wonder at this vista rising in her backyard.

"Took a couple of fat-cat tourists on a spin out there, in our little Bell JetRanger helo. We spotted bear, moose, a couple herds of elk. Gonna be some good hunting for the larder this fall. Good photo safaris, too—we're marketing those heavy this year. You should come on out, Cass. It'll be a good time here at the ranch."

"I don't think that's what Cass is asking, is it, Colonel?" Emily gave Mark the hint, but he missed it. "Six years since the last time we flew a mission."

Then she caught the look in Mark's eye. He'd known exactly what he was doing. Instead of scowling at her for spoiling his game, he offered her one of his broad conspiratorial winks, including her in his play. He'd always enjoyed his games but never been particularly attached to the winning or the losing. Less so with each passing year. The ranch had mellowed him so much that it was occasionally hard to spot the former 5th Battalion D Company commander of the Night Stalkers' regiment.

He pulled out a hip flask. After taking a sip, he offered it to Cass seated on Rollo, reaching over from atop Wind Runner. His big black gelding hadn't slowed with age, but the years had made Mark a better rider—at least he rarely fell off anymore.

"Sorry, didn't get you were talking about *flying*, not flying. Well, why didn't you say it plain, old son?" His horsemanship may have improved; his phony Texas accent hadn't.

Cass was looking at the flask as if there was something wrong with it, or the fact that it was still early afternoon. The early summer finally warm enough for no more than a light jacket.

"None of us on duty out here, Cass, and 'tain't poison. Licensed distiller from just down the valley a piece. All local: water, grain, even the oak for the casks and the cooper who knocked them together—seriously hot, by the way. I'd introduce you, but don't want to tick off your wife." Well, his Texas was a little better, even if she'd never understood why a Navy brat turned Montanan kept toying with it. As far as she knew, neither he nor his SEAL father had ever been so much as stationed there and his mother was pureblood Cheyenne from Wyoming.

"He also has a beard down to his solar plexus, except when he singes it while charring a barrel. You might object to that even more than your wife would." Emily felt it was only fair to warn him.

Cass laughed and took the flask. The whiskey was too harsh for Emily's palate, any whiskey was, but Cass seemed to like it well enough to take a second taste before returning it to Mark, who tucked it away.

It might be Mark doing most of the speaking, but it was Colonel Cass McDermott she watched carefully. He hadn't brought his wife on this trip, which meant he was here on business—the Army's business.

"Did you say six years, Emily?"

"You're thinking eleven." She kept her smile to herself.

"I admit I was."

"The last five were under a different classification, Cass." Meaning operations that her former commander hadn't been cleared for. Always a bitter taste, one that showed clearly on his face.

"Yeah," Mark said in his normal voice. "Classified mission compartmentalization sucks. I always found it as annoying as hell, too."

Cass made it halfway through a nod of acknowledgement when a rabbit bolted from practically under the nose of Cass' horse. When Rollo ran, he had a habit like no other horse she'd ever seen. The gray dropped low and bolted so fast that Cass looked as if he floated in space for a moment before plummeting to the thick Montana grass.

"Goddamn it!" Mark swung his reins over and gave Wind Runner a hard kick. He didn't need it; his horse also loved to run, and he was the fastest on the ranch—because, of course, that's what Mark had insisted on when they moved here, not realizing as a rank beginner what he was asking for.

Rollo offered an easy ride, good for a beginner like Cass—usually. Wind Runner? Not so much. Mark and the two horses raced out of sight over the bluff.

Knowing her own level of incompetence, she'd requested the friendliest of mounts and never regretted her choice. Chesapeake watched the others race away as she chewed her latest mouthful of the lush grass before reaching for another bite. Emily patted her on the neck.

She hoped that she wouldn't have to go rescue Mark next.

Dropping the reins over her mare's neck, she slid to the ground. Nothing much bothered her horse, and she wouldn't run off even if it did.

"Anything hurt other than your pride, Cass?"

"Not much." He remained seated in the foot-tall grass of the July prairie.

The rains had come late—late enough in June to strike fear into every rancher's heart, even a Jane-come-lately like herself. But the so-called million-dollar rains had finally come on strong and set the crops. It had also turned the entire Front Range into a magic carpet of bluebells, buttercups, and windflowers. Their bright colors danced on the air lush with the scent of green. July's typical dusty dry taste had been pushed out into August, making every Montanan walk a bit sprightlier, whether from the prairie or the town.

Cass picked up the cowboy hat they'd given him against the sun, but he didn't put it back on. Instead, he worried the brim around in a slow circle through his hands as he remained seated on the grass. "Six years? Thought you were flying to wildfires."

"That's one way to look at it." They'd also been flying black ops missions under the cover of being helitack firefighters, reporting only to the President and the Secretary of Defense.

She sat down on the grass beside him. Emily felt Chesapeake come up behind her, but she didn't react.

Her mahogany mare picked the hat off Emily's head without catching her long blonde hair in its teeth.

"See? They don't tell me squat simply because I'm the 160th SOAR's commanding officer."

She let her silence tell him that it was going to stay that way, too. Her years flying for the Night Stalkers of the Army's Special Operations Aviation Regiment had been the highlight of her career, but that hadn't been the end of it by a long stretch.

Chesapeake flapped Emily's hat up and down, laughing through clenched teeth. It was an old game between them, since back when they first met and the only thing Emily rode was Black Hawk helicopters. She waited for the horse to hang her head over Emily's shoulder so she could scrub Chesapeake's cheek. The horse sighed happily, dropped Emily's hat in her lap, then turned her attention to ripping up grass.

Cass was thinking hard about her flying career...and something else as well. Didn't matter, Emily was dug in here, but she was curious at what had dragged him all the way to Montana from Fort Campbell, Kentucky.

Picking up her hat, she slid it on. Not for Chesapeake to steal again, but her light blonde hair and matching complexion didn't offer any defense against the Montana summer sunshine even wearing a serious SPF number and sitting in the broken shade of the swaying birches.

"Six years is still too long for us to go airborne again, Cass. A single month off blunts that fighting edge in a top pilot. Six years..." she let that hang.

It would take a minimum of half a year of retraining to regain that edge, if she even could. Flying a Night Stalkers helicopter into a battlespace was *not* a bicycle that your body simply remembered how to fly.

"You knew that before you came here. What's really going on?"

Rather than answering directly, he appeared to be watching the snow-capped ranges behind her. "I saw that you're still listed as active duty."

She was. Mark had finally retired when he'd hit his twenty years—*Same as Dad is plenty good enough for me*—his final four years as a trainer at the nearby Malmstrom Air Force Base. He'd flown and taught leadership courses before finally standing down as a lieutenant colonel. Getting the silver oak leaf had tickled him no end. But when she'd pointed out that a few more years' service might get him a bump to being a bird colonel, he'd scoffed.

Think I'm after Cass McDermott's job? Not even a little interested.

And he hadn't been.

Done my tour.

In the two years since, he'd settled in as if he'd never been anywhere else. His dad still ran the place. Though pushing seventy, Mac was a retired SEAL and wouldn't stop until he was six feet under the sod, if then. But Mark and the ranch had started to fit each other in ways he'd never managed even as commander of the most elite SOAR company.

As the commander of the 5th Battalion's D Company, he'd been a driven hard-ass. The only quality that was good enough for Viper Henderson was perfection—setting the gold standard himself. On the ranch, he was the one behind the scenes making sure everything kept ticking along. It was easy to miss where he slipped in unless she watched for it.

He was also Superdad. Tessa and Belle loved her, but they worshipped their dad—two seriously daddy's girls. Which was okay, she worshipped Mark a little herself.

Cass *knew* Mark had retired; he'd come out to the ranch for the retirement party. Whatever he was after…

I saw that you're still listed as active duty.

"Oh, no. Wait a minute, Cass. I don't want back in the service."

"Saw you earned the same silver oak leaf as Mark, same year too, though you're a couple years younger. Don't seem to recall any invitation to *your* retirement party...unless there never was one. Still on active duty without any missions or any posting showing up in your records at all, at least not any I get to see."

Emily had already answered that one. Five years technically flying to fight forest fires. At least that was the wider perception. By which time, she'd had it running so smoothly that she was able to hand it off.

For the six years since, she'd created and led a clandestine intelligence operation at the behest of the former President. Though now that she thought about it, that operation had finally matured as well. There was little that Lauren, Claudia, and Michael actually needed of her anymore. She been chomping at the bit for a while now, worse than Chesapeake when she scented the barn coming in range after a long ride.

Fully retire like Mark? Leading yet another trail ride didn't exactly fill her cup past a quarter full. Chasing down yet another attack on the Executive Branch sounded equally uninspiring no matter how good she had become at it.

She'd always been a pilot first and last.

Cass smiled. "Eddie Arnson wants to make you an offer."

"Then why are you here?" The Chairman of the Joint Chiefs of Staff, the top-ranking military officer in the nation, knew how to find her. He was Mark's uncle, after all. Only the second Marine Corps general to ever be named to the post. She still wondered what crowbar the President had used to pry him loose from his beloved HMX-1 post commanding the Marine helicopters responsible for Presidential-lift missions.

"Because I asked to make the pitch."

"So pitch."

The ground vibrated slightly beneath her butt. A discontented snort from Rollo announced that Mark had caught the runaway horse unfairly and far too soon into a glorious gallop over the thick summer pastures.

Cass waited for the two of them to come up.

"You hitting on my wife, Cass? Gotta warn you, Emma gets *more* dangerous with age. And she started out plenty dangerous to begin with." He rubbed his jaw where she'd planted his face into an aircraft carrier's ready-room table for stealing a first kiss. A dozen years and a lifetime ago.

Though he never missed an opportunity to mention it, they shared a smile at the memory. She remembered the kiss with searing clarity but had to take Mark's word on what she'd done to him after that.

He also kept the outer bezel of his watch permanently set to the precise minute of that first kiss. She'd tested him a few times; he never had to hesitate longer than a single breath to tell her years, days, hours, and minutes since.

Despite the memory, Emily's smile felt tight on her face.

"Can't say that my missus would take it much better than yours," he winked at Emily, but kept looking up at Mark on his horse. "How do you feel about being outranked?"

"You've always outranked me, Old Man. Simply being older seems questionable grounds for such a thing, but..." Mark shrugged it away.

"You can double that barely concealed envy now. They're bumping me upstairs, commander of USASOAC, giving me a star for my troubles." He tapped his shoulder where it would go.

"Head of the whole Army's Spec Ops Aviation Command? Very fancy, *General* Cassius McDermott, sir." Mark offered a salute sloppier than a recruit fresh through the gate. "Congratulations, Cass, seriously. You're a hundred percent the man for that job. Who's taking over the 160th?" Command of the 160th SOAR called for a colonel, not a brigadier general.

Emily felt the blood drain from her face. Robbed her of the power to speak.

"Funny you should ask that." Cass pulled a small box out of his pocket and tossed it at her.

Emily caught it by reflex. Though it burned against her palm, she opened it. Then turned it to show Mark the winged silver collar insignia of a bird colonel.

He slid down off his horse but didn't say a word. Instead, he stepped up and rested one of those big strong hands on her shoulder. That was good, or the gentle breeze rippling over the grasslands might waft her away easier than an errant bumblebee, never to be seen again.

"There's the pitch. You going to be making the catch, *Colonel Beale?*"

Emily couldn't react as Chesapeake stole her hat again.

The only comfort she found was that, for once, Mark was struck as speechless as she was. Not a single Texas drawl to be heard on the wide Montana prairie.

The sole sound on the wind? Her horse's laughter.

Buy now at fine retailers everywhere to continue reading
Guard the East Flank

ABOUT THE AUTHOR

USA Today and Amazon #1 Bestseller M. L. "Matt" Buchman started writing on a flight south from Japan to ride his bicycle across the Australian Outback. Just part of a solo around-the-world trip that ultimately launched his writing career.

From the very beginning, his powerful female heroines insisted on putting character first, *then* a great adventure. He's since written over 75 action-adventure thrillers and military romantic suspense novels. And more than 200 short stories, and a fast-growing pile of read-by-author audiobooks.

PW declares of his Miranda Chase action-adventure thrillers: "Tom Clancy fans open to a strong female lead will clamor for more." About his military romantic thrillers: "Like Robert Ludlum and Nora Roberts had a book baby."

His fans say: "I want more now...of everything!" That his characters are even more insistent than his fans is a hoot.

As a 30-year project manager with a geophysics degree who has designed and built houses, flown and jumped out of planes, and solo-sailed a 50' ketch, he is awed by what is possible. He and his wife presently live on the North Shore of Massachusetts. More at: www.mlbuchman.com.

Other works by M. L. Buchman: *(* - also in audio)*

Action-Adventure Thrillers

Dead Chef
One Chef!
Two Chef!

Miranda Chase
*Drone**
*Thunderbolt**
*Condor**
*Ghostrider**
*Raider**
*Chinook**
*Havoc**
*White Top**
*Start the Chase**
*Lightning**
*Skibird**
*Nightwatch**
*Osprey**
*Gryphon**

Science Fiction / Fantasy

Deities Anonymous
Cookbook from Hell: Reheated
Saviors 101

Contemporary Romance

Eagle Cove
Return to Eagle Cove
Recipe for Eagle Cove
Longing for Eagle Cove
Keepsake for Eagle Cove

Love Abroad
Heart of the Cotswolds: England
Path of Love: Cinque Terre, Italy

Where Dreams
Where Dreams are Born
Where Dreams Reside
*Where Dreams Are of Christmas**
Where Dreams Unfold
Where Dreams Are Written
Where Dreams Continue

Non-Fiction

Strategies for Success
Managing Your Inner Artist/Writer
*Estate Planning for Authors**
Character Voice
*Narrate and Record Your Own Audiobook**
Beyond Prince Charming: One Guy's Guide to Writing Men in Romance

Short Story Series by M. L. Buchman:

Action-Adventure Thrillers

Dead Chef

Miranda Chase Stories

Romantic Suspense

Antarctic Ice Fliers

US Coast Guard

Contemporary Romance

Eagle Cove

Other

Deities Anonymous (fantasy)

Single Titles

The Emily Beale Universe
(military romantic suspense)

The Night Stalkers
MAIN FLIGHT
The Night Is Mine
I Own the Dawn
Wait Until Dark
Take Over at Midnight
Light Up the Night
Bring On the Dusk
By Break of Day
Target of the Heart
Target Lock on Love
Target of Mine
Target of One's Own
NIGHT STALKERS HOLIDAYS
*Daniel's Christmas**
*Frank's Independence Day**
*Peter's Christmas**
Christmas at Steel Beach
*Zachary's Christmas**
*Roy's Independence Day**
*Damien's Christmas**
Christmas at Peleliu Cove

Henderson's Ranch
*Nathan's Big Sky**
*Big Sky, Loyal Heart**
*Big Sky Dog Whisperer**
*Tales of Henderson's Ranch**

Shadow Force: Psi
*At the Slightest Sound**
*At the Quietest Word**
*At the Merest Glance**
*At the Clearest Sensation**

White House Protection Force
*Off the Leash**
*On Your Mark**
*In the Weeds**

Firehawks
Pure Heat
Full Blaze
*Hot Point**
*Flash of Fire**
Wild Fire
SMOKEJUMPERS
*Wildfire at Dawn**
*Wildfire at Larch Creek**
*Wildfire on the Skagit**

Delta Force
*Target Engaged**
*Heart Strike**
*Wild Justice**
*Midnight Trust**

Night Stalkers Reload
*Guard the East Flank**

Emily Beale Universe Short Story Series

The Night Stalkers
The Night Stalkers Stories
The Night Stalkers CSAR
The Night Stalkers Wedding Stories
The Future Night Stalkers

Delta Force
Th Delta Force Shooters
The Delta Force Warriors

Firehawks
The Firehawks Lookouts
The Firehawks Hotshots
The Firebirds

White House Protection Force
Stories

Future Night Stalkers
Stories (Science Fiction)

SIGN UP FOR M. L. BUCHMAN'S
NEWSLETTER TODAY

and receive:
Release News
Free Short Stories
a Free Book

Get your free book today. Do it now.
free-book.mlbuchman.com

www.ingramcontent.com/pod-product-compliance
Lightning Source LLC
Chambersburg PA
CBHW022034120726
47899CB00001BB/266